ANOTHER CASE OF MURDER

Ray pitched his notepad open. "A woman's body was found last night at the Augustin Community Garden."

"Poppy Robinson." Sherry shook her head. "Has any cause of death been pinned down yet? She seemed the picture of health last time I saw her. I expect you're going to say cause of death was heart attack, unless there was a bizarre accident at the garden, but I can't imagine what that could have been."

"Poppy Robinson was murdered."

"Murder? Poppy Robinson was murdered?" Sherry's heart knocked hard. "How do they know it was murder?"

Ray turned back the pages of his notepad. "A shovel was alongside the body in the raised garden bed she was discovered in. The trauma to her head was consistent with having received blunt force from the blade of the tool. There was a subtle indentation in the thick metal of the shovel head, so she really got whacked. Very hard to bend that grade of steel. Whoever did this took the time to square her body up perfectly within the bed's frame with the shovel parallel to her. Coroner's report confirms the find[...] can say Poppy Robins[...]

Books by Devon Delaney

EXPIRATION DATE

FINAL ROASTING PLACE

GUILTY AS CHARRED

Published by Kensington Publishing Corporation

GUILTY AS CHARRED

Devon Delaney

KENSINGTON BOOKS
www.KensingtonBooks.com

KENSINGTON BOOKS are published by

Kensington Publishing Corp.
119 West 40th Street
New York, NY 10018

All Kensington titles, imprints, and distributed lines are available at special quantity discounts for bulk purchases for sales promotion, premiums, fund-raising, educational, or institutional use.

Special book excerpts or customized printings can also be created to fit specific needs. For details, write or phone the office of the Kensington Sales Manager: Attn.: Sales Department. Kensington Publishing Corp., 119 West 40th Street, New York, NY 10018. Phone: 1-800-221-2647.

Kensington and the K logo Reg. U.S. Pat. & TM Off.

First Printing: July 2019

ISBN-13: 978-1-4967-1447-3
ISBN-10: 1-4967-1447-4

ISBN-13: 978-1-4967-1448-0 (ebook)
ISBN-10: 1-4967-1448-2 (ebook)

10 9 8 7 6 5 4 3 2 1

Printed in the United States of America

Acknowledgments

I want to thank my husband, Chris, for believing I could write a mystery series people might find entertaining and supporting me as I made my dream a reality.

Thanks to my fellow cooking contest competitors, who consistently encourage each other to explore the next step in a hobby that celebrates the love of food.

Deep appreciation and thanks to my tireless agent, Dawn Dowdle, who saw something in me and took a chance.

Thank you to my fabulous Kensington editor, John Scognamiglio, whose enthusiasm for great writing is contagious.

Thank you to the entire team at Kensington, who keep my name out there on social media, edit my manuscripts with pinpoint accuracy, and create the most eye-catching book covers.

Finally, thank you to my friends, who told me I inspire them to try something new.

Chapter One

"Ma'am, sorry to wake you, but a fellow passenger would like a pillow from the overhead compartment and your trophy is resting on it. Would you mind if I pull the statue down from its comfy spot so I can get the pillow for her?"

Sherry's eyes opened to the sight of a stewardess hovering over her. Before Sherry could respond to the question, the woman in the blue and gold uniform removed her hand from the storage bin and waved the shiny replica of the United States map mounted on a pedestal.

"Sure," Sherry answered as she blinked the sleep haze from her eyes.

A man seated across the aisle exclaimed, "Now that's what I call a trophy."

Sherry delivered a smile his way. Blushing, he elbowed the woman sporting a navel-orange-size knot of hair on the crown of her head seated beside him.

The woman gasped. "I recognize that trophy.

You must be Sherry Oliveri. My husband and I were in the audience at the America's Good Taste Cook-off and Sherry Oliveri was the name they called to receive that winning trophy. Such a fun name. I must say, even though you were sitting right there, I wouldn't have known it was you. You don't look familiar without your cooking apron on. Your hair looks different too. Not as stylishly coiffed as you wore it onstage."

Sherry reached up to locate the direction her bedhead locks might have oriented themselves during her nap.

"We were so excited when our state won. And excited for you, too, of course. Can I get a picture with you? Herb, get up and take our picture, will you, please?" The woman jabbed Herb's shoulder repeatedly with the tips of her fingers as if she were poking an avocado to test for ripeness. After Herb hauled himself out of his seat, the woman followed her husband out to the plane's narrow aisle.

"Me too. I'd like a picture with the winner," exclaimed a female voice in the neighboring row. She waved her hand frantically.

A man beside the waving woman catapulted out of his seat. The headphones he wore took flight and landed on one of the stewardess's black flats. He scrambled to collect them and cozied up behind Herb in the increasing queue.

In the midst of shaking off her abbreviated nap hangover, Sherry was helped to her feet by the stewardess, who had taken the liberty of unfastening the seat belt that was the last line of defense against the gathering crowd. Sherry was handed her trophy and guided into the aisle, where she squeezed herself in amongst the bodies. She fidgeted with a snarl of hair that tumbled across her forehead, in hopes of detangling the mess, but gave up the effort when her fingers became ensnared. She crouched down toward the line leader, whose arm stretched skyward to reach around Sherry's shoulders.

With Sherry's back wedged painfully against the edge of another passenger's seat, Herb clicked his phone's camera. He pumped his arms in triumph. "Perfect picture. Thank you so much. My wife had us fly all the way down to Florida to watch the cook-off, and we were so tickled one of our fellow Augustinians took home the grand prize. We've been following your cooking career for years. Herb McDonald's the name, and the woman clutching you like you were the sole remaining slice of bacon at the hotel's continental breakfast is my wife, Bea. Guess I should learn to be a better cook and she'd hold me that tight more often."

"Herb, that's enough. Sit down so Sherry can give her other fans a chance for a picture."

Herb let loose a boisterous chuckle before returning to his seat. His wife crawled over his legs to reach hers.

"I shouldn't have postponed my highlight appointment at Hair Force One." Sherry sighed as she imagined the unflattering images the camera phones captured.

"You have a very natural look," the stewardess offered. "Cooks are supposed to spend time in the kitchen not at the beauty salon."

Sherry peered back over her shoulder and met

a line of people that clogged the plane's aisle as far as she could see. She jerked her head toward the stewardess, who cradled a pillow under one arm. "I'll cater your next get-together if you announce mealtime right now."

"Ladies and gentlemen, this is the captain speaking. I've been advised of severe turbulence in the airspace ahead of us. Please return to your seats and fasten your seat belts until further notice."

A collective whine reverberated throughout the plane's cabin.

The captain's ominous words sent a cold vibration through Sherry's core. As passengers dispersed, Sherry sighed and tucked her trophy back in the overhead bin. The intercom speaker crackled to life as she slammed the compartment door shut. She nestled in her seat, pulled her seat belt tight, and settled her arms into a self-hug.

"This is the captain again. I have an update, not weather related. I've been advised we are flying today with a celebrity onboard."

Sherry pinched her eyes shut and held her breath.

"The winner of America's Good Taste recipe contest is among us. I'm honored to be transporting Sherry Oliveri home, along with her winnings. I'm told she is an Augustin, Connecticut, native, who prepared New England Crab Cake Sliders for the big win, and I'd like everyone to join in a heartfelt round of applause for representing the Northeast so well in the national contest."

"Please don't give out my address," Sherry whispered as her eyes widened. Heads rotated her way and Sherry gave the queen's wave in all directions.

The plane dropped, along with Sherry's stomach.

"Sorry, folks. I shouldn't try to walk and chew gum at the same time. Or make that, I shouldn't try to steer the plane to a calmer altitude and applaud for a celebrity passenger at the same time. Better keep my eyes on the road, so to speak. But the rest of you, put your hands together for our winner."

After the brief but robust clapping ended, Sherry leaned her head back and peered out the window.

"Would you mind if I took that middle seat until the plane finds calmer air? It's a long way back to row six."

Sherry looked up and was eye level with the belt buckle of a man in dusty rose-colored shorts, white tube socks, and black sneakers. "Of course. I'll move my purse." Sherry gathered her overstuffed bag from the empty window seat to her left. She scanned the floor for any unoccupied space to set the tote down in. Seeing only enough room for her feet, she nestled the bag on her lap. She pulled her knees up against the edge of the seat cushion and the man maneuvered by.

"For the price of these seats, you'd imagine they'd offer a bit more room." As the plane shuddered, the man lost his balance. He steadied himself by clutching Sherry's headrest. "Pardon me as I nearly crush you. For your sake, I'm glad I showered this morning." He removed his chest from Sherry's face.

"Doesn't help that I've been eating and drinking nonstop for the past three days." Sherry patted her core. "I'm trying to suck in my stomach so you can get by, but that's asking the impossible."

The plane danced across another turbulent patch.

"I don't like this one bit." She rubbed her moist palms together, unzipped her purse, and checked her phone. "Another hour and a half to go. I'm not sure I'll survive."

"Don't waste your time worrying. These planes don't go down easily." He wrapped his seat belt around his waist and pulled tight.

Sherry turned her head in the man's direction and was struck by the fact he was in need of a shave. His lips were curled into a smile. Being in such close proximity, Sherry saw the whites of his eyes, though rather bloodshot, were the foundation for the remarkable blue color of his irises. His hair was graying, which seemed inconsistent to his overall youthful, sturdy appearance.

"I'm never convinced until I set foot back inside the terminal." Sherry looked at her phone again and clicked on her email's inbox. She had received two messages before boarding but hadn't enough time to read them. She opened the first from Romie Green.

Subject: Terrible News
   The rumors can't be ignored any longer. Count on this being the final season of the Augustin Community Garden. We should have joined the board sooner. Maybe we could have done something to stop that woman. No official announcement as of yet, but I'm positive her decision's coming. You've probably heard I tried to talk her out of her decision after the board

meeting with disastrous results. Not my best showing—the scene escalated to yelling, cursing, and obscene gestures. To no avail. She stonewalled me. So frustrating! I wish you had been at the meeting, but I'm sure the cook-off was way more fun. Call me when you get back. I hope you won. I have no doubt you did!

In the midst of digesting the email content, Sherry recoiled when she felt a weight on her shoulder. Her seatmate was quick to retract his hand.

"I didn't mean to startle you. I thought you were feeling sick. That was a deep-from-the-gut groan you let out."

"A reaction to some bad news. Luckily, not nausea, although I can't rule that out in the near future if this free-falling metal tube doesn't get on a smoother path." Sherry extended a hand. "My name's Sherry."

The man embraced her hand in his. "Sherry Oliveri, I know. I couldn't help but notice the line of admirers waiting to take a picture with you. I was in that line, by the way. My name's Nolan. I'm also from Augustin, and I was lucky enough to be in Orlando during the cook-off, so I bought a ticket. I was in the audience cheering you on. Nice job.

"Thanks. I'm the one who got lucky. The judges were in the mood for crab yesterday, I guess."

"I hope the news wasn't too rough." Nolan jutted his chin in the direction of Sherry's phone.

"Unfortunately, not good news. You say you're from Augustin?"

Nolan nodded. "Born and raised."

"Are you familiar with the Augustin Community Garden? It's a lovely piece of land smack in the middle of town. You've probably been by the property a million times without knowing what bounty was being produced inside the gates. The sign at the end of the driveway is very inconspicuous. We don't want to rile up the neighbors by attracting unintended looky-seers." Sherry searched Nolan's face for a glimmer of awareness, but he remained solemn. "I joined the board this year because it's a perfect combination of two of my passions, gardening and food. We grow the most magnificent vegetables. Not we, exactly, more like the members who have joined for various reasons. Some people don't have access to a plot of dirt to create their own garden. They might live in public housing or whatever, with no backyard space."

"Isn't that nice." Nolan's voice took on a distant, preoccupied quality.

"The bad news is, the woman who generously lends out the land to the town seems to be reconsidering. She hasn't said so in public, but the word is getting around. That word has come from a woman I work with on the board who emailed me and that prompted the groan you heard."

"Maybe there's something that can be done to stop the woman? The generous-lender woman, not the emailing-with-bad-news woman."

"My young friend on the board has youthful ambitions to convince her otherwise, but I'm not sure the attempt is possible or even advisable. I mean, at the end of the day, the land is hers. She has every right to do as she pleases. She and her two siblings, that is. All three own the property jointly since it was passed on to them when their father died. I'm sad, though, because Romie, that's my friend's name, and I devised the garden's association to Augustin's food bank and that organization really counts on the harvested veggies supplied to fill their pantry. We've fed a lot of people."

"Doesn't sound like a done deal quite yet, if the owner of the land and her siblings haven't made any kind of announcement," Nolan added. "I can see by the look on your face the garden means a lot to you. I hope things work out the way you'd like."

"Me too." Sherry returned her attention to her phone. She opened the second unread email. She sat up straighter when she read Amber Sherman's name attached to the message.

Subject: Mystery package delivery
Hi, Sherry

I figured you'd be easier to reach by email rather than texting while you were in transit. A box was delivered to you here at the store, about half the size of a shoebox. Let's call it a baby shoebox. What's inside makes a soft rattle, like a bag of popcorn kernels, when I pick it up, so I wanted to peak your interest. I'm always excited to get a delivery, so I thought you might be too.
All for now,
Amber Sherman, Assistant Manager, the Ruggery

Sherry cocked her head, which, combined with the plane's bucking, sent her equilibrium for a ride. She dropped her phone.

Nolan kicked his leg out and saved the phone from a rough landing with a foot deflection. "More bad news? Maybe you should stop reading your email. It might be putting a damper on what should be your time of celebration."

"Good news this time. Either way, I'm trying to keep busy so I can get my mind off this blasted plane ride."

"Anything you care to share?" Nolan took a peek out the window. "Ugh, look at that storm."

The view was a solid wall of clouds. Nolan lowered the shade.

"Thanks for shutting that. Out of sight, out of mind is wishful thinking." Sherry exhaled. "I'll try to give you a short introduction so the story makes sense. Along with competing in cooking contests for more years than I care to admit, I work part-time at my father's hooked rug store. At a cook-off I was in, I made a wonderful friend, who, for various reasons, was in a perfect time of her life to make a location and career change, so she moved to Augustin to become an assistant manager at the Ruggery. That's the name of the store. While I was at the cook-off this week, Amber, that's her name, pulled double-duty taking on my hours as well. Anyway, she emailed to say I received a package at work, which I'm assuming contains seed contributions for the Community Garden. Probably doesn't sound as exciting to you as to me, but I can't wait to add them to my growing collection."

"Funny you should mention seeds. I've always

thought of having a garden and I've made up my mind to start one this year. I've decided I'll start with growing my own lettuce and tomatoes. Imagine heading out the back door at dinnertime to pick whatever's ready. Seems like a great idea."

"I highly recommend gardening. The satisfaction of tending little seedlings as they grow into gorgeous vegetables will cure what ails you. When I put out the call for seed contributions, I didn't have much hope people would respond but, so far, so good." Sherry tucked her hair behind her ears and searched Nolan's eyes for any signs of interest in what she was saying.

He lowered his gaze when they exchanged glances.

"If you don't have space where you live, feel free to fill out an application on the Community Garden's website."

"Maybe I will. I'll take a look when I get home."

"You're not getting nervous about the storm, are you? I mean, you're playing that armrest like it's a bongo."

Nolan smiled. "No, no. Bad habit that drives my girlfriend crazy. She's always telling me to sit on my hands so she can have some peace and quiet. Sounds like you're a busy lady. You cook competitively and work at your father's store. You sit on the Community Garden board. I read the entire cook-off brochure cover to cover, and your bio mentioned you were a pickle purveyor at the Augustin farmer's market last summer too. I won't get personal and ask about a husband and kids, but if you have those, you're certainly swamped."

Sherry noted Nolan peered at her hand, presumably to check for a wedding ring.

"My pickle stand went the way of my husband. Both are in the hands of someone else. We divorced. My husband, not the pickle stand. Although, after a brief honeymoon period, my pickle stand and I parted ways, also. And, no kids. The woman who was grooming me to take over her pickle business came out of retirement and decided to take back the reins, which opened the door to me joining the garden board. You're right. I'm plenty busy."

"The cooking competition circuit seems an active mix of creativity, sport, challenge, and excitement. How do you keep from losing your motivation over the years?"

"I admit I may have. Only once or twice. I was involved in two mishaps at cook-offs. Each time I reconsidered continuing entering contests, but that feeling lasted about as long as it takes me to peel a butternut squash."

"I'm not sure. Is that a short amount of time or a long time?"

"Sorry. Short amount of time. I'm very fast at the task, even though there's a lot of muscle involved getting through the vegetable's tough skin and muscle strength isn't my forte. So, in a flash I picked my spatula back up and returned to work creating recipes."

Nolan lifted the window shade. "I was thinking, a huge team must be required to coordinate a cook-off as big as America's Good Taste. Fifty cooks, each representing their state. Do you have any idea what goes into getting a cooking competition up and running? I imagine the process is as complicated as a space shuttle launch."

Sherry tucked her phone back in her purse. "Could be. Every time I'm in one, I pick the organizer's brain, after the fact. I appreciate their efforts to make the competition a good experience for everyone involved. I don't know how they get the job done. The task of narrowing the field of entrants down to the finalists takes a panel of experts months. For instance, for yesterday's contest, I submitted my crab cake recipe online almost six months ago. After the contest received my entry, and hundreds maybe thousands more, a group of reviewers weeded out ones that had too many typos, weren't organized well enough for an average home cook to be able to replicate, any duplicates, plain awful recipes, and on and on. At the same time, a venue for the contest had to be found, sponsors attracted, advertising created, travel arrangements made, not to mention all the stoves set up, ingredients purchased at the last minute, and aprons and gift baskets provided. The list grew every day until the event day arrived. There always has to be some emergency contingencies in place like what to do if there's a last-minute contestant cancellation, while addressing the obvious, like planning first aid for burns and cuts, etcetera. I'm forever fascinated talking to the officials after a cook-off when they finally can exhale. They let their hair down and spill the beans on everything that went on to get the event to appear smooth as coconut cream. All I know is how to be a contestant. I wouldn't want the coordinator's job. Behind the scenes, I imagine they deal with unforeseen disaster after unforeseen disaster. At the end of the day, I'm always so impressed that no catastrophe occurred." Sherry lowered her voice to a near whisper. "Except for the occasional murder."

Nolan's eyebrows merged and he blinked hard. "I don't think I heard you right. Did you say murder?"

"That was the mishap I was referring to. Twice there's been a murder associated with a cook-off I've been a part of. You probably read about the incidents if you've been anywhere near Augustin over the last year or so. There was nonstop coverage by all the news outlets."

Nolan leaned forward and planted his elbows on each of his armrests. "Come to think of it, that was my first introduction to cook-offs. I didn't know a thing about them until I read the news articles. I've certainly never attended one, so when I found myself with some extra time in Orlando, I bought a ticket to see what goes on. I really had a good time and there was no murder. That's a plus." Nolan let loose gentle laughter. "I was on the edge of my seat watching you cooks do your thing. The way the event was set up, the audience could mill around from competitor to competitor, but we had to stay behind the roped-off work area. We were close enough to see how focused you all were on getting out your best effort." Nolan paused before adding, "Funny, I would much rather be on the organizational end of things than go through the tension of competition."

"That's what a lot of people tell me."

The intercom crackled to life. "Ladies and gentlemen. Thank you for your cooperation. We have passed through the rough air and there's blue sky up ahead. It's safe to leave your seat, if nature calls."

"That's my cue to return to Nine B." Nolan unbuckled his seat belt and stood as best he could, with limited headspace. Sherry shifted her legs toward the aisle, providing him with an extra few inches to maneuver by.

"It was nice talking to you, Nolan. You made the bumps tolerable." Sherry waved as he wiggled past her. After a flex of one leg, followed by the other, Sherry yawned, pressed her cheek against the back of her chair, and closed her eyes.

"Pardon me, I hope I didn't wake you."

Sherry raised her heavy lids to the sight of the stewardess with her arm around a woman in a beige cardigan and jeans. "This nice lady would like a photo with you before we land, if possible."

"Patti. You don't really need another photo of me, do you?"

Patti Mellitt, food journalist and restaurant reviewer, winked at her friend. "No, no. I got hundreds at the awards ceremony. I wanted to tell you, you're the talk of first class. I admit I might have made the suggestion to the stewardess to alert the captain you were on the flight. Hope you don't hold that against me."

"No hard feelings. Wonder how I can get the contest sponsors to upgrade my ticket to first class next time so you and I can sit together." Sherry returned a wink.

"I had no choice. The plane was nearly booked and the only choices of seats were in first class. I had to follow my favorite cooking contester on her way to further success. You don't disappoint. Oh, and I emailed a press release on the cook-off and there's tons of interest in interviewing you."

"Thanks, I think." Sherry watched the woman, who'd covered many contests over the years for various media outlets, make her way up the aisle before disappearing behind the curtains that separated the pricy seats from economy class. Sherry stifled a developing yawn and stretched her arms until they slammed into the headrest in front of her.

"The life of a celebrity," Herb called out from across the aisle. "No rest for the weary."

"When you get home, dear, try to get some rest. You do look dead tired," Bea added.

Chapter Two

"Right this way, Ms. Oliveri." The twenty-something young man ambled down the radio station's hallway. His pipe cleaner arms and legs were too long for his torso and flailed in all directions with each stride. His bristle-brush hair jostled from side to side in time with his snappy gait. "The studio is at the end of the hall." The robust voice echoed off the walls lined with framed black-and-white photographs.

Startled by the human megaphone, Sherry stubbed her shoe on the edge of the carpet runner but was able to save herself from a full stumble. "You'd make a great announcer. Your voice is very commanding."

"My plan is to get my own radio show. After I finish my internship here at WAUG, I hope to get a job in a bigger market. Not that this radio station is small potatoes. I'd like to live in a more urban setting where I have a better chance of reaching my age demographic. Getting a gig on-air would

be the pinnacle of my career. That's what I'm shooting for. Management's not my thing. Too suit and
tie, no creativity. Delegation of tasks isn't for me.
I'm a doer." He spun on his heels to face Sherry.
"I'm not saying your interview this morning is for
old people listeners. That's not what I'm saying."
He lowered his head and scuffed the linoleum floor
with one canvas slip-on. "First lesson, be careful
what you say. You don't want to offend listeners."

"No offense taken."

"I'm sure people that tune in this morning to
hear you sharing your experience competing in
the America's Good Taste Cook-off will be of a
more life-experienced age group, but you never
know. The next generation of cooking contestants
is lurking out there somewhere and may tune in, if
we're lucky."

Sherry glanced at each photograph lining the
walls, from political figures to pop culture icons, as
they continued to the end of the hall. "Have all
these people been on the show?"

"Every single one. Your picture will be up there
soon."

Sherry ran her fingers through her hair. "I wish
I'd had time to wash my hair."

The young man, whom the receptionist at the
front desk referred to as "the intern," in lieu of a
proper introduction, stopped in front of a door
with a sign reading, "Studio 2A."

"That's the beauty of radio. Heard but not seen.
No one listening ever needs to know your hair is
dirty. And you can send us your best photo, if
that's what you prefer. When you're having a good
hair day. Maybe wearing your contest apron."

The intern opened the door to a tiny waiting room and swept his arm forward. "If you'd wait in the blue room until the commuter report is done, Kayson will come get you. The traffic reporter is in studio today, due to car trouble, ironically. Normally, he would be doing a remote for this station and others, but if the van's engine won't start, he's stuck inside. Anyway, the studio isn't big enough for more than two adults, so that's why you have to wait out here. The joys of small-town radio."

Sherry went inside and took a seat on the only piece of furniture in the room, a denim blue love seat. She set the trophy she brought down at her feet. Scanning the room, her gaze settled on a framed award for "Best Original Programming— Kayson in the Morning." A few inches away was a framed article brandishing the headlines, "Kayson Bradshaw—WAUG Radio's Highest Rated Talk Show Host Takes on the Tough Issues Facing Augustin's Future." The tiny letters of the article strained Sherry's capability to read from a distance. She crossed her legs, uncrossed them, and recrossed them. She pulled her phone from her purse and checked her email before remembering the receptionist insisted the phone be turned off.

The door opposite the love seat burst open. A statuesque man opened his arms wide and smiled in Sherry's direction. "I'm sorry for the delay. You must be Sherry Oliveri."

Sherry stood, knocking her trophy over. The man's high cheekbones constructed the perfect base for hazel-green eyes that sparkled with warmth. His salt-and-pepper eyebrows were wild and untrimmed, nearly meeting each other at the top of his Roman nose's bridge. His square jawbone was divided at the chin by a pronounced cleft that danced as he spoke.

"Let me help you with that. This beauty is none too subtle, right?" The man, who was nearly a head taller than Sherry, bent over and collected the toppled trophy off the floor. He extended his free hand. "Hi, I'm Kayson Bradshaw."

Sherry winced as Kayson squeezed her hand. "Very nice to meet you. I enjoy listening to you. On the radio. Well, I guess you know what I meant."

"Thank you for coming on my food segment, *Bites*, under such short notice. Our program manager read a press release about your win and couldn't book you fast enough. Although, I admit, even though I consider myself a foodie and love to promote all things food related, especially featuring our locals, when my producer told me you, a home cook, had bumped celebrity chef Winnie off the show, I was skeptical about the decision. Winnie has taken food trends to new heights in New England this year, and she doesn't make herself available for many interviews, but she'll be back in town in six months, my producer assured me. Besides, any recommendation from Patti Mellitt gets top billing by me. She's a big fan of yours."

"Patti Mellitt and I go way back. She's been very kind to me in her articles. I'm honored, but I feel like the listeners are getting the raw end of the deal. I love Winnie's recipes. Have you tried her bacon-infused blackened sea scallops with lemon caper foam? A little fussier than my simple concepts, but she's a New England gem and probably much more interesting than me."

"Now you're peaking my curiosity, about you and Winnie. I guess we'll find out soon if you were the right choice to have on today." Kayson's glance strayed to the trophy. "You do have a unique spin on cooking. Honestly, cooking for cash and prizes doesn't seem like the purest of reasons to create a delicious meal. Where's the love? That's what drove my mother's cooking. She put heart in each bite, never striving for recognition or profit."

Sherry's jaw dropped. *Is it too late to turn and run?* Sherry estimated the distance between where she stood and the door that led to the hallway. If she attempted a full sprint, the element of surprise would be on her side, and she could be down the hall and out of the building in twenty seconds, tops.

"This way. We're on in two minutes." Kayson waved Sherry forward with a swing of the statue of the United States. She steeled herself and followed him into the studio.

"Have a seat. Put on this headset and talk into the mic and you're golden. Don't respond to anything you hear in your ear, except my voice. Most importantly, have fun." Kayson set the trophy on the desk that separated the interviewer and interviewee. He placed headphones over his ears and pulled a boom mic closer to his face. On Kayson's desk, the front edge of a massive computer screen was partially visible. After he made an adjustment, all Sherry saw were plugs and cables. Beneath the monitor, Kayson rested his hands on a board busy with blinking lights, protruding knobs, and colorful buttons.

Sherry secured her headset over her ears. Her

heartbeat resounded in her eardrums. She lowered her chin when Kayson pointed his index finger at her.

Kayson announced, "Welcome back, listeners, to another edition of *Bites*. Last week we discussed one of the current food trends sweeping the northeast, savory maple syrup recipes. I'm told local sales of the amber liquid gold rose after many viewers shared their recipes and tricks on how to turn the sweet sap into a savory sensation with the addition of spices, herbs, and various condiments. Let's see how today's discussion will affect the taste buds of Hillsboro County.

"I am pleased to have as a guest today a woman who excels at preparing a meal in the winner-take-all food sport of cooking contesting. Not only can she stand the kitchen's heat, she burns the competition with her intensity. Sherry Oliveri is joining me in studio this morning, fresh off her win at the America's Good Taste recipe contest held this week in Orlando, Florida. Sherry beat out forty-nine other competitors, each representing their home state, to come out victorious for Connecticut."

Kayson gave Sherry a thumbs-up. She forced the edges of her mouth upward. Silence. Kayson jutted his head forward and deadlifted his bushy eyebrows.

A woman's voice came through the headset. "Sherry, your turn. Speak."

Sherry cleared her throat. "Yes, hi, everyone." She directed her gaze at Kayson, who was fixated on his computer. "Thank you for having me."

"Sherry, I think our listening audience would be interested in how you got into recipe contesting, if that's the correct term. Quite an unusual hobby, to say the least, where your recipe competes against others for a reward of varying value. And a second question popped into my head. I realize television has promoted competitive cooking for years, but don't you think the concept's become a bit over-done?"

Sherry rolled her eyes, an immature gesture she would never admit she was reduced to.

Kayson didn't appear to see it, nor did the listeners, so her secret was safe.

"To answer the first question, about seven or eight years ago, I was reading a magazine in a doctor's office waiting room. In the back of the magazine was an advertisement for a recipe contest, the theme of which was 'make something unique with the sponsor's sliced bread.' Honestly, I'd never considered myself competitive. My sister, Marla, was the athlete and competitor growing up, and I didn't see the attraction of trying to run faster than the next guy or kick the soccer ball in the net more times than your opponent. Even when I decided to enter a recipe in my first contest, I was more interested in displaying a talent rather than kicking butt, as Marla would say. That was until I was notified I was the winner of the bread contest, chosen over thousands of entries. The feeling I felt to have beaten everyone else was so exhilarating. Even all these years later, I'm uncomfortable admitting that."

"So, it's the rush of the crush, in a sense." Kayson

lifted his head and stared into Sherry's eyes. "Squashing the competition is the cherry on the sundae for you."

Sherry held her gaze on Kayson. "It's not a bad thing to be good at something you love to do, and I love to cook. There's the added bonus to receiving compensation for your efforts if the judges choose you as the winner. Similar to you getting a raise if your boss thinks you're doing a good job. To answer your second question, until cook-off attendance numbers are down and the ratings drop off for TV cooking contests, both will continue to thrive, and I'm happy about that. People seem to enjoy the rush of the crush, as you put it."

Kayson cocked his head to the side. "Fair enough. The judges obviously thought your recipe was the best in Connecticut, and, beyond that, the best in the United States. This giant trophy sitting on the control panel between us says it all. I wish you all could see it. The inscription reads, 'America's Good Taste Begins in the Kitchen.' Before we open the phone lines to callers, do you have any tips for anyone in the listening audience who might want to try their hand at recipe contesting?"

"That's probably the question I get asked most frequently. My best advice is to pick a contest with a theme you have a passion for, whether that means the sponsor's product is a favorite or, say, the theme is make a healthy breakfast in thirty minutes or dessert using five ingredients or less, something along those lines. That's a great place to start. From there, the sky's the limit in terms of what you may come up with. Check what recipes have won in the past and don't duplicate. Innovate."

"Great advice, Sherry. Let's see. My dream contest would be a grill-off. Grilling in the summer brings out the hunter-gatherer instinct in me. Instead of hauling my spiked caveman club out to the forest to hunt for dinner, I trek to the butcher. I'd go in a loincloth if I didn't think I'd be arrested. Butcher Bruno cuts me a slab of what looks best in the meat case that day and when fire meets meat, I'm as happy as a dog beside a fire hydrant."

"I can see by the twinkle in your eyes you'd do well in a grill-off. Here's a true story I've never shared with anyone but your listeners today. I learned one of my most useful competitive cooking skills at the hairdresser getting my blond highlights put in. As a matter of fact, I used the concept this week."

"Well, that shocks me on many levels. First of all, I'd never know your hair isn't your natural color. The hue reminds me of a roasted fingerling potato." Kayson looked up and smiled.

Sherry ran her fingers through her hair, scraping the lighter front locks up over the darker roots. "I'm overdue for a touch-up, hoping for more of a Yukon Gold color. I ran out of time before going to Florida. Freshening my look wasn't a priority. As your intern reminded me, luckily this is radio, so I can be heard and not seen. Believe me, after all the recent travel, early wake-up alarms, and intense cooking over the last few days, I sound better than I look." Sherry peered over the console at Kayson, who had his eyes on several blinking lights.

"The hairdresser story?" Kayson beckoned Sherry, with a twirl of his hand, to pick up the pace.

"I'm not sure you're aware of the process, but when a hairdresser applies highlights, she paints on the slower-acting formula first on the perimeter because that's where the goo sits on your hair the longest. She works her way around your head, applying the faster-acting agent last and somehow your hair magically ends up the perfect matching color. Using the same technique, I approached my one-skillet recipe in the limited time given at the cook-off. Ingredients that require the least heat and longest cook time are on the perimeter of the pan while the hottest center spot is reserved for the heartier ingredients. That way the food's all evenly cooked and hot for the judges at the closing bell."

"That's a cute story, Sherry. Nice that you can get your inspiration from the unlikeliest of places. I'm being told in my ear it's time for a commercial break, during which we'll open the phone lines. So please call in with your questions and comments for Sherry Oliveri, Augustin's premier cooking contester. She will be here for the next twenty minutes." Kayson clicked a button and turned a knob, and the show went to commercial. He removed his headset and placed it next to the trophy. "Keep your eye on that light. When it turns green, we're back on the air." He pointed to the top of the console, where a light shone red.

"Why did you have to start the conversation on a sour note? That comment about contests being overdone?" Sherry asked.

"Don't pay any attention to me. I'm having a bit

of fun. No harm meant. You held your own and then some. I admire that. Lights on, we have five seconds before air." Kayson replaced his headphones. "Welcome back to *Bites*, my weekly segment covering all things food. Sherry Oliveri, home cook extraordinaire, is in studio with us sharing her secrets to devising recipes that win cash and valuable prizes." The tip of Kayson's head, accented with a broad grin, sent Sherry's posture snapping backward a fraction. She pursed her lips in an effort to suppress a return smile but was unsuccessful.

"We have a caller. Good morning, you're on air with Kayson and Sherry. To whom am I speaking?"

"Hi, I'm Marla Barras, and I'm here with my dad, Erno Oliveri. Hi, Sherry."

"That's my sister. Marla, I didn't know you were coming to town. Is everything all right? Is Dad okay?" Sherry leaned in, elbows planted on the table.

"Everything's great. Thought I'd make a surprise appearance for Dad's birthday. Why didn't you tell us you were going to be on *Bites*? Say something, Dad."

"Hi, sweetie." Erno's voice was at a near shout. "I didn't even know you were back from Florida."

"She can hear you, Dad. You don't have to yell." Marla giggled. "Kayson, I wanted to share that Sherry has been the family's best cook since I can remember, and she's even tried to mentor me in cooking contesting. I live in Oklahoma now and work on our family's ranch so my time in the kitchen is limited, but her encouragement got me to the finals of a cook-off last year so, if I can get there, everyone has a chance."

"That's some testimonial from Sherry's sister. Remember, Marla's the competitive one." Kayson winked at Sherry.

"Thanks for calling in, Marla and Dad. I hope I see you both later. How long are you staying, Marla?"

"I'm leaving tomorrow," Marla answered. "Call me when you're done over there, or I can meet you at the Ruggery. Bye, bye."

Kayson clicked a button on the console. "We have another caller. Incendio. I hope I'm pronouncing that correctly. Very interesting name. You know, I'm somewhat of a student of names and their origins. Means fire, if I'm not mistaken. Incendio, you must have a hot topic question or burning comment."

The man on the line coughed. Sherry cringed.

"Good stuff, Mr. Bradshaw. Yes, I'd like to ask Ms. Oliveri which one of her recipes is her favorite to prepare."

Kayson hummed a descending scale. "I'd like to know that too. Maybe Sherry would be willing to prepare that recipe for me at some point."

"After all these years competing, I can safely say my favorite recipe to prepare is always the last one I won a contest with. The winning recipe holds a special place in my heart until the next one comes along and bumps the old recipe off its pedestal. Plus, I've most likely practiced the darn thing so many times I can go through the prep steps in my sleep. On the other hand, I can get tired eating the same recipe over and over. I've been known to knock on my neighbor's door and hand her dinner at five minutes to six without any warning if I've sampled the darn thing too many times."

Kayson's waving hand caught Sherry's eye. "Sorry to interrupt, Sherry, but I'm sure you can hear my producer trying to break in with news."

Sherry mouthed, "Oops."

The studio went quiet as Kayson's hand hovered over the console. He poked the flashing purple light. Sherry scooted back in her chair and crossed her legs.

"We interrupt your regularly scheduled programming with breaking news. Police have released information of a woman's body discovered on the grounds of the Augustin Community Garden early this morning. Positive identification has been made as Augustin resident Poppy Robinson. Her next of kin have been notified. Further details are pending while the investigation is underway. Stay tuned for updates. You will now be returned to current programming." With a click and a squeal, the deep voice dissolved.

Sherry rubbed her bare arms to smooth the goose bumps that sprouted halfway through the newsflash. "Oh my God, Poppy."

"You okay, Sherry? Was the deceased an acquaintance of yours?" Kayson asked. "Ladies and gentlemen, bear with us as Sherry collects her thoughts."

Sherry put her hand over the mic. "I didn't know her well, but yes, she was an acquaintance."

"Seems Sherry knew the deceased woman. I am sorry for your loss." Kayson lifted his palms skyward as the producer asked them in their earpieces if they were able to continue.

"Poppy is, was, a member of the Augustin Community Garden board, as am I, so we have spent time together at meetings and out in the field. But I didn't know her beyond that. My deepest sympathy goes out to her family."

Kayson punched another button. "My deepest sympathy to the family, also." Kayson held his gaze on Sherry until she shifted in her seat. "Are you okay to finish out the interview?"

"I'm fine to continue if we have any more callers," Sherry whispered.

"We will forge ahead. Live radio can certainly be unpredictable. The midday news will have more details forthcoming. We'll take a right turn here and answer another call. Good morning. To whom might I be speaking?"

"Good morning. This is"—the caller paused—"Charlotte from Augustin. I wanted to know what Sherry thinks is the ingredient du jour. If maple syrup is out, what's in?"

"Hello, Charlotte. Without hesitation, I'd say anything fermented. Kimchi, which is fermented cabbage, is a fantastic addition to soups, stir fries, and salads, and even makes a great hamburger topping. Or if kimchi isn't your thing, try sauerkraut. Both are really good for you in many ways. A little tangy and pungent, but not overwhelming. For some, an acquired taste that takes some getting used to. Use either sparingly and enjoy how they complement whatever they're served with."

"I have that in common with fermented food," Kayson added with a snicker. "Sometimes I come on a bit strong, but, hopefully, I grow into an acquired taste." He pushed the button again. "Welcome to *Bites*. Who do we have on the line?"

"Hi. I wanted to tell Sherry I'm a huge fan. If I could travel to all your cook-offs, I would. Keep up the good work."

"Thanks. I'm sorry, I didn't get your name."

"I also wanted to say, as much as I feel it's bad karma to speak poorly of the dead, that bitter woman, Poppy Robinson, had it coming to her." With that the caller hung up.

"Well, that was harsh." Kayson sighed. "We have one last caller I'm told as we near the top of the hour. Welcome to *Bites*. Please, give us your name."

"Hi, my name is Camilla. Sherry, I've seen you at the grocery store."

Sherry waited for the next sentence, which never came. "Not surprisingly, I consider the grocery store my second home." She chuckled. "Come say hi to me next time."

"The last time I saw you there you were eyeballing the different olives in the olive bar," the caller explained.

"That definitely sounds like something I would do." Sherry snickered. "I was probably contemplating the subtleties of using green olives versus capers in my tartar sauce. I'm sure I looked pretty silly, but I can spend countless hours studying my ingredient choices."

Across the table, Kayson's shoulders rose and fell with silent amusement.

"I would never want to bother you, but I always try to get a look at what you're buying. I think I may try a cook-off one day if I can get my courage up. You've inspired me. And I'm sorry that last caller was so harsh. I knew Poppy Robinson and, while she was no charmer, no one deserves to die before they're good and ready. I'm assuming, since she was only in her forties, she wasn't ready. But I would say it wouldn't have killed her to be nicer to her fellow man while she had her time here on Earth. One day at Vinnie's Deli, as I was parking my car, she knocked on my window and told me people who park over the line, like apparently I had that day, should do community service garbage pickup as a penalty. I thought that was uncalled for and vowed if I saw her again, I'd challenge her to admit she'd never missed the mark when pulling her car in."

"Thanks for saying I inspire you, Camilla. That means a lot to me. Hard for me to comment on Poppy until I collect my thoughts. Thanks for calling in."

"Must feel good to have so many admirers. Food really is the universal glue that binds everyone together. Food is love, one bite at a time. Folks, this is a good place to put the segment to bed. Sherry Oliveri, I have thoroughly enjoyed our time together and know the listening audience has too."

"Thank you, Kayson. I've had a very nice time talking to your listeners." Sherry smiled at the man across the console.

"Stay tuned for news, traffic, and weather, and thanks for listening to *Bites*. Join us again next week." Kayson removed his headphones and Sherry followed suit. He reached across the console and lifted the trophy. "I'll take you back to the lobby." Kayson paused and studied the statue. "I was serious about sharing a meal, if I'm able to convince you. I could show you the softer side of Kayson Bradshaw."

"I don't know. Maybe." Sherry picked up her purse and extended her hand toward her trophy.

Chapter Three

Sherry trotted from her car to the Ruggery's back door. Her hand slipped off the knob on the first turn. She regripped and the wooden door's ancient hinges released, but not without screeching complaints. She made her way through the break room, past the storage room, and down the narrow hallway. As she entered the store's showroom, Marla, Erno, and Amber applauded.

"Hi, everyone. Thank you, thank you. You are too kind." Sherry bowed at the waist.

"I knew those salmon cakes would win," Erno stated.

"They were crab cakes, Dad." Sherry sighed. "But I appreciate your vote of confidence. How is everything going here? Thank you so much for watching Chutney while I was gone, Amber."

"Everything is fine, and you're most welcome. Chutney and Bean had a great time." Amber peered around the room. "For a senior dog, your guy is full of energy. They're here somewhere."

Sherry joined the search for the pair of pint-size pups. "I thought my faithful companion would greet me at the door. Jack Russells continually have to prove, despite their size, they're the keeper of the gate."

"Last I saw him, he had chased Bean into the supply closet. Might be nap time for them now. I'll go check." Amber sauntered to the back of the store.

"Hello to you, Marla." Sherry stepped up to her sister and shared a hug. "A surprise visit for Dad's birthday is the best present, right, Dad? Are we all going out to dinner?"

"You're the one with the surprise. Why didn't you tell someone you'd be on the radio this morning? We had to find out from your neighbor Eileen, who called Dad the minute she heard your name announced as an upcoming guest." Marla wagged her finger at her sister.

"Sorry. I got in just before dinner and I was so exhausted my brain shut down. I RSVP'd the request to appear and then it was lights out for me. Are we on for dinner tonight?"

"Apparently Dad has other plans. So, if you're free, you could be my dinner date." Marla pursed her lips.

Erno scuffed his loafer across the wooden floor. "I'm sorry, girls. I made plans before I knew Marla would be here."

"Wait. Didn't we make plans to celebrate your birthday tonight before I left for Florida?" Sherry asked.

The front door burst open. Chutney and Bean

scampered in from the back room like a canine tsunami. Once their legs stiffened to a halt, they continued to slide across the smooth floor until finally coming to rest at the feet of the three who'd entered the store. Frances Dumont and Ruth Gadabee crouched to pet the furry welcome wagon. Bev Van Ardan remained upright.

"Never gets old receiving such an enthusiastic canine reception." Frances groaned as she straightened up. "I do wish these two were a little taller, though. Say, standard poodle height. That way I wouldn't have to dip my knees to pet them. It's a long way down and a longer way back up." The tall woman in the floral day dress adjusted her handbag until it rested high on her forearm. She handed Sherry's father a jar of Dumont Farm Perfect Storm pickles accessorized with a curly ribbon tied around the lid. "Happy birthday, Erno. You're so lucky to have your lovely daughters here on your special day. Do they want to join us this evening?"

"Such a nice offer, Frances, but I think Marla and I will have a quiet dinner together." Sherry checked Marla's expression for her approval.

"That's right. I'm heading back to Oklahoma in the morning, so I think I'd like to catch up with my sister tonight," Marla added. "Where are you all eating?"

Bev Van Ardan stepped forward. "We've been invited to Mayor Obermeyer's." She cocked her head and the silk scarf around her neck shimmered as it caught air. "He has some very important business to discuss and has sought out our valuable opinions on the matter. But before we get into that, what was all that commotion about a local woman named Poppy Robinson and her death that cast a shadow on your appearance on WAUG. I regret I wasn't able to listen in, but, on my way over here, my driver mentioned some callers got a bit testy?"

"A few of the callers were a bit heated. Bev, you should have been listening to the interview. That way you wouldn't have to rely on others' misguided hearsay. Although, I admit, we almost missed the interview ourselves because one Sherry Oliveri didn't feel the need to inform her own family she was to be on the show. Thank goodness for Sherry's neighbor Eileen. You will thank her for us again, won't you?" Ruth Gadabee spoke softly. "Bev, my dear, let me say something, and I hope you don't take this the wrong way. You've really only been part of the community for about a year now and you may not understand the mentality of an Augustinian. We are a passionate group of citizens who band together when we have a united cause."

Bev released a note of indignity. "What are you getting at?"

"I agree with you, Ruth," Frances stated. "Bev, since you and Erik brought your MediaPie Corporation into town to acquire Channel Twelve television, you've been a wonderful addition to the fabric of the town, but let's face facts. You still commute from your penthouse in New York to lunch with us, so you can't claim you know what makes this town tick until you settle here. Ruth and I have roots that go back so far I can remember she was the first person to have a television in town. I was so proud, then, to call her my best friend. Remember that, dear?"

"Of course, Frances." Ruth squinched up her forehead. "Do you think the television's why we became best friends?"

"That's neither here nor there," Frances stated. "Point is, our friendship is as mature and rock solid as the Grand Canyon because this town nurtures togetherness."

Bev adjusted her scarf and set her shoulders square. "What does any of this have to do with what went on today during Sherry's interview? And, may I add, you're making me out to be some sort of alien creature from another planet. I may not be the Pickle Maven of Augustin as you're known, Frances, or the matriarch of one of the oldest families in town, like you Ruth, not to mention the girlfriend of the owner of one of the oldest businesses in town . . ." Bev winked at Erno. "But I'm as close to being a part of Augustin as can be. What does any of this have to do with why there was a dispute during Sherry's radio interview?"

"I'll answer that." Ruth used her fingertips to fluff her chin-length, graying hair. An entire section moved in unison, abundant hair spray presumably providing the adhesive. "Breaking news interrupted the interview. As you said, Poppy Robinson was found dead in the Augustin Community Garden."

"I'm so sorry. Her name sounds awfully familiar. I wonder if she's had dealings with Erik and Media-Pie. I can't put my finger on where I've heard the name before. Did you all know her?" Bev questioned.

"We knew her all right. That's where the contro-versy comes in." Frances's tone was sour. "I'll give you an example of the woman's character. Poppy was a fair bit younger than Ruth and I, but that didn't stop her disrespecting us by denying our ap-plication for a Community Garden bed the year she established the communal plots. When Ruth talks about the collective mind-set of the town's res-idents, Poppy's denial strikes a chord. We all watch out for one another. The foundation of the Com-munity Garden is neighbor helping neighbor, and she abused her authority. We don't judge unfairly and exclude."

Sherry put her hand up to her mouth to mask a smirk.

"Please, Frances. If you and Ruth were any more judgmental, you two would be nominated for the Supreme Court," Bev stated.

"Why would you need a bed at the Community Garden?" Sherry asked. "You both have plenty of property for gardens of your own, not to mention a working farm where the Dumonts produce the county's best pickles under Frances's watchful eye."

Frances didn't miss a beat. "The state's best pickles, dear."

"Agreed. It's not about what women in our posi-tion need, it's about what we deserve." Ruth trans-ferred her vintage purse from one forearm to the other. "To be part of a movement and she inten-tionally excluded us. When we demanded an expla-nation, Poppy's response was, 'This is something that can't be bought into. Donations are encour-aged, though.' That stung. I, for one, was on the side of a few of the more insistent callers who claimed Poppy was, shall we say, difficult."

"She's rubbed many people the wrong way," Frances added. "Take my friend's daughter, Hildie Bulte, for example. When she and Poppy were fresh out of college, sorority sisters mind you, Hildie applied for work at Poppy's father's company, Robinson Investments. Hildie interviewed and was all but guaranteed the job. In the twelfth hour, Poppy went to her father and nixed the offer. Guess who got the job instead? Yes, Poppy. She seems to have left a trail of destruction in her wake most of her life."

Marla scoffed. "I'm sure Poppy was the better person for the job and that you're not seeing both sides of the big picture. Hilde Bulte is a lovely woman. I've been in her store, but I wouldn't hire her to watch over a large sum of cash either. Have you seen her new face-lift? I ran into her at the drugstore on my way here, and she was nearly unrecognizable, and not in a good way. I mean, whoever she paid a fortune to rejuvenate her looks got away with murder. What a waste of money."

"Hildie did okay for herself after Poppy ripped the job opportunity out from underneath her. She went on to meet her husband, Otto, and they're co-owners of Bulte Bedtime Tails, a dog and cat sleep cushion emporium. I'm sure they have to hire a team of bean counters to watch over their mountain of cash now. The cost of that face-lift is a drop in the bucket compared to the couple's his and hers Teslas they motor around in. When one door closes, another opens," Frances said. "It's a safe bet to wager Hildie wasn't one of the disgruntled callers this morning."

"Okay, bad example, but I overheard a couple behind me at the checkout line at Au Natural market comparing rumors Poppy had plans to pull her funding of Augustin's animal shelter if the organization wasn't renamed after her. They claimed she's also been seen taking more than one free sample at the grocery store, and they think she parked her car in a handicap spot without a sticker," Ruth added. "Too bad the woman who called in and said Poppy harassed her for parking over the line didn't know that."

Bev pinched her lips. "The couple should take a closer look at the parking signs before they label her a parking pirate. Au Natural has a number of select spots designated for energy efficient cars right up front next to the handicapped spots. Doesn't she drive a hybrid?"

"And, if taking more than one free sample is a major infraction, handcuff me right now and throw away the key." Erno extended his wrists. "Guilty as charged."

Bev shook her head. "If all those accusations are true, I can understand why callers who knew that Poppy woman would vent, but it seems a bit heartless so soon after the body cooled. That's what happens when you open up a radio show to callers. You get opinions from people who don't have to show their faces. Were all the callers living saintly lives? I dare say most likely not. Don't throw stones if you live in a crystal house."

"So that's what your driver was referring to when

he said things got heated during the interview," Marla added. "I didn't hear you give away any of your top secret recipes, Sherry."

"You didn't and you won't," Sherry answered.

Erno tsked his tongue on the roof of his mouth. "You never should, sweetie. As I like to say, close the garden gate before a weasel gets in."

"I think I know what you mean, Erno," Amber remarked.

"I've never heard you say that, Dad. Have you, Marla?" Sherry shot a sideways glance at her sister, who subtly shook her head.

"Speaking of top secret recipes, at least Poppy Robinson's death had nothing to do with a cook-off. Right, Sherry?" Marla's gaze cross-examined Sherry. "It didn't, did it?"

"Don't even suggest such a thing. I feel bad enough it was my fault Poppy's death was discussed on-air after the breaking news was reported. Talk of the woman's death spilled over to the interview when I made the mistake of saying I knew her. I didn't exactly know her. I only worked alongside her for a relatively short while. Hard to guess whether her health was poor or some accident occurred that night. We'll have to wait and see what the news is on cause of death."

"What was she like to work with?" Bev asked.

"Poppy had strong opinions and shared them at our board meetings. She had a very specific way she wanted things done in the garden, and she let everyone know any deviation from her ways wouldn't be tolerated. For example, she only allowed a certain type of hand shovel to be used in the raised garden beds because she felt the wrong size or brand would damage the cedar planks that contained the dirt. At one board meeting, she brought in a tall shovel she'd confiscated from a gardener and waved it in front of us as she made her point. She stated, in no uncertain terms, she would take away the member's privileges and banish him from the grounds for a full season."

"Sounds more like a dictatorship than a democracy," Erno scoffed. "Goes to show, don't dig in the dirt if you don't want to find worms."

"May the poor woman rest in peace. That's what I say." Sherry leaned down and picked up Chutney as he sniffed her pant leg. "You never told us what the dinner meeting with Mayor Obermeyer is all about. Who wants to spill the beans?"

Frances unlatched her purse and unfurled a colorful flyer. "I'll spoon out the beans."

"The correct term is spill the beans, dear, not spoon out the beans," Ruth corrected. "So, spill away."

Frances waved the flyer. "This is a mock-up of the brochure for Augustin's proposed Fourth of July celebration. Right now, all we have are photos of fireworks from last year." She pointed to the inside third of the tri-fold. "This entire blank section will be printed with an enticing description of the newly revamped festivities that will draw paying crowds from near and far to fill the town's coffers with revenue that's been seeping in Hillsboro's direction over the last couple of years as Augustin's Independence Day celebration has fizzled out. What hasn't been decided is what the revamped festivities will consist of. So, tonight, the planning committee, on which we sit, is having a brainstorming session to come up with a captivating concept."

"That's quite flattering the mayor chose you four to come up with an idea. I'm impressed," Sherry remarked.

"The man recognizes our value to the fabric of Augustin." Frances raised her chin high.

"I'll take credit for forming the alliance," Bev added. "Cooper and I have mutual interests now that my husband's company, MediaPie, has become a presence on local cable. Cooper's possible bid for mayoral reelection is coming up in the fall, and he has reached out to my Erik for airtime on Channel Twelve. Erik, of course, has to give all candidates equal visibility, but some can be more equal than others. In return, you never know when a permit or ordinance may be needed for our expanding business entities. Change doesn't come without a struggle in Augustin, we've discovered. Must have something to do with the tight fabric. I mean, what other town on the East Coast still has a day dedicated to well water? Maybe two houses in the entire county still use well water. Can be quite useful to have friends in relatively high places so we can move this town into the new millennium."

Ruth scowled. Marla tapped Sherry's ankle with the toe of her sneaker.

"Yes, thank you for your concern. Bev's bringing the rest of us along for the ride because she's more of a nouveau honorary citizen, while the rest of our family trees can be traced back to the onion farmers who settled this scenic coastal town hundreds of years ago. Cut us and we bleed Augustin onion juice." Frances laughed.

"A bit dramatic, dear," Ruth said to her taller friend. "Any ideas for making Augustin the best destination to spend the Fourth, you young gals? We're interested in attracting back your age group." Ruth paused. "Your peers, although primarily the ones with husbands and children especially."

Sherry and Amber exchanged glances.

Marla shook her head. "I won't be able to attend, but I would think amping up the fireworks show is the first step. If they're anything like they were when I was here two years ago, the show could use a hit of adrenaline. That show lasted a good twelve minutes and there was more dead air of anticipation between rockets than there were actual aerial bursts of color. There were so many intervals where the audience, thinking the show was over, applauded and packed up their picnic baskets, only to have another round begin minutes later. Kind of a hurry up and wait situation. Kids were whining, parents had headaches, and the rest of us drank too much. The town can do better, I'm sure."

"I have an idea," Amber remarked, "that may or may not be well received. How about a cook-off preceding overhauled fireworks? Who doesn't love a live cooking contest on a beautiful summer evening? Sherry can attest to their popularity. I could hear the excitement in the callers' voices this morning when they knew they were talking to such a decorated competitive cook. She's sparked a lot of interest in food sport, why not have one in the hometown of the goat."

"Goat? Isn't that a bit harsh, Amber?" Erno asked.

"G-O-A-T stands for greatest of all time." Amber giggled.

"A cook-off could be a nice idea except for one sticking point. No one would want to enter if they knew Sherry was in the contest. Let's face that reality," Frances said.

Amber nodded. "I was thinking more along the lines of Sherry designing and organizing the event. She's an expert, wouldn't you all agree?"

"Where can I hide for the next couple of months? By then, the idea will have blown over."

"I think you've come up with a fantastic idea. Sherry, don't deny your fans their fondest wish. This is your time to shine. Who wouldn't love a local cook-off down at the Town Beach pavilion with the smell of salt water and libations wafting on the warm July breezes? The event doesn't have to be as elaborate as your national extravaganzas. The fundamental requirements are a fun theme, alluring prizes, and judges who know what they're doing. What do you say, Sher? Can we run Amber's suggestion by Mayor Obermeyer?" Erno interlaced his fingers in the prayer position and posed them in front of his face.

Sherry lowered her head. "I was looking forward to a little free time before the summer, but I guess that's not going to happen. Remember, guys, not only do I have my hours here at the Ruggery, I'm volunteering at the garden, and I've taken on editorship of the municipal newsletter, the *Augustin Sound*. All those part-time jobs add up to one full-time commitment. Plus Amber, who seems to have become my time management director, has me signed up for a doubles tennis league."

Marla pumped her fist. "That sounds like a yes to me. Quick, guys, get out of here before she changes her mind." Marla rotated her father around by his shoulders and gently pushed him toward the door. "And have a wonderful birthday, Dad. Thanks for putting me up last night. I'll take a bed at Sherry's tonight, if that's okay with her. But I'll see you in the morning, before I head to the airport."

"Brilliant," Bev added.

"Great work, Amber," Ruth tacked on.

"We'll keep you posted on the mayor's reaction. Erno, we will be by your place later to pick you up," Frances said as she, Ruth, and Bev exited the Ruggery.

Chutney and Bean jumped down from their owners' arms and scampered under the hooking demonstration table, their preferred play area.

Amber slid her arm around Sherry's back. "I put you on the spot and now I feel guilty."

"No worries. I'm a bit panicked because I know all there is to know about competing in cook-offs, but putting one on and having the event be a success is another story. If the mayor likes the idea and gives the go-ahead, I'll be entering uncharted waters."

The antique brass bell mounted on the doorframe tinkled as the front door brushed against the metal. In sauntered two men, one in a moss-green baseball jacket and khakis, sporting a weathered, wide-brimmed hat, and the other undeniably attractive in an overeducated go-getter sort of way.

Sherry's eyes widened. "Ray. Detective Diamond. This is an unexpected surprise."

Chapter Four

Detective Bease removed his hat and tucked his signature accessory under his arm. He held a notepad in the other hand. Detective Diamond remained a step behind.

"Hello, Sherry. Mr. Oliveri. Amber. It's been a while." Ray embellished each name with dip of his head.

Sherry's traveling gaze stalled on Ray's face, which was clean-shaven last she'd laid eyes on him. A reddish-brown mustache lay across his upper lip. She pointed in her sister's direction. "You remember my sister, Marla? She's in from Oklahoma for my dad's birthday, although the timing of her surprise visit is a little off."

Ray glanced in Marla's direction. "Yep. Nice to see you too, Marla. Everyone here should know Detective Cody Diamond."

Sherry was unnerved by the fact Cody's eyes were shielded by mirrored aviator sunglasses camouflaging the direction of his sight. The younger detective, dressed in a mini-me version of Bease's outfit, only crisper and wrinkle-free, remained stone-faced.

"Diamond was my partner during the OrgaNick's Cook-off murder investigation. He's shadowing me because he's been named Criminal Intelligence Analyst Supervisor, and I am currently his pet project."

Cody raised his sunglasses and laid them to rest in his wavy blond hair. Cody's steely guise softened. "Promoted to, not named."

"Right, promoted." Ray opened his notepad and lifted it to eye level. "Seems my insistence on gathering information the old-fashioned way is rubbing my commanders the wrong way. Diamond's been assigned to observe me in order to assess the situation." Ray wrestled a pen from his blazer's breast pocket. "Waste of time, in my opinion. My way gets the job done. If I have to enter the information into a computer I do, but my notepad has never let me down by running out of battery at the most inconvenient time. You, of all people, should agree, right, Sherry?"

Cody's lips parted, unveiling gleaming white teeth. "Information needs to be shared in a timely fashion to as many channels, departments, and personnel involved as possible. Tablets get that job done, wouldn't you agree?"

Sherry's cheeks warmed. "Don't put me in the middle of this. I've got my own problems to sort out. I need to clone myself to get all my jobs done."

"Can't help you there." Cody carried his computer tablet to the checkout table and held the machine inches above the flat surface. "May I put this here?"

Sherry sidestepped the group and met Cody at the table. "Of course. But what exactly are you two here for?"

Ray pitched his notepad open with the ease of a trained chef flipping a skillet omelet with one flick of the wrist. "A woman's body was found last night at the Augustin Community Garden."

"Poppy Robinson." Sherry shook her head. "Has any cause of death been pinned down yet? She seemed the picture of health last time I saw her. I expect you're going to say cause of death was heart attack, unless there was a bizarre accident at the garden, but I can't imagine what that could have been." Her words were delivered with increasing speed until she noticed both detectives puffed out their cheeks. "Oh no. Please don't say what I don't want to hear."

"Poppy Robinson was murdered." Cody delivered the news, blanketing Sherry's plea.

"Murder? Poppy Robinson was murdered?" Sherry's heart knocked hard. "How do they know it was murder? I mean, I realize you guys know what you're doing, you're the trained experts, but are you sure?"

Ray turned back the pages of his notepad. "A shovel was alongside the body in the raised garden bed she was discovered in. The trauma to her head was consistent with having received blunt force from the blade of the tool. There was a subtle indentation in the thick metal of the shovel head, so she really got whacked. Very hard to bend that grade of steel. Whoever did this took the time to square her body up perfectly within the bed's frame with the shovel parallel to her. Coroner's report confirms the findings. So, yes, with certainty, I can say Poppy Robinson was murdered."

Sherry alternated her gaze between the two detectives in short bursts. "This is going to sound so selfish, like I don't care about the woman's death, but because of past circumstances, I want to state I wasn't even in Connecticut until late afternoon. After that, I was nowhere in the vicinity of the Community Garden."

"Take it easy. No one's making accusations. We're only in the fact-gathering portion of the investigation. For starters, we toss the net wide to see what we can snare. Seems your name is on a short list of board members, of whom Ms. Robinson is the chairwoman, and I'd like to ask you a few questions to assess the woman's character." The tip of Ray's pen was poised to scratch across a page. "Did Ms. Robinson handpick you to work with her?"

The detective had yet to write down a word, while Cody Diamond was tapping on the tablet, as if being paid by the letter.

Sherry pointed to Ray's pen. "Is that New Jersey? I see blueberries enameled on the barrel. Last time we spoke, you had almost completed your fifty-state pen collection."

Ray waved the pen. "Don't tell New Jersey, but Michigan thinks they're the blueberry capital of the United States. New Jersey would probably sport a tomato. You'd think I'd have that one by now, the state being so close. Sometimes the things closest to you are the ones you take for granted."

"Huh, well, anyway, back to your question. Poppy

didn't handpick me. My friend Karenna Kingsley recommended me. She's the daughter of Poppy's father's secretary. I was helping Karenna with her backyard garden, and she mentioned her cleaning lady lived in an apartment with no access to a yard but always boasted she grew the most wonderful vegetables. I asked how that could possibly be, and her answer was my introduction to the Augustin Community Garden. I'd probably passed the property a million times driving around town without ever giving the place a second thought. When I found out their mission statement was to provide growing space and gardening education to those who lacked either or both, along with providing food to the town's food bank, I was interested in volunteering as quickly as they would accept me. I didn't meet Poppy until the first meeting I attended, back in the summer. She gives her fellow board members the right to interview applicants, and she does the ultimate choosing without ever having a face-to-face meeting. She says a better method is letting your application speak for itself. Once accepted, by the time you attend the first meeting, you've filled out reams of paperwork selling your qualifications. If you misrepresented yourself, she'd quickly make you regret the faux pas. That was a guarantee."

Cody looked up. "Think about the members of the garden. Was there anyone in particular you'd single out who had a beef with Ms. Robinson? Or was there anyone on the board you believe would murder the woman?"

"Diamond. Slow down. Let the woman think clearly without pressure."

Cody lifted his hands and flexed his fingers. He softened his tone. "Do you have an answer to my question? Was there anyone on the board or a garden member who may have had a reason to want Poppy Robinson dead?"

"On one hand, I can't think of a soul. She ran the meetings with an iron fist, often not letting others express their opinions without being challenged constantly. It's true. I can think of more than one occasion where someone abruptly walked out, stating they weren't given the floor so why should they stay, but the proceedings never got heated to the point of violence, thank goodness."

"Sounds like Ms. Robinson wasn't there to make friends, though, would you agree with that?" Ray asked.

"Making friends wasn't a priority," Sherry answered.

Cody typed furiously. "Okay, then, if you can't pinpoint an enemy, who do you think was her strongest ally?"

"I remember she referred to her father, Rohan, quite often," Sherry suggested.

"Deceased father," Ray interjected.

"Yes, deceased but his presence lingered. She reminded the board often that his wish was the land he bequeathed to his three children be used as a garden, with the purpose of enriching a segment of the town that wouldn't otherwise get firsthand knowledge of planting, nurturing, and harvesting their own food. She said, 'Rohan wouldn't want that' or 'Rohan's wishes are what's most important.' Kind of hard having a ghost run the show, but that's what it felt like. I'm making her sound kind of nutty, but I'm telling you the truth."

"Did you ever think of quitting?" Cody asked. "I mean, yours is a volunteer position. Why would you submerge yourself in her idea of how to please her father postmortem for zero compensation? Seems like the garden was more of a self-serving tool for her than a benefit to the town."

Marla walked around the checkout table and eyed Cody's computer screen. He, not too subtly, adjusted his posture, shrouding the device. Marla huffed and returned to her sister.

"I was never on her bad side. Despite all Poppy's foibles, she was determined to stick to the mission statement, and I liked that. Her style was abrasive, but so far, her approach to things hadn't undermined my confidence in the organization. I made a mental decision to stick the position out through one full year. I think I have a lot to offer the garden's education program. I was hoping to give some cooking demonstrations and seed-saving seminars, too, when the harvest begins next fall."

Erno approached Sherry and put his arm around her shoulders. "That's my girl. I didn't raise a quitter."

"The garden board is very small. There are only six of us, now five, and each is doing the work out of the kindness of their heart. You're going to have to look somewhere else for the murderer. That person isn't on the board, I would stake my life on that." Sherry hummed and reconsidered. "Bad choice of words. But you understand what I mean. I'm so sorry for the Robinson family. Is there anything I can do for them? I know she has two siblings who co-own the piece of property the garden sits on, but I've never met them."

Sherry watched as Ray and Cody exchanged glances. Cody picked up his computer, and Ray closed his notepad. "I'm sure they would appreciate flowers or, better yet, a casserole at this time of grief. Isn't that what people do?"

Sherry shrugged her shoulders. "That's a nice gesture. I'll do that. I'm sorry I can't provide much useful information."

"Useful is a relative term." Cody lowered his sunglasses over his eyes.

Sherry added, "There was one more thing I forgot to mention. Rumors have been swirling that Poppy had done an about-face and decided to sell the land the Community Garden sits on. You can imagine there's opposition to that idea. So many people have committed time and resources to making the garden a success, and if she pulls the plug, everything disappears in a nanosecond, leaving a lot of disappointed members and volunteers. She never made any formal announcement at our meetings, but the anticipation that the rumors were true has some on edge."

Cody parked himself next to Ray. "Interesting."

Ray dipped his head, put on his hat, and pulled the door open. "Thank you for your time. I'll be in touch." He closed the door behind him as he followed Cody out of the store.

"If you have things under control here, I might head home and take a rest before dinner. Today's my birthday, you know, so I deserve the afternoon off." Erno chuckled.

"No need to remind me, Dad. Every year we consider the entire month of March your birthday. Marla and I might go back to my place, too, if that's okay, Amber. I don't know about Marla, but I could use some downtime. You're invited to join us for an early dinner. All this talk of murder is dredging up some bad memories and my stomach acid is churning. The saving grace is I'm many, many steps removed from being involved in any aspect of Poppy's murder. See you later, Dad, and happy birthday."

Her father strutted out the front door, whistling a tune she couldn't identify.

Amber strolled up beside her coworker. "Wasn't too long ago you helped Detective Bease track down the murderer of Channel Twelve's young anchor. You really showed some sleuthing talents when your dad became the main suspect from the get-go, and you took matters into your own hands to direct the investigation the right way. Was that the last time you had any contact with Detective Bease?"

"Not exactly the last time. Whatever you do, don't remind Ray about my so-called sleuthing. The subject's a touchy one with him because I found myself deeply involved in one investigation, and then a second. I'm sure he was hoping to be rid of me after the OrgaNick's Cook-off murder investigation concluded. Who would believe there would be another so soon after. Two cook-offs, two murders. Ray certainly didn't heap a ton of thanks on me for my efforts that nearly got me killed. On the contrary, he doled out 'stay out of the sleuthing business' warnings more often than I dole out snick-erdoodles at Christmastime."

"You've seen him since all that settled down?"

"For a reason I don't want to get into, I owed him a meal and we met up for dinner about a month ago."

"Really?" Marla let the word drag out as if she were singing a song lyric. "Do tell."

"Nothing to report. He was very pleasant company and he ordered the cod with lemon-caper sauce. I had crab cakes, which weren't nearly as good as I can make them, may I add. We talked about his pen collection, his new yoga regimen, and cooking, of course. He's beginning to dabble in recipe creation and asked my advice on a few flavor combinations. That's it. Haven't seen him since." Sherry took a step toward the front door.

"What was all that about the way Bease takes notes?"

"He's a dinosaur, so set in his ways. I admit I was surprised to see Detective Diamond with him with the sole purpose of updating the man to detective two point oh. Ray has always had a strong aversion to incorporating technology into his work. Feels the applied science removes the intuitive street smarts from the equation and that's what he relies on to get the job done. Diamond worked with him throughout the OrgaNick's Cook-off murder investigation and never succeeded in replacing that notepad Ray uses with the shiny new computer tablet issued by his department. If I were a betting woman, I'd put my money on Ray and his notepad to prevail. I'd wager a happy Ray on the police force is more important than a high-tech Ray, but you never know."

The corner of Sherry's mouth lifted. "I meant to give Ray a pen I got in Florida at the cook-off to add to his state pen collection. I know he already has a Florida pen, but I found another I don't think he has yet."

"That's nice of you to think of him while you're in the throes of a cooking battle," Marla said with a rolling lilt.

Amber let out a hum. "You two should get out of here and go do something sisterly. Everything is under control here. There are a few scheduled appointments this afternoon. Mrs. Rosenberg is coming in to choose a blue yarn for her seascape rug and Dorothy Staffenfelder is stopping in to pick up the canvas Erno designed for her next project. It's a gorgeous fall produce cornucopia of cabbages, apples, onions, and squash. She's going to love the design. It may take all spring and summer to complete, but she's up for the task."

"Perfect. We'll be on our way." Sherry rotated before freezing in her tracks. "I almost forgot to pick up the package you said in your email was delivered for me. I'm pretty excited to see if there are more seeds to add to my growing collection. Do you have that handy?"

"Right, one second." Amber trotted to the back of the store and disappeared through the doorway. She returned a moment later, wide-plank floorboards of ancient wood creaking with her every step. "Here you are." She handed Sherry the package.

Sherry studied the front of the brown-paper wrapped box before turning it over. No return address was provided in the top left corner. Sherry's name and address were written in block letters. True to Amber's word, the contents of the box rattled when tipped. The jingle was music to Sherry's ears.

"That's the sweet sound of seeds for the Community Garden. The seeds that come from the strongest and most productive of last season's plants are the highest quality, besides the fact the local gardener donations don't cost a cent and that makes them extra special. I consider them priceless. These'll be much appreciated by the gardeners and the food bank. I'll bring them home and add to the growing collection."

"Amber, I hope you come for dinner so I can say good-bye with a glass of wine in hand." Marla backed toward the door. "Are you set, Sherry?"

"Let me see how tired I am when I close up shop, but I think a meal with good company sounds like an offer I can't refuse," Amber answered. "I'll text you guys."

Chapter Five

Amber clutched the reclaimed wood door's cast-iron knob. Bean was draped across her arm. "Such a good dinner. Thank you again. Marla, always so nice to see you. Have a safe trip back to the ranch and let me know when you're back in Augustin."

"Thanks for coming. I'll see you next time I'm in town." Marla threw Amber a wave.

Amber blew an air kiss and let herself out.

"Your phone's ringing, Sher. I'll grab it. When did you change your ringtone to 'Cheeseburger in Paradise'? The last I heard your phone ring it was playing the song 'American Pie.'" Marla walked from the kitchen to the front hall, phone in hand. "Here you go. I'll tackle the dishes."

"Very perceptive of you. I liked the story behind the Jimmy Buffet song. The lyrics spoke to me. I'll explain after I grab this." Sherry settled herself on the living room couch and clicked the call accept key. "Hello?"

"I'm looking for Sherry Oliveri. Are you her?"

"Yes, hi. Who am I speaking to?"

"Hi, Sherry. I got your name and number from my sister's contact list. My name is Tessa Yates. My sister is Poppy Robinson."

Sherry pulled the phone from her ear and studied the display. The area code was one she recognized from the city. Bev Van Ardan had the same area code.

"I'm so sorry for your loss, Tessa. I didn't know your sister well, but what I knew of her spoke to her love of gardening." Sherry proceeded with caution. "What can I do for you?"

"Thanks, I appreciate that. Sherry, everyone knows you're Augustin's most accomplished cooking contester. I don't even live there, and I'm aware of how many cook-offs and recipe contests you've won. You've been in magazines, on television, and on radio, and if you google, 'Sherry Oliveri, recipe contest,' the results are in the hundreds." Tessa paused.

"You're too kind, thank you."

As Sherry spoke, Marla poked her head through the living room doorway. Sherry flagged her sister down with a fan of her hand. Marla accepted the invite and wedged herself in between her sister and the corner of the couch. Chutney leapt up and secured a spot between the sisters.

Sherry mouthed, "Tessa Yates, Poppy Robinson's sister."

Marla replied softly, "Did you say, 'Hello to Poppy's robot son'? What does that mean?"

Sherry covered the phone. "No. I said, 'Tessa Yates, Poppy Robinson's sister,' is on the phone."

Marla's mouth formed a large O.

Sherry clicked on the speaker setting button.

"All that being said, what I really am interested in are your sleuthing skills. I'm aware you have been instrumental in tracking down two murderers in two different investigations. Come to think of it, how do you find yourself in those situations anyway?"

Sherry's hand went limp and the phone plummeted to the floor. Marla rescued the device and positioned it in front of her sister's face.

"Are you there?" Tessa's voice trembled. "I hope my inquiry isn't too bold."

"Yes. No. Sorry, you took me by surprise."

"What I'm asking is, can you help find the person who took my sister's life? I fear the investigators will move too slowly and this needs to be addressed posthaste. You have a proven track record of success. Soon, when people google Sherry Oliveri, the recipe contest results will be secondary to your investigative prowess."

"Tessa, I have no idea who may have taken your sister's life. I wouldn't even have the foggiest notion where to begin. I can't really do much for you in that department, but I'd like to bake you a casserole if you're having a memorial service in town."

"Only a fool would turn down that delicious proposal. How thoughtful. But the pressing matter is a Detective Ray Bees has been in touch with my brother, Gully, and myself, separately. After a short round of questioning, he gave me the impression Gully is at the top of the suspect list. The detective didn't say as much, but the implication was strong."

Tessa began to whimper. She sniffed a few times. "Are you familiar with Detective Ray Bees?"

Marla nudged Sherry with the point of her elbow.

"The name's pronounced Bease, rhymes with grease, not bees as in honey bees. And, yes, I am," Sherry replied.

"That makes sense. Naming your child Ray Bees is a cruel joke, if you ask me. The detective was pressing me about our family dynamics, particularly the relationship between Gully and Poppy. I'm afraid the truth doesn't do my brother any favors. Poppy was eight years older than Gully, so they weren't terribly close. Their interests were quite different."

Sherry lowered her head. "It's none of my business, but were there difficulties between Poppy and Gully? If not, I don't believe your brother has much to worry about. I know Detective Bease, and he would never rush to judgment without a thorough consideration of all clues, facts, and evidence. As a matter of fact, you're reminding me, his thoroughness can be a bit aggravating. I was the main suspect, for a while, in one of those previous murder investigations, and the speed of light wouldn't have been fast enough to clear my name. But that was a completely different situation."

Tessa's voice brightened. "Is that why you began snooping around on your own for evidence to someone else's guilt? If so, you can surely see my point why I can't sit back and let my brother be falsely accused. You've found a killer before. I have no doubt you can find my sister's."

"That was different," Sherry repeated, strain

present in her voice. "Circumstantial evidence put me at the top of the suspect list. But I knew I didn't poison the judge at my cook-off, and that was a perfect jumping off point for me to start snooping, as you call my attempt to expedite an otherwise tediously slow process. Honestly, I have no idea if your brother, you, or the man on the moon killed your sister because I wasn't there."

"Let me answer your question about the dynamics of Poppy and Gully's relationship. The friction between the two was started by our father, Rohan. No doubt there, Poppy was his favorite. The proof came when Gully and I were excluded from the management board of the land he left us when he passed away. Granted, he did leave his property to all three of us, but not without restrictions. The will states if Gully and I joined the garden board, the legal trust would be broken and the land would be solely Poppy's. I admit Poppy has done nothing to remedy that injustice, but I'm not in the same financial situation as Gully, so I have to sit back and scratch my head over Rohan's decision. He gave Poppy complete control over the purse strings, with the exception of a meager cash inheritance for each of us. He left the bulk of his fortune to various charities, like Last Chance Rescue."

"That's nice he loved giving animals a fighting chance at a long life," Sherry said.

"Not animals. The charity funds the rescue and renovation of statues in various New England locations that have fallen into disrepair and are too expensive for the budget of some towns."

"That's nice too, I suppose."

Tessa's flowing voice slowed to an intense drip. "Luckily, I am in no way dependent on my inheritance to live a comfortable life. Being an acting coach in the city is a very lucrative career."

Sherry tipped the phone toward the light so she could read the time. Marla tapped her sister on the shoulder and gave the "let's speed things up" hand roll gesture.

"Yes, Gully squandered the money he inherited, which irked Poppy to no end. I was hoping she would never utter the phrase Rohan often spoke"— Tessa deepened her voice—" 'I could have predicted that.' Poppy's never been one to camouflage her feelings. The day Gully admitted he was nearly broke, Poppy blurted out those words and you should have seen the look of devastation on my brother's face. What did anyone expect he'd do with any funds that came his way? Gully decided on pursuing his dream of being a competitive rock-wall climber and painter. Not a coincidence the timing of him quitting his new office job came the day after the will was read. Thing is, both of Gully's interests have major start-up and running costs and ultimately not much earning potential, so a lot more cash flowed out than came in."

"Did you tell Detective Bease all these details?"

"For the most part, give or take a few omissions." Tessa's voice softened. "I didn't feel the need to go into detail. He said the session wasn't a formal questioning, merely touching base as a preliminary step in the investigation."

"What leads you to believe Detective Bease even has Gully on the suspect list? Sounds as if you're describing benign family spats. Unless you're skipping a detail, like anger issues or prior arrest records, I personally wouldn't draw the conclusion Gully is guilty from what you've told me."

"Detective Bease filled in a few of the blanks concerning where Poppy's body was discovered. She was found laid out in one of the garden boxes. Next to her was a shovel and under the shovel was a note allegedly from Gully. The note spelled out, in no uncertain terms, that he didn't like the direction Poppy had taken our gift from Rohan. He wrote that if Poppy cared anything about her siblings, she would sell the land and split the profit equally between the three of us. The detective made a point of telling me the note ended with 'You're dead to me. Period. Gully.' "

"That's a bit damning." Sherry's words, intended only for her sister, were spoken with more than the necessary emphasis. She placed a hand over her mouth but the accusatory words had escaped.

"I understand, and I agree, but he didn't kill anyone. I know Gully. He says things out of passion, but they're the passionate words of a free-spirited artist not a killer. What I'm asking you is, can you find the killer and get my brother off the hook? I know you tracked down the killer of Augustin's local TV anchor, I think her name was Carmell Gordy. The police will take too long. Gully's the only family I have left. Please, Sherry. I'm begging you." Tessa garnished her plea with a single sob.

Sherry pinched her eyes shut for an instant. "If I come across anything, I'll call you, but if I were you, I'd leave the investigating to the detective.

He's very good at what he does." Sherry checked her phone screen. "Is this a good number to reach you at? I'll put you in my contact list."

Tessa's tone took on a creamy richness. "Yes. Thank you so much for agreeing. Keep me posted, would you? Good-bye."

"Wait, I didn't agree to anything. Hello? Tessa? Ugh."

Marla shifted her muscular legs toward Sherry's more sinewy ones.

"If she wasn't already an acting coach, I would suggest she look into becoming one. During that phone call she played more characters than Bette Davis in one of her classics."

"Are you really going to help that family after all the things I've heard people say about Poppy? They might *all* be a bunch of crazies." Marla twirled her finger around by her temple.

The corner of Sherry's mouth curled up. One of Marla's strengths was putting things into perspective.

"I feel for Tessa because, when Dad was on the suspect list during the Channel Twelve murder investigation, I'd have done anything to get him off that list pronto. But, for a total stranger? Why would I put myself through that ordeal again?"

Marla stood. "Why did Tessa say Gully was the only family she had left? If her last name isn't Robinson, wouldn't you assume Yates is her married name? Where's her husband?"

"Who knows? What do you say we take a look and see what we can find for an after-dinner snack?"

As they headed to the kitchen, Sherry caught sight of the package she brought home from the

Ruggery resting on her worktable. "I need to cata-
logue these seeds too. Another item for my to-do
list." She carried the box to the kitchen counter.
She pushed it to the side to make way for snack
preparations.

"You're getting a text." Marla left the room and
returned with Sherry's phone. "You're so popular.
That reminds me, I haven't had a chance to ask
you about any new dating prospects. You're always
so evasive on the phone. Face-to-face you have to
give me the full story. There's no escape."

Sherry took the phone from her sister's calloused hands. "You need a manicure."

"What's the point?" Marla presented her ragged-
edged fingernails. "My nails don't stand a chance
against roping a calf, hauling a hay bale, or cor-
ralling a renegade piglet. See? You always manage
to change the subject when I ask about your private life."

The screen on Sherry's phone displayed three
missed texts, each sent in the last few minutes.

"Anything exciting? Not that we want any more
excitement. I think a bit of calm would be preferred." Marla surveyed the contents of the refrigerator. "Definitely a fruit and gelato dessert night.
You're low on much else."

"What did you say?" Sherry willed her gaze off
her phone and over to Marla.

"Gelato. Fruit. Dessert." Marla turned to her sister. "Since you won't tell me anything about your
love life, maybe you can tell me about that text
you're reading. You look like you saw a ghost."

"Three texts, actually. An older text from Dad

says he left his reading glasses at the store. Apparently he can barely text either because most of the words are autocorrected and don't make sense. Listen to what he typed: 'I'm on my way to the major's horse and hope I don't need red smell pants because he can't.' Yikes! I think he meant he's on his way to the mayor's house and hopes he doesn't need to read small print because he can't. I've been interpreting his texts for years now, so I'm getting pretty good at it.

"In the second text a fellow member of the Community Garden board named Romie Green wrote she would be attending the emergency meeting called to discuss the garden's future."

"And the third?"

"I hesitate to mention this one. Don't overreact. The third is a dinner invite from the man who interviewed me at WAUG. I'm not sure we're exactly compatible. You know how first impressions can stay with you?"

"Sure. What was your first impression?"

"Within the first few minutes of meeting, Kayson had given me quite a hard time about cooking contesting and that went over about as well as telling me ovens are electric not gas when I arrive at a cook-off after I've practiced on the latter for weeks. Do I want to spend a couple of social hours with a guy who called cooking competitions overdone? Yes, I agree the contests you see on TV are more game shows than cooking contests, with weird twists and turns to entertain the otherwise easily bored viewing audience. Those aren't the ones I prefer. The ones I choose to compete in are skill-based contests. Live cooking competitions are inherently exciting done in only the simplest of formats."

"Forget the cooking contest for a minute. Let's focus on your potential date with Kayson Bradshaw. Give the guy a chance. If he set the tone one way, and you're not happy, guess what? That can be changed. Like the way you take a tired bland recipe and add your Sherry spin and suddenly the flavor is ramped up to spectacular. Besides, trying to get him to know the real you would give you two something to talk about on your date. How exciting." Marla clapped until Sherry swatted her sister's hands.

"A frightening proposition for the poor guy. He did take the time to write a poem, so that's a check in the 'makes an effort' column."

"A poem? Are you kidding me? Don't tease me. Let me hear what my possible future brother-in-law wrote."

"'A cook is defined as someone who
    prepares
Food using heat, but *you* don't stop there
You burn the competition in every sense
You're there to win, the others have no
    defense
So my offer is a night off from your hot
    oven
Dinner, wine, dessert—one course or a
    dozen
Please say yes and leave your recipes
    behind
Someone else is cooking while you relax
    and dine.'"

"How can you turn the man down after he spent countless hours writing those words?" Marla puckered up and blew the whistle holler Sherry recognized as the way her sister called her hogs in at night. "Let's get down to the nitty-gritty. What does Kayson Bradshaw look like? I'm always curious about radio personalities."

"He's tall, has a nice voice, that sort of thing," Sherry suggested.

"Getting information out of you is like pulling teeth. Maybe it's because your ex-husband, Charlie, is a hard act to follow. I can see why you're not too keen on dating yet. Although, didn't you say Charlie's seeing someone?"

"Charlie does have a very nice girlfriend. They seem like a perfect match. She loves golf as much as he does. He and I are on very good terms, and I'm really happy for him." Sherry measured each word for equal weight, giving them a robotic quality. "After seven years being married to me, he deserves an easygoing girlfriend, and if she's letting him play as much golf as he says he does, she's in that category." Sherry sent a quick tilt of her head toward her shoulder. "You'll have to judge for yourself when it comes to Kayson."

"Fine. Maybe it's too early in the game and you haven't made up your mind about the guy. In case you decide to act, don't you think you should touch up those dark roots? Two-tone hair was so last year. But, wait a minute. You haven't been entirely single since your divorce. Didn't you date Detective Bease?" Marla kicked the refrigerator door shut with her barefoot and carried a box of blackberries and a box of blueberries to the counter.

Sherry's mouth dropped open. A muffled wail escaped. "I didn't date Ray. We went to dinner. Once. Which is exactly the number of times I'll probably go to dinner with Kayson Bradshaw. Once. Ray is a nice man. I enjoyed myself. We run in different circles, and I don't see the point of a second dinner. He fits in the boy-space-friend category not boyfriend. Although, I have to admit we do have some very similar interests, surprisingly. Dating anyone right now is low on my priority list."

"Keep your options open. That's all I'm saying."

"I'm too busy with my volunteer job with the garden, my cooking, working at the Ruggery, and my newest venture, editor of Augustin's online newsletter. As a matter of fact, I need to press Mayor Obermeyer to submit the content for his column or he's not going to be included in this latest issue. I'm pretty sure, if he's running for office again in November, he'll want to stay relevant." Sherry studied the berries on the counter. "Speaking of the mayor, wonder what will come of the cook-off suggestion for the Fourth of July."

"I predict the concept's a go. A brilliant idea with you as culinary captain at the helm. Now, can we please get a move on with dessert? I'm dying of sugar deprivation."

Chapter Six

The morning sun faded behind the wall of ominous thunderstorm clouds. The arrival of the inclement weather was punctuated with a rumble of thunder and a flash of lightning.

"Better get inside," Eileen called from across the street. "Spring lightning storms are Mother Nature's way of shaking off the winter chill. She may also be angry with the way humans have been treating her treasures and warning us to shape up and behave." Sherry's neighbor picked up the stack of branches she'd trimmed from her forsythia bush border and carried them to the edge of her driveway. "See you later. Great job on the radio interview." Eileen waved and went inside.

"Come on, boy, finish your business, or I'm going to have to run home for an umbrella and a lightning rod." Chutney obeyed. Sherry picked up his deposit, and the mission was declared a success. She tossed the bag in the trash and ran back inside as the first raindrops began to fall.

"I'm relieved Marla's plane took off before this weather came in. Delays are the worst." Sherry pulled her phone from her back pocket. She found her contact list and hit a key before plunging down on the couch.

"Thanks for calling Augustin Town Hall. How may I direct your call?"

"Am I speaking to Tia?"

"Yes, you are. Oh, listen to that thunder. Mother Nature is on the warpath. And you are?"

"Tia, this is Sherry Oliveri." Sherry yanked the phone from her ear when a shrill scream violated her eardrum. "Tia, are you okay?"

"Sherry, you won the America's Good Taste recipe contest."

Sherry waited for any follow-up, but there was only heavy breathing. "Yes, I know."

"I'm so excited for you. That means you're the best cook in America, right? And you belong to us. I'm talking to the best cook in America, everyone," Tia shouted.

"Tia, Tia. Hold on. America's Good Taste is a name the sponsors drummed up for a big contest. I don't think winning means I'm the best cook in America."

Tia's voice deflated to the appropriate energy level for a receptionist's professional greeting. "You'll always be the best in my mind. I suppose you'd like to talk to Mayor Obermeyer. He just stepped back into his office."

"Yes, please. And thank you for your kind words."

"If you ever need a taste tester, I'm your gal. Hold while I transfer you."

"Good morning. Mayor Obermeyer speaking. How may I help you?"

"Hi, this is Sherry."

"Hi, Sherry. So nice to speak to you. I had a very nice dinner with your father last night, along with Ruth, Frances, and Bev. Erik Van Ardan had a conflict and canceled, so Erno and I were outnumbered. But that's the way us men like to better the odds." The mayor snorted. "I suppose you're calling to see where the final draft of my article for the newsletter is. The good news is I'm emailing it to you right after we hang up. I've made the changes you suggested. I feel I've taken the pulse of the average Augustinian and my column addresses the most pressing issues on their minds. Speed bumps, shade trees, and library fines. Hot button topics and I have covered them all. Improving Augustin boils down to the following—people need to slow down, find leafy cover from the blazing sun, and read more but pay a bigger fine if they don't return their books on time."

"And would you still like to change the title of the column from 'What's on the Mayor's Mind' to 'Getting the Job Done'?"

"That's the plan. If you'd like to add a blurb about your latest cook-off win, by all means do. A win for you is a win for all of Augustin." The mayor paused and Sherry heard papers being shuffled. "On to a different topic, I have a personal matter to address with you before we get to last night's dinner discussion. I'm in the process of deciding whether to run for a third term in the fall. The last time I ran, one of the promises I made the citizens of Augustin was supporting a Community Garden whose longevity would span generations. The food bank depends on the garden during the spring, summer, and autumn months. But now the garden has a black eye. Finding Ms. Robinson's body in the mulch has deep repercussions. People who once saw the garden as a sanctuary of nature and nurture now see a space that harbors maniacs who hit people with shovels."

Through the picture window behind the couch the sky was the color of smoked salt. A flash of brilliant white filled the room and she turned her head in time to witness a bolt of lightning zigzag across the horizon. A chill traveled through Sherry.

Sherry studied her phone. "Do you think I'm safe talking on my cell phone during a thunderstorm? I've heard you can get electrocuted."

"That wouldn't be the way I'd want to leave this earth, but don't worry, it's perfectly safe. Don't believe everything you hear. As a precaution, I'm on speaker phone, so can you keep your voice down, I'd prefer this conversation stay between you and me. The office chitchat can spread like wildfire."

Sherry clicked on her speaker setting and balanced the phone on the arm of the couch.

"As I was saying, with your recent history of successful sleuthing, I would like you to hurry Poppy Robinson's investigation along and find the killer. Please."

The glass in the window behind Sherry vibrated as thunder rattled the house. "Mayor Obermeyer, you realize you're asking an awful lot of me. This murder is different. I only knew Poppy for a short while. I had very close connections to the two other murders I became involved with. As a matter of fact, I was the main suspect in one for a time when the judge of a recipe contest died after having sampled my recipe. I had no choice but to become involved. My father was a suspect in the other and I had to help clear his name. He's my father!"

"I understand, but consider this. Poppy Robinson has been a resident of Augustin her entire life. So have you."

"That doesn't mean much. A lot of people, including yourself, are lifelong Augustin residents."

"Hear me out. Before Poppy and her brother and sister inherited the land the Community Garden sits on from Rohan, she was CIA at Robinson Investments."

"CIA?" Sherry whispered. "What does that stand for?"

"Chief Interior Associate. Not sure what the responsibilities are but sure sounds important. Robinson Investments made Rohan a wealthy man, and I'm sure Poppy was secure financially, but, upon his death, the outfit was dissolved. The man didn't feel anyone could run the company as well as he, and that included his own offspring. Anyway, Poppy's last duty as CIA, as stated in Rohan's will, was to donate a sum of money to the Augustin Library to fund their cooking section. Cooking. Sherry, can you understand what that means? Were you aware her father was very inspired by your creativity in the kitchen and felt the library's food and cooking section had been overlooked for too long? We, as citizens, are very grateful for that bequest. Did anyone ever divulge that nugget of information to you?"

Sherry opened her mouth to reply.

"Probably not. Poppy mentioned the story to

me as she handed me the check but felt it should be kept under wraps if there weren't specific instructions from Rohan to go public. I'm only telling you now so you'll understand you have a responsibility here."

"No, she never mentioned anything like that to me. But, as I've told Detective Bease, Tessa Yates, and anyone else who'll listen, I didn't have many conversations with Poppy. She wasn't the most approachable person. I guess I should've tried a little harder to get to know her. I had no reason to consider I might never see her again after our last meeting and, suddenly, something like this happens. I'm certain I never did more than shake hands with her father, but I do remember exactly where I met him. I did a grocery store demonstration a few years back for a chicken recipe contest I won. Maple Chipotle Chicken Thighs with Sweet Potato Pancakes was my recipe, if I'm not mistaken. Rohan came over to the table I was preparing my recipe on, introduced himself, and tried a sample. He gave me his business card for his private client group, and I was very flattered he thought I might be wealthy enough to invest with him. I believe the minimum investment was five million dollars, and I wasn't then, and most likely will never be, close to qualifying for that unless cookoffs really enter a new stratosphere of prize money. I remember reading his name on the card and thought, 'very catchy.' Rohan Robinson. I love alliteration."

"So, you'll find the killer?"

"I didn't say that."

"But, you'll try?"

"If something pertinent presents itself, of course I'll go right to Detective Bease. Honestly, if I had to act this very minute, I wouldn't even know where to begin." Sherry softened her tone. "Seems like you know more about the woman than I could ever hope to."

"In all honesty, between you and me, Poppy's sister, Tessa, and her brother, Gully, possess the strongest motives. Poppy was a real obstacle to their financial freedom."

"I think you may want to speak to Detective Bease if you have any suspicions. He's the lead investigator on the case."

"I can't waste time with those investigators. They have to turn over every stone and ruffle every feather before they take two steps forward. I can't wait for them to move along at a snail's pace. Yes, as mayor, I am privy to some inside information, but knowing how to sort fact from fiction is your specialty."

"Hardly. I've heard from a reliable source, Tessa made a very good living as an acting coach. I don't think she was dependent on any money from her father."

"That may be the case, but because the decision to keep or sell the land was in Poppy's hands alone, I'd think Tessa would be angered by her exclusion in the decision-making process. I mean, that would be like you handing one of your fabulous recipes over to another contestant in a cook-off for he or she to prepare and serve to the judges. If the outcome is completely out of your hands and the recipe isn't made correctly, wouldn't you consider blaming the cook?"

"Yes, that would sting. What does Tessa's husband do for a living?"

"No husband," the mayor replied in a clipped tone.

"Do you know why Tessa and Gully didn't seem to have the Rohan seal of approval regarding making decisions concerning 7 Whale Watchers Avenue?"

"When Poppy came to Town Hall with Rohan's idea for the garden, what was clear was she was the only Robinson onboard with her father's plan. She hinted a disagreement over the financial side of the issue was looming. She avoided any talk about Tessa and Gully specifically, and I didn't press. As for Gully, who's known to be unemployed more often than employed, any hope of further inheritance lay in Poppy's hands because Rohan left most of his money to various charities. I'm guessing the idea of honoring Rohan's wish to have the Community Garden flourish soured in Gully's mind when his bank account dried up."

"Do you know for a fact Gully's strapped for cash?"

"Definitely. The family's campaign contributions dried up the year Rohan died," the mayor hissed.

"Could be the kids don't support your agenda."

"Don't be ridiculous. The two with money clearly didn't want to make Gully feel bad about not being able to equally contribute, so they ripped the donation rug out from underneath me. Anyway, finances, or lack thereof, can make a person turn on his own family. All in all, I wouldn't trust any one of them as far as I could throw them. Regardless, whether the perpetrator is a Robinson family member or not, I want he or she found pronto so the garden continues on the way old Rohan would have wanted."

"I'll try," Sherry murmured. She turned back toward the window. The sun broke through the storm clouds. "Have you considered even if the murderer is found there's no guarantee the Robinson property won't be sold sooner rather than later? I don't think you should put all your campaign eggs in one voter's promise basket."

Mayor Obermeyer released a grumble propelled by a lofty exhalation. "I appreciate your input, but when you read my article for the newsletter closely, and as the editor I sure hope you do, you'll know that beyond the Community Garden I'm also passionate about upgrading the sidewalks in town and planting shade trees, which will up the quality of life for all my constituents."

"Not exactly *all*." Sherry grimaced. "A very specific location and demographic is benefiting and, in no way, are those folks the neediest. On the contrary, the twenty-five percent of the town that has no sidewalks or shade trees beautifying their crumbling neighborhoods are getting nothing while the improvements are being made on the highest median-priced properties who may have complained about a crack or two on their already existing bucolic sidewalks located under magnificent shade trees. There are lots of squeaky wheels out there that you're not greasing."

Mayor Obermeyer sniffed. "And what about the library. Give me some credit for my desire to improve the fine system so readers will read faster or pay up, which, in turn, adds to the coffers, which, in turn, will buy more shade trees."

"My job isn't to criticize your accomplishments, or lack thereof, Mayor. Does make for interesting reading, though."

"If I didn't know any better, I'd think your friend Kayson Bradshaw has put a bug in your ear about me and not in a good way. I heard the interview you did with him."

"Not at all. And he's barely someone I consider a friend. The interview was our first meeting. Why would you say that?"

"Just a notion. Thank you for your insight, Sherry. I'll give your suggestions some consideration. Now, one more piece of business. I'm beyond excited the Augustin's inaugural Star-Spangled Grill-off will be the headliner on the new and improved list of July Fourth activities. I expect the contest will draw unprecedented crowds to Town Beach to celebrate, spend money, and watch the fireworks. As soon as people see the event was masterminded and developed by you, they'll race to submit entries."

"I'm hoping I'm up to the task. I've participated in more contests than I care to count but being on the organizing side is a new experience for me." Sherry heaved herself off the couch. "I'll put together a list of steps needed to get the show up and running and send the instructions over to you."

"Sounds great. I have some good news. I have

the perfect partner to work with you on the cook-off so you're not flying solo."

Sherry opened her mouth to speak, but once again, her hesitation lost her the opportunity.

"The woman has cooking contesting experience, is a lawyer I have worked with many times, and she volunteers on our Grass is Greener in Augustin council." The mayor hummed a note of approval.

"She sounds more qualified than me. I look forward to meeting her." Sherry pulled her phone closer to her face and checked the time. Her empty stomach argued with her brain when she calculated there was still another hour until lunch.

"Actually, she said she already knows you. That can't be a surprise. Nearly everyone in town knows you or at·least knows of you. Anyway, her name is Madagan Brigitti."

"The name sounds familiar. I can't think where I know her from." Sherry pulled the phone away from her ear and tapped her forehead. "I remember now. She was in a cook-off with me. Because I always do a bit of internet research on my opponents prior to the competition finals, I learned her husband is a cookbook author. I thought that gave her an unfair advantage. I went in with a bit of a chip on my shoulder and made it my business to show her how real talent prevails under pressure."

"That's great. All the more reason she's a good choice. Her husband's still successfully writing cookbooks. Yet another resource to be tapped. I've set up a meeting between you and Madagan for this afternoon. Presumptuous of me, but no time like the present. I know the schedule you gave me says you're working at the Ruggery this afternoon, but if you meet Madagan at noon at Town Beach, you can go over details, like times, rules, theme, sponsors, and prizes and then divvy up the work. Shouldn't take long."

"Easy for you to say," Sherry said under her breath.

"I'll work on the needed permits. I may have to pull some strings." The mayor snickered. "Oh wait, I almost forgot. Being mayor, I'm in charge of permits." He snickered again. "She'll meet you in the parking lot. Good luck. Got a call coming in. Better go. Check your email for my newsletter article in thirty minutes. Bye."

Sherry stared at her phone. "When will I learn to say no? Can you tell me that, Chutney?"

The little white dog folded his legs underneath him and curled up on the hooked rug outside the living room. "I'm not looking forward to meeting up with that woman again. She left a bad taste in my mouth at our one and only meeting."

Chapter Seven

When Sherry arrived at Town Beach, she found the parking lot was sparsely occupied. Not many beachgoers on a day when the clouds were thick with the threat of forecast rain. April showers were coming early. Sherry parked her SUV next to a silver Mercedes.

"I bet that's Madagan's fancy car," Sherry commented under her breath. "Being a lawyer must be lucrative, but are the material gains worth throwing your ethics out the window? I wouldn't hire her, that's for sure."

After Sherry turned her car off, she gathered a windbreaker off the passenger seat and tucked the garment under her arm. She strained to see if the luxury vehicle next to hers was occupied. The car appeared empty. As she opened her car door, she recoiled when she heard a thud.

Sherry pushed with care. "I'm sorry. I didn't know you were there." She slid out of her seat. "Madagan?"

"Yes, hi, Sherry. So nice to see you."

Sherry gazed at Madagan's face and on down her tall, lean frame. "I didn't see you get out of your car."

"No car for me today. I rode my bike. I was working from home, so I thought I'd save some gas and get some exercise at the same time."

"That makes sense. The mayor mentioned you were on the Greener Augustin committee. Nice to see you practice what you preach."

Madagan sported black bike shorts and a clingy thermal shirt. Her never-ending legs were a faded bronze, and she wore a visor that propped up her chestnut-hued ponytail. "Of course. I make it a habit to."

Sherry smoothed the front of her blue fleece sweatshirt, but the oversized cover-up bulged and puckered, despite her efforts. She plunged her arms through her windbreaker's sleeves and zipped.

Madagan grinned. "It's been maybe four years since we cooked off against one another, is that right? The Spring Fling Cook-off was the one and only cooking competition I've ever been in. I would choose to deal with litigation all day long rather than try to get the perfect sauce or flavor balance accomplished under pressure. I don't know how you manage to keep up your winning ways year after year."

"I do what I enjoy. To each her own, I guess."

Without waiting for a rebuttal, she headed toward the beach pavilion. Sherry steeled her stance when she reached the pergola. The structure shielded the picnic tables soon to be set up when the beach officially opened for the summer season.

Sherry surveyed the area, searching for the best location to find the pitch of the beach that was most level. "I imagine the July Fourth cook-off should take place in front of the pavilion. The audience can stay up here. There's no need to provide cover for the cook-off contestants because, if the weather is inclement, the fireworks get pushed back a day and so would the contest. Once the recipe entry period expires, I envision narrowing down the entries to a finalist group of ten, mostly because that's the number of cooks plus all the needed equipment this space would tolerate. Prior to the actual cook-off, usually there's a semi-final round of say twenty-five recipes that are prepared by a panel, taste tested, and narrowed down to the ten that will participate in the live cook-off. Wouldn't be hard to find volunteers for that task. What do you think? Maybe your husband would volunteer his expertise."

Madagan took a step closer to face Sherry. "You know, after all these years, I want to confess I was told at the time of the Spring Fling Cook-off you thought I had an unfair advantage because of who I married. I can sense you're still harboring those feelings about me. Am I right?"

"What's done is done. But if your husband is a cookbook author, speculation that he wrote your recipe seems inevitable."

"As a lawyer, I've witnessed false accusations on a regular basis, and I've made a few myself, thinking I was in the right. Let me say two things in my defense. First of all, yes, I did ask Vaughn to taste my recipe, why wouldn't I? And he did give me a few suggestions. All his years in culinary school refined his palate to such a degree the quick and convenient theme of that contest actually offended him. His recipes have a minimum of twenty ingredients and can take up to three hours to complete. If you recall, the contest required the recipe be completed in one hour. His suggestions didn't apply, and I didn't use any of them. And second, my feelings and integrity took a beating that day, in a number of ways, so I never entered another cooking contest. I guess you got the outcome you were looking for. But, in conclusion, Your Honor, I do believe I have been falsely accused of cheating, when, in fact, I didn't even place in the winner's circle because, left to my own devices, my cooking was only good enough to get me to the finals, where I was soundly beaten by you. The better cook prevailed. By the way, have you ever been falsely accused of something? If so, imagine if a resolution took years because someone wouldn't even make an attempt to see your side of the facts."

The pit of Sherry's stomach ached. She hoped her face wasn't advertising full-blown embarrassment, but, judging by the scalding prickles that danced across her cheeks, she was certain she was flushed redder than marinara sauce. "I was all ready to get an apology out of you, now I'm the one who has to say I'm sorry."

"You didn't know me, but you'd already made up your mind I was a bad apple. Hopefully, you've come to realize that's very unfair. You know what they say about assuming. Can we start over on a better note?"

"I'd like that," Sherry said.

"New beginnings start this minute. Now, back to the point at hand. I agree this is a great venue and ten finalists would provide a captivating show for the viewing audience." Madagan fished a small notebook and pen out of her waist satchel. As she wrote, she dictated. "Venue: Town Beach, check." She began a diagram rendering. "The audience will be here, the grills here, and the backdrop with sponsor signage, here."

"I have a feeling you're going to be amazing to work with." Sherry watched Madagan fill the first page with notes and a drawing. "We also need to go over contest rules, get at least one sponsor, preferably two, choose a catchy theme, decide on first, second, and third prizes, provide contestant aprons, pick two judges, and get the online entry composed. Listen to all that. What did I get myself into?"

"I'll email you a copy of the rules of a very similar contest I found in my research that was run in Michigan last July. I can get my office to make the necessary changes to fit our contest. That should be a breeze. As for the Grand Prize amount, second-place prize, and on down to third runner-up, I believe five hundred dollars, two fifty, and one hundred are sums the town can easily afford to spend this first year, while still making a tidy return. If all goes well, the town can up the ante for the following year. Vaughn would be the perfect judge and has consented to the task. To avoid any possible suspicion of insider influence, I will, of course, not be submitting an entry." Madagan tapped the pen on her paper. She flipped a page on her notepad. "A theme to consider for the cook-off could be best grilled patties on a bun. Whether a salmon burger, a buffalo burger, or black bean burger, the entry has to be a recipe for a patty-shaped, grilled burger of the cook's liking, sandwiched between two halves of a bun. I am, for example, a vegan, so if I entered, I would make a cremini and white bean burger served on a whole-grain English muffin with chipotle-honey mayo and pickled vegetables.

Sherry's thumb jutted skyward. "Wait. You said your husband was offended by the quick and easy theme of the Spring Fling Cook-off. Why wouldn't the relatively simple theme of a grilled patty on a bun insult him?"

"With age comes acceptance. After all these years, he's come to the realization no one cooks like him, so he's had to tone down his holier than thou attitude or lose the following his livelihood depends on. I don't want to say he's sold out, but if the shoe fits. There's a one hundred percent chance he admires how you are able to win big with a simple recipe concept. You're lucky professional cooks can't enter amateur cook-offs because they'd be crawling out of the woodwork to compete for those great prizes."

"Gosh, thank your husband for me. I feel honored."

"My husband suggested bringing onboard a woman he admires greatly for her New England culinary articles and her new podcast, Bone Soup. Her name is Patti Mellitt. I read she was a judge at the Channel Twelve appetizer cook-off you competed in recently."

Sherry opened her mouth to add her thoughts but was left mute.

"If any or all of these ideas appeal to you, we are off to a good start. It's a matter of designing a logo for the aprons, attracting sponsors, and finalizing the entry form." Madagan flipped the cover to her notebook over and stuffed it, along with her pen, back in her belted zipper bag.

"I'm blown away by your efficiency. I've got a lot to learn from you. That all sounds wonderful. I'll take on the apron design and entry form, although the workload seems a bit out of balance in my favor."

Madagan dusted the palms of her hands against each other. "I'm obsessed with details, always have been. Drives my hubby nuts. He's such a creative genius, who believes good things come to free spirits and that I'm a nitpicky compulsive organizer. I'll never change, so bear with me. I get a lot done in a short amount of time. That's my best attribute. But beware, I'll steamroll over you if you can't keep up, even organizing a cook-off."

"Sounds like we have more in common than you think. I hear you loud and clear. Lead, follow, or get out of the way. I'll get on my assignments ASAP, ma'am." Sherry saluted before extending her hand toward Madagan. "No hard feelings, then?"

Madagan's hand enveloped Sherry's. She pumped vigorously. "No hard feelings. We'll make a good team." She unzipped her bag and presented Sherry with a business card. "Reach out to me anytime. Mayor Obermeyer gave me your email."

Madagan was quiet while she closed the zipper. "Mayor Obermeyer mentioned you're on the trail of Poppy Robinson's killer."

Sherry cradled the business card in her palm. "I'd say the mayor is greatly exaggerating. I'm feeling compelled by certain outside pressures to see if there's any information I can uncover. I'm starting from scratch with a ton of trepidation and have gotten nowhere, but if that's his idea of being on the trail, well, then, yes, I am."

"If you need any persuading to continue your efforts, I'd also like to see the murderer brought to justice in a timely fashion and, from what I've read about your sleuthing skills, the mayor couldn't ask for better assistance than what you can provide. On the other hand, I, for one, wouldn't make your intentions public knowledge, in case someone is out there looking for more victims."

Sherry groaned. "I'm curious. Why would you be interested? Did you know Poppy? A lot of people knew *of* her, but not many seem to really know her. The woman wasn't exactly Augustin's reigning Miss Popularity. On the contrary, her list of enemies is growing as we speak."

"Count me in the minority of those who saw the woman in a different light. Poppy Robinson was a sheep in wolf's clothing. She had a soft side. She's been my client for years now. She hired me when the family was preparing to turn their inherited land parcel into a Community Garden. I can't discuss the details but, as I am an environmental lawyer, she had me look into the prior use of the land, the intended future use, and the previous owner's use of contaminants and pesticides. Shouldn't offer tainted garden space to the public. That's begging for trouble. What people didn't understand was Poppy's goal was not only to provide space for those who otherwise had no access to productive land but also fresh produce for the food bank and an education program for special needs children. She wasn't a fan of most adults, and she made that perfectly clear, but she would do anything for a child in need. I believe the perception of Poppy as a villain is fabricated by someone for some reason I can't fathom."

Sherry watched a seagull in flight skim the surface of the water. "If I could trace back to the source of the rumors she was to sell the land out from under the gardeners, maybe I could get to the reason behind them and what was to be gained by demeaning the woman's character."

Over Madagan's shoulder, Sherry eyed a speeding motorboat whipping the subdued waves of the Long Island Sound into a tumbling frenzy, sending them crashing into the shoreline. "As far as I know, Poppy never publicly stated she was selling out. The word was hearsay that kept building momentum until finally accepted as truth. But I think people might be as wrong as marshmallows on sweet potatoes. I don't think she was selling the land willingly, if she was."

Madagan waited until the boat's belching engine faded away in the distance. "Has anyone ever told you talking to you makes them hungry?"

Sherry stretched her arms over her head. "That's the nicest thing anyone could ever say to me."

"I'm going to speak out of turn here. Poppy was drafting her letter of resignation to the garden board. She was planning on presenting her intentions at a board meeting within the next two months. Her action was surprising to me because the goals her father spelled out for her to fulfill upon his death, plus her own interests in keeping the garden alive, weren't entirely realized, but I agree, something was forcing her to act quickly and most likely against her will. My guess is one or both of her siblings were pressing her."

"That's becoming a popular sentiment," Sherry added.

"If family pressure was too great, Poppy may have shut down and complied rather than fight for what she and her father wanted. What a shame. The garden did a lot of good for the town." Madagan craned her head toward the water as two power-boats raced along the horizon. "Those speedboats are such noise polluters. Motorless boats and paddleboards should be the only mode of transportation on the water, but not everyone has enough time on their hands for a long, lazy day of leisure. And adrenaline junkies have a need for speed."

"Sounds like the garden's demise was a foregone conclusion before Poppy was murdered. But, you say she hadn't made her decision public, so how did word leak out she was 'selling out'? Tessa? Gully? And if they knew, that fact wouldn't make sense for them to, you know, take her out if she was going to do what they wanted with the land."

Madagan shook her head. "The logical question is, did the information leak out or was the word put out prematurely for some reason? What I do know is this. Tessa and Gully never attended the meetings between Poppy and me. Never. Poppy was adamant about waiting for an opportune time to tell them and had chosen the upcoming anniversary of her father's death, May thirteenth, as the right time. Some would say creepy, I know, but I don't judge my clients' personal preferences, I make them legal. She might have chosen that date to make Tessa and Gully regret the decision she was forced into. I'm not certain what the effect on Tessa and Gully would have ultimately been. Personally, I doubt they'd feel much remorse for a man who held them in lesser regard than he did Poppy."

"Sounds complicated. I'm agreeing with you that Poppy's gotten a bad rap she most likely doesn't deserve. I'm aware she's philanthropic, generous, and, in the end, yielding to her family's wishes. Yet, around town, her legacy is as spoiled as week-old sushi. Would Tessa or Gully have tarnished their sister's reputation in haste because they were frustrated she wasn't acting fast enough to give them what they believed they deserved, namely the land inheritance turned into cash?"

"Even if Tessa and Gully were behind the slander of Poppy, what ultimately happened to her is what has to be focused on. Because of my commitment to client confidentiality, I can't elaborate, but, suffice it to say, nothing is as it seems." Madagan walked over to her bike and flung her leg over the crossbar. She unclipped her sleek purple and black helmet that hung from the handlebars and secured the protective headgear tight. "I'll be in touch." A robust push off with her foot got the bike rolling and Madagan pedaled away.

Chapter Eight

"Good afternoon," Sherry called out as she shut the Ruggery's back door behind her. "I picked up sandwiches on my way back from my meeting at the beach." She placed a bag of food on the table in the break room and continued on to the main showroom. "I'm here to relieve you for the afternoon, Dad. I know Amber's at a doctor's appointment, so I'm here a little earlier than usual."

Erno carried an oval rug to the cash register. "Hi, sweetie. I won't be needing a sandwich. I've got a midafternoon late lunch date with Ruth at the Sound Effect restaurant and you've just made it possible to move the time up to early afternoon. Thanks. She insists on treating me to a one-day-late birthday lunch. I've been craving a lobster roll all week and Sound Effect makes the best around."

"I had no idea you were eating out, so I thought I'd surprise you with a tuna and goat cheese melt, but I can eat my gesture of kindness for dinner, I guess. . . ." Sherry's voice trailed off to a whisper. "You know lobster roll ingredients are lobster meat, butter, bread, and more butter. Not sure that's so great for you."

Erno set the rug on the counter and kissed his daughter on her forehead. "A special birthday treat, then I'm back on my healthy eating regimen, I promise. Before I head out, Ruth made me promise I'd come armed with the latest news on who killed Poppy Robinson in your garden. We're all a little unnerved by the situation. Do you have any developments to share?"

"First of all, the Augustin Community Garden isn't my garden. And no, there isn't any news as far as I know."

"Okay, then. Do you have any idea who found the body?"

"News reports say she was found by a homeless man staying in the shelter off Oyster Drive. The man's known to take morning walks around the garden almost every day. No crime in that as long as he stays out of the fenced-in area. He's quoted as saying the garden uplifted his spirit so much he recently partnered with four others from the shelter and submitted an application for a garden box. They've been approved for this season. Witnesses attest to him being at the shelter all night before finding Poppy in the morning, so he's not under suspicion. Her time of death was put somewhere around eight that night, Ray said."

Erno began rummaging through a basket of tags and twine on the checkout table. "Ruth and I were talking, and we think you should investigate whether the remaining Robinson kids have alibis. Common knowledge around town confirms they wanted no part of that garden. It only stands to reason they'd prefer the land be sold so they could cash in. Poppy was the only obstacle to that happening, thanks to Rohan's will shenanigans. That's why you should never play favorites with your children, even if you want to. Messes with their heads and they may go after one another, like baby lion cubs do if their mother feeds the biggest chunks of wildebeest to the same cub at every meal. Sibling rivalry is no joke if there's too much at stake. As I always say, 'if kids were flags, they'd be easier to raise.'"

"Dad, I've never heard you say . . ." Sherry let the words fade away. "Poppy's brother and sister did have a lot to gain if the property was sold, you're right. I'm sure Detective Bease is taking a look into where Tessa and Gully were that night." She eyed the rug on the counter. "Is this for a customer?"

Erno rolled the rug up and secured it with twine. "Sam Pringle is buying the rug for his new granddaughter's nursery. He'll be in later this afternoon. Don't you love how new generations will be enjoying our rugs for years to come? There'll be a little piece of me in that baby's life, or at least under her tiny feet soon, and that warms my heart."

"I know. Kind of amazing." Sherry ran her fingers across the exposed loops of colorful lamb's wool that peeked out the ends of the bundle.

Erno lifted his barn coat off the wall hook. "See you tomorrow, sweetie. Wait. You're not in tomorrow until the afternoon and I'll be gone by then, so

I'll see you the day after." Erno blew a kiss, jettisoned with a sweep of his hand, and disappeared from the room.

"Looks like I'm serving lunch for one at the cash register," Sherry muttered as she headed to the back room. She opened the brown paper bag containing a "number three" and a "number five" from Chowdas, Wraps and Rolls daily menu specials. "I think I'll go for the goat cheese. Dad doesn't know what he's missing." She unwrapped the sandwich and placed it on one of the floral design melamine plates she kept a set of on hand at the store. She opened the mini fridge and took out a glass jar of her secret sandwich sauce.

The local eatery's lunches were good, but some homemade improvements were never a bad thing. Sherry had perfected a combination of mango chutney, grainy mustard, and vegan mayonnaise, and a splash of champagne vinegar that went well with baked chicken, burgers, and paninis. She dolloped some sauce across the insides of the sourdough bread and returned to the front of the store. Chutney and Bean emerged from under the table and gathered at Sherry's feet. Any crumbs that fell were dealt with in orderly canine fashion, usually involving a growl, a faux scuffle, or a standoff. May the best canine prevail.

With a bite of her sandwich in her mouth, Sherry jerked her head toward the door as her peripheral vision caught movement. Usually the copper bell dangling from the doorframe tinkled when the door swung open, announcing a customer's arrival, but the door barged forward with such aggression the only sound was a muted thud.

Sherry swallowed prematurely before she'd finished chewing.

"Sherry, thank God you're here." Romie Green hurdled forward as her foot grazed Chutney, who had scurried to the door. Unkempt wisps of her stick-straight hair, the color of clarified butter, were splayed across her cheeks. As she righted herself, she used her knuckle to nudge her tortoise-shell-framed glasses back into place. Behind the lenses her doe-like brown eyes glistened with excess moisture.

"I ran all the way here from the library. I was checking out a book, which I think I left on the counter, when Mayor Obermeyer appeared and told me the most upsetting news." The woman's voice was shrill, like a fire alarm, yet oddly delicate at the same time.

"What is it? What did he say?"

"He said he heard I had words with Poppy Robinson in the parking lot at the last board meeting. He stopped short of saying I was a suspect in the investigation, but I know what he was thinking."

"You had words with her, didn't you? The email I got from you on my way back from Florida said you screamed at her."

Romie's tone took on an air. "I'm not proud I lost my temper. Poppy was so arrogant. To pull the plug on all the good the garden does for the town is criminal. The notion kills me. I was so hoarse after that evening I had to suck on honey lemon lozenges for the next two days."

Romie's wispy voice was difficult to hear under

normal circumstances and seemed to require the greatest effort for her slight stature to produce.

Strained to the uppermost volume limits, Sherry could understand the need for soothing lozenge relief. "I wouldn't be too upset. If everyone who had words with her or hard feeling toward her stepped forward, there'd be a line of suspects around the block."

Romie lifted her chin higher. The woman swiped at her runny nose with the cuff of her shirt.

"I don't know if the mayor understands his opinions have bite to them. As far as I can fathom, she hadn't made the final decision about selling the land, and if she had, she hadn't made the news public." Sherry eyed the remainder of her inviting sandwich like a pastry chef eyed an expensive bottle of Madagascar vanilla extract. "Did Poppy make her plans to officially close down the garden known at the last meeting?"

"Well, not exactly, but I've heard things. And that's only the start. Mayor Blabbermouth said he wouldn't be surprised if a Detective Beast tracked me down sometime soon because he may have mentioned to him my unfortunate parking lot tantrum during questioning."

"Bease."

"What?"

"Bease. Not Beast. His name is Detective Ray Bease. And who exactly have you heard quote, un-quote, things from?"

Romie groaned, which, born from her delicate stature, sounded more like a mouse being stepped on than an adult expressing displeasure. "What-

ever. Who cares what the detective's name is? And
who cares who told me Poppy was shutting down
the garden? You have to help me, Sherry. You got
yourself off a murder suspect list once. You told
me so. Can't you do the same for me? You have to
find out who killed Poppy Robinson. I regret letting myself get so enraged the thought actually
crossed my mind for a split second to make her
pay for her selfishness, but I would never act on it.
You have to believe me."

"Okay, take a deep breath. You're getting yourself worked up. Logically, you must have an alibi if
you didn't commit the crime. The good news is,
when you supply one, all suspicion ends. Let's start
there. What were you doing at the time of Poppy's
death, which the detective told me was around
eight p.m. It's as easy as that and you're off the
hook."

"I was parked in the Community Garden parking lot."

"So much for an alibi. I'm sure you had a good
reason to be in what is essentially the wrong place at
the worst time. Can you share that reason with me?"

"I can't say." Romie lowered her head. "I'd be
breaking a promise if I told you. As long as the
killer is found before the detective formally questions me, everything will be fine, right?"

Sherry moaned. "That's like saying as long as I
turn on the stove tonight dinner will be ready. Lots
of things have to happen in between start and finish for everything to be fine."

"Can you try? Please?" Romie reached for
Sherry's hands and gripped them in hers. "I have
to go. I teach at the Outreach Center in an hour.

They would miss me if I were hauled off to jail. Who else in town has the necessary degree in Flora and Fauna Relevancy and Remediation but me? Without me, the course, and the fifty-three students invested in the program, goes down the tubes. I'll check in soon. Thank you so much." Romie dropped Sherry's hands and left the Ruggery.

Despite her dwindling appetite, Sherry zeroed in on the second half of her lunch. She transported the savory delight to her mouth at the exact time the metallic tone of the door's bell sounded. She rushed a bite and set her jaw in fast motion.

"Am I interrupting anything important? The look on your face says 'speak at your own risk.'" Ray entered and removed his tan hat. Fibers from the hat's frayed edge broke off and dropped to the floor. Detective Diamond trailed behind at arm's length, sporting a smirk.

"Hi, Ray. I'm having a hard time finishing my lunch, that's all. Hello, Detective Diamond." Sherry wedged the remaining portion in her mouth.

"Take your time. Diamond and I have a couple of follow-up questions for you concerning Poppy Robinson." Ray slid his hand inside his blazer and removed his notepad. At the same time, his associate set his briefcase on the counter and removed a computer tablet. He swiped the screen before handing the computer to Ray. Ray tucked his notepad back in his blazer and accepted the device. Ray studied the screen. "Can we make the type bigger? These are fifty-year-old eyes."

"You'd think they were eighty-year-old eyes the

way you carry on." Sherry crumpled her empty sandwich wrapper. "I'm with him." Sherry tipped her head toward the tall blond detective. "Ray, you need to get with the times before they pass you by. If you need a computer lesson, I'd be happy to oblige. Don't you want to make fifty the new thirty-five? Or do you say it the other way around, thirty-five is the new fifty? No matter. You know what I mean."

"I'll consider your offer. I'd rather you give me cooking lessons, though." Ray pointed to the corner of Sherry's mouth. "You have some sauce right there." He reached in his pocket and produced a tattered tissue.

"No thanks. I have a napkin." Sherry dabbed secret sauce off her lip.

Ray peered over his shoulder at Cody. "Speaking of sauce, I have a question concerning the cook-off you attended in Florida, but first, let me ask you, off the record, about the Augustin Community Garden board you've recently joined. It's an obvious place to begin when reconstructing the current events of Poppy Robinson's life. What are your thoughts about Poppy's brother, Gully, and sister, Tessa, not being members of the board or the garden, for that matter? In the very least, makes sense they'd be interested in any decisions concerning the land they own."

"I have some thoughts, if they're off the record."

"They're off the record." Ray poked at the tablet with his right index finger while his nine other fingers were curled in a ball.

"If our conversation is off the record, what are you typing?" Sherry took a step closer to Ray.

Ray tilted the screen toward Sherry. "I'm getting ready to search for your winning recipe from that contest and you're going to tell me what website to search. But first things first, Poppy's siblings?"

"I'm the newest member of the board, and, in the short time I've been active, the subject of her brother and sister has never come up. I've learned Tessa Yates is an acting coach in the city and I believe Gully Robinson is pursuing painting. Maybe they're too busy. Gardening isn't everyone's obsession." Sherry's shoulders began to ache. She found relief when she rolled them backward. "The reason they don't sit on the board would be something Tessa might be able to answer. Have you talked to her?"

"I'm not at liberty to disclose that information."

"Well, there might be some things I'm not at liberty to disclose." Sherry shifted her gaze to Detective Diamond. "I have a suggestion for you two if you do talk to Tessa further. I believe chapter four of *The Effective Detective* spells out how far preliminary questioning should proceed in order to keep the witness comfortable and agreeable. One question too many and you've lost access to valuable information."

"I'm impressed," the young detective mumbled, barely moving his lips.

"I heard Detective Diamond refer to the manual so often I was intrigued. I bought a used copy online for six ninety-nine. Great reading right before bed."

"I believe chapter six outlines how to recognize when a witness is giving the investigator the runaround." Ray checked his wristwatch. "Can we

stay on topic here, please? I've only got a few minutes. One board member's name, Romie Green,
has come up during questioning of other members
as having had a substantial argument with Ms. Robinson after the most recent board meeting concluded."
Ray was nudged aside by Detective Diamond as he
reached toward the tablet.

"That episode occurred on a Thursday evening,
exactly two days before Poppy was murdered," Detective Diamond stated. "Were you in attendance
at the meeting that night?"

Two furry creatures chased each other across
the room behind Ray.

"I was not. I was in Florida for my cook-off. I didn't
even hear about the argument until . . ." Sherry held
her breath to slow her racing heart.

"Until?" Ray asked.

"Until Romie emailed me during my flight back
from Florida. She wouldn't have mentioned the
argument if she had anything to hide. I'm sure of
that. She's a good person who's passionate about
the garden's mission statement. She's interested in
protecting its future."

"Passionate," Ray repeated. "Speaking of which,
were you aware of the fact Romie Green has a romantic involvement with Gully Robinson?"

*Oh, Romie. You may have left out one important de-
tail when you asked for my help.* "She never mentioned that." Sherry pictured Romie's expression
as the need for Sherry's assistance was explained
and could only visualize the desperation conveyed.
"I would never have guessed. At the meetings,
Romie wasn't given any preferential treatment by
Poppy. As a matter of fact, she received the same

coolness the rest of us were served, so I would have never surmised they knew each other socially. Poppy was a tough nut to crack."

"We're done here for now," Ray announced.

"I don't think we're done." Detective Diamond looked at Ray. "Didn't you have a question about Ms. Oliveri's cook-off?"

"Thanks. Yes. My assignment is to use this computer every day for work or otherwise to familiarize myself with all it can do. I'd be grateful if you'd share a link to your winning recipe I've heard so much about. I don't know if I'll be able to recreate the dish, but if I can make some sort of crab cake close to yours, I'll be satisfied. I consider the exercise part of my technology education. By the way, today is Diamond's last day assigned to me. My boss thinks I'm ready to be left alone with this flip-top electronic brain. I'm celebrating a graduation of sorts."

"Congratulations. How about if I email the link to you?" Sherry shifted her gaze from Ray to Detective Diamond, who nodded toward his colleague. "That way you exercise a few computer skills at the same time. Multitasking capabilities are what make a computer most useful."

"Good idea. That's an efficient use of resources. Chapter three in *The Effective Detective*," Ray added.

"I never thought I'd hear you utter those words. Detective Diamond must have brainwashed you." Sherry's grin stretched from cheek to cheek.

Ray hummed a brief bass note. "We'll be in touch." He picked up the tablet and rotated toward the door.

"Ray, I've nothing more to add to your investigation. This should be the end of the questions, right?" Sherry's final word insisted upon itself.

As Detective Diamond passed by Sherry, he settled his aviator glasses over his eyes. "An investigation is an ongoing process. A series of steps taken to achieve an end. Where those steps lead is anyone's guess right now." He followed Ray out before securing the door shut behind him.

"I was afraid of that." Sherry sighed, accompanied by the tinkling of the bell over the store entrance door.

Mr. Pringle, a portly man with a hairless head, slipped through the opening door.

"Hello, Mr. Pringle. I have your rug right here. Your daughter and granddaughter will love it. My father was bursting with pride that a new generation of customers will own his rugs. Family is why Erno Oliveri does what he does. He's taught me that from day one."

Chapter Nine

Sherry stretched her arm overhead before bring-ing the phone back down to her ear. "What a day. I'm so happy to be home. After the detectives left, I had back-to-back customers until closing time. I couldn't even get to the ladies' room. I had to exercise mind over matter, or should I say mind over bladder, until I could get that door locked and find a moment for myself. How was your doc-tor's appointment?" Sherry put her feet up on the green and gold tufted ottoman.

"Fine. I'm sorry the doctor's office was running so far behind. Sounds like a good sales day. That's a plus." Amber's tone grew cautious. "Doing any-thing special on your date tonight? Don't overdo. The tennis league starts soon and you'll need your energy."

"When's the last time I overdid any nighttime activity? And I don't even consider tonight a date. I might be regretting my decision to accept a friendly meal with Kayson Bradshaw because I'm not even sure we're friends. I was going to back out, but, after I gave it some consideration, I thought he might be sitting on some useful information. I just don't know if I'm up for his aggressive wit. I'm meeting him at Rip Currant in about twenty minutes. My goal is to be home by nine. Don't worry, I have the tennis on my calendar. Looking forward to the battle of the fluffy yellow balls, I think."

"Good luck tonight. Bye."

Sherry's phone went silent. She hauled her legs down from their elevated position and made her way to the door. A check in the mirror as she passed didn't impress. "See you in a bit, boy."

Chutney, sprawled out on the front hall area rug, lifted one eyelid.

Rip Currant's hostess, dressed in a white oxford shirtdress and sporting a severe wedge hairstyle, ran her finger down the restaurant's seating chart. Her finger stopped at a table that appeared menacingly close to the kitchen's doors.

As Sherry parted her lips to deliver an argument against the undesirable seating location, Kayson Bradshaw materialized alongside her.

If the hostess's double take had been any more blatant, she might have inflicted whiplash upon herself. "Good evening, sir. You must be Mr. Bradshaw. I've seen your face on the side of the metro buses. I was so excited when I saw your reservation on the guest list."

Kayson nodded and returned a smile.

"Would you mind saying something for me? I think you have the most captivating voice I've ever heard." The hostess didn't risk blinking her eyes and missing a moment of the captive celebrity.

Kayson stole a sideways glance at Sherry. "I would be most appreciative if you would show me to my table, please."

"Sounds better on the radio, but that'll do," she uttered, nearly breathless. The hostess stepped around her stand, collected a menu, and burrowed between Sherry and Kayson. "Excuse me, ma'am. I must seat our VIP guest. Your dinner companion hasn't arrived yet, Mr. Bradshaw, but I'd like to bring you a complimentary cocktail while you're waiting."

Kayson peered at Sherry, whose mouth was agape. He issued a grin that could melt an ice cream sandwich instantly. "This beauty right next to you is my dinner date. Good evening, Sherry."

The hostess backed away from Kayson. "I'm terribly sorry." She retrieved a second menu from her stand. "Please, follow me. Best table in the house is waiting for you." The hostess glanced at Sherry. "Both of you."

"What a view. The river at night is lovely." Sherry took her seat and opened her menu.

Kayson's menu lay unopened in front of him. "No cocktail? Just jumping right to the main course?"

"Pinot grigio, please." Sherry looked up from the menu. "What are you looking at?" Sherry inspected Kayson's face for signs of envy, sarcasm, or boredom with the company he was keeping.

Kayson held a steady gaze over Sherry's shoulder. He leaned in tight. "Isn't that the mayor behind you?" Kayson made a cryptic hand gesture to the far corner table. "Word is he's a confirmed bachelor for life but looks like he doesn't mind entertaining the ladies, no commitment required."

She craned her neck around in the direction Kayson was fixated on. "That's our mayor. By the way, he's probably thinking the same about you."

"Touché."

"I can't make out who he's with, from the back of her head. I should probably go say hi. I edit the municipal newsletter and he's been struggling to meet the deadline for submission, so we've been talking back and forth for the last couple of days. I don't want him to think I'm avoiding him."

"The last article authored by him showed signs of urgency and desperation. His reelection bid is faltering and he's grasping at straws, clearly trying to pander to the wealthiest sector of Augustin. His actions are despicable, if you ask me. If a candidate's not interested in representing the entire town, he or she shouldn't be on the ballot. That would be my suggestion to him."

"My job is to edit the newsletter, not pass judgment on the content. Don't shoot the messenger." She scooted the chair with the back of her knees harder than she intended. The resulting squeal of the chair legs across the floor quieted the room for a split second. "I'll be right back. Order me a large pinot grigio if the waitress comes by, please. I'm ready for a drink. I'll be back in a flash."

"They don't come in large, medium, and small. That's only for sodas."

"That man is infuriating," she whispered as she turned tail. "He goes after my hobby, now he's bashing my newsletter job. Rude is what I call him. Makes me want to get a move on finding the killer so the Community Garden is deemed safe and Mayor Obermeyer has a better shot at reelection. A third term in office would really get under Mr. Radio Celebrity's skin."

The man at a nearby table raised his head and cupped his hand around his ear. "I'm sorry, are you talking to me?"

"No, no. Only to myself." Sherry picked up the pace as she maneuvered between tables.

"Sherry, how nice to see you." The mayor lifted his stout body from his chair as she approached. His blue plaid blazer popped open as his midsection heft resettled itself. His dinner napkin floated off his lap. He extended his bloated hand.

"Hope I'm not interrupting. I saw you across the dining room and wanted to say a quick hello." Sherry pumped the mayor's hand and turned to face his dinner partner. "Hi, I'm Sherry Oliveri. I work part-time for Town Hall editing the newsletter."

The woman dressed in a drapey silk shirt placed her manicured hand on Sherry's forearm as she tossed her wavy hair aside with a graceful head bob. "So nice to meet you. My name is Tessa Yates. What a lovely cardigan you have on. Lavender is a gorgeous spring color. Have a wonderful dining experience." The words were delivered with such enchantment Sherry envisioned cartoon rainbows could next come cascading from the woman's parted lips. Tessa retracted her hand and placed it on the nape of her neck with practiced elegance.

"Have a nice dinner, Sherry, and thanks for stopping by." The mayor lowered himself into his chair and gathered up his fork.

"Same to you. Have a nice dinner." Sherry shimmied her way between tables back to her seat across from Kayson.

"Listen, I want to apologize for coming off harsh concerning the mayor. I need to temper my opinion outside the radio station."

"And inside, too," Sherry added.

"I'm sure Mayor Obermeyer's a nice man to work with. I don't agree with his policies and methods, which basically means I don't agree with how he's doing in office." Kayson picked up the menu lying in front of Sherry and handed the leather bound list to her.

"I don't appreciate you forcing your opinions on me. I can make up my own mind who I work for and who I vote into office and they may or may not be mutually exclusive in this case."

"Message received. Now, let's order. I'm going to have the seared Branzino with preserved lemon and pistachio couscous. When I saw that on the menu, I didn't even bother reading the other choices."

"I'll have the seared scallops and a Caesar salad. I like to order the dish I can't make well at home. I'm not able to sear scallops at the high heat a restaurant's grill can reach without my smoke alarm going off. Soggy scallops are the worst, so I don't even bother trying anymore. At twenty-nine dollars a pound, those sweet round delicacies are too expensive to serve incorrectly." Sherry drummed her fingers on the menu's cover.

"Is something bothering you? I apologized for coming on too strong once again. That was the right thing to do, I hope."

"Something is bothering me. I don't know what to think. Mayor Obermeyer is dining with Tessa Yates."

"Tessa Yates?"

"Poppy Robinson's sister. When I spoke to her, she was acting so weird, like she had never met me before."

"Poppy Robinson, the woman murdered at the Community Garden?"

"Yes."

"I've been reading snippets of news release updates on her case as they dribble in. Not much has been uncovered." Kayson shrugged. "I'm guessing it's not unusual for the pair to be dining together. Seems about right. If the mayor would ally himself with a wealthy family, such as the Robinsons, they might make beneficial contributions to his run. Do you know Tessa?"

"Well, no, I've never met her in person."

"So it's not weird that she would act as if she's never met you because she hadn't, is that right?"

Sherry ran her fingers down the stem of her wineglass. "She and I have never met in person. We've talked on the phone. Tessa reached out to me, in fact, but when the mayor introduced us two minutes ago, you'd never guess she placed the call. She did a great job of acting as if she had never heard my name before."

"You've lost me." Kayson helped himself to a warm roll and a pat of butter before handing the bread basket to Sherry.

Sherry selected a dinner roll. As she spoke, she wielded her bread-laden hand like a samurai to punctuate her words. "What I want to know is why the mayor told me the entire Robinson family was untrustworthy and that Tessa and her brother, Gully, had every reason to want to eliminate Poppy, yet he's over there breaking bread with someone he believes is a possible murderer? Tessa may be an acting coach by profession, but is the mayor the better actor?"

Chapter Ten

"I'm at home finishing up the newsletter this morning. Madagan texted she'd like a quick meeting at lunchtime outside the library and after that, I need to work on pinpointing where three people in particular were at the time of Poppy's murder. Tessa Yates, Gully Robinson, and the mayor." Sherry balanced her phone on the edge of the kitchen counter while she dipped her tea bag in the mug's hot water.

Erno said, "Why are you bothering giving this investigation any extra thought? Poppy's death was tragic, but you barely knew her. The scowl the woman wore on her face was enough to scare my tail between my legs and make me retreat in the opposite direction whenever I saw her. I wouldn't give her death another moment of your time, sweetie. She was a bad egg."

Sherry pinched her lips as she considered her father's words. "You know the saying, 'driest leaves, juiciest fruit'?"

"I prefer, 'you have to open the oven door to get the cake out.' "

"That'll work too, Dad, but maybe not in this case. The point is there was more to Poppy than the peppery persona she projected. She took her father's dying wishes to heart, and, as much as I hate to admit it, one of them has an indirect involvement with me. My cooking accomplishments inspired Rohan to make a big donation to the library to improve their cooking section. I'm getting a strong urge to sift through the murder muck to try and separate fact from fiction."

Erno hummed a note of consideration. "Trust your gut. Do what you gotta do. I'm a firm believer in honoring your father's wishes. You mentioned Tessa, Gully, and the mayor. Tessa and Gully, that makes sense they should be under some suspicion, but you're not saying Cooper Obermeyer is a suspect, are you? What would the mayor's motive be to murder that woman? Her father was probably one of his most prolific campaign contributors throughout his political career." Erno clicked his tongue against the roof of his mouth, a habit Sherry knew all too well meant he didn't approve.

"I don't want to speculate without evidence. I can still hear Detective Bease's scolding words from the last time I did that. There are things I can't ignore, though. Red flags are waving because, in public, the mayor has nothing but negative things to say about every member of the Robinson family, yet he was all cozy with Tessa at dinner. I can only wonder what his relationship with Gully is like behind the scenes."

"Sounds like the mayor's as two-faced as honey mustard."

"Guess you could say that, Dad. I'm gonna get going. Have a restful day off. Talk to you soon." Sherry put her phone down and brought her mug of tea over to her computer. Instead of opening the final draft of the *Augustin Sound* newsletter, she typed "Gully Robinson, Augustin, CT" in the search box.

After clicking on a few links, Sherry settled on a business-networking website. She sipped on the warm liquid sweetened with lavender honey as she absorbed the details of Gully's professional life.

> Previous employment experience: Trail Guide—Shoreline Park, Tour Guide—Hudson Valley Art Museum, Professional Rock Wall Climber, Artist In Residence—Art Village, Florida, Assistant Manager—Rock Solid Sports Equipment.

Sherry copied and pasted the list into a new spreadsheet and saved the file under the name "S-Info."

After an hour, the Augustin newsletter was edited, formatted, and emailed to Tia at Town Hall to be attached to the town's mailing list and sent off to enlighten and entertain citizens who took the time to read all six pages. Sherry even found a spot to put in a blurb about her latest recipe contest win. Editor's prerogative. When she was done, Sherry hooked Chutney up to his leash and together they exited her small colonial house, only to immediately be greeted by neighborly Eileen.

"Hello again, you two." Eileen straightened up from her weeding crouch. "The day's warming up. Sure was chilly earlier."

"Spring is here. Won't be long before we're complaining about the heat," Sherry teased.

Eileen smoothed down her baggy floral-appointed pant legs as they hiked up her calves. She made her way to the edge of her property and met Sherry and Chutney on the sidewalk. "I heard you may have involved yourself in trying to find Poppy's killer. I think that's a good idea, given your newfound sleuthing expertise."

Sherry sighed. "On a limited basis. Word does get around in this town fast. If Detective Bease gets wind of any interest on my part, he'll shut me down faster than you can say Poppy Robinson didn't have many friends."

"The woman liked you, dear. If you need proof, word came in this morning's mail delivery. Hold on, I have it right here." Eileen returned to her front porch and shuffled through a pile of letters and publications. She came back to Sherry with a newspaper. She laid the paper flat against her chest and displayed the back page of the *Nutmeg State Of Mind.* "The article's a call for contributions to the food bank's garden bed, plants, seeds, cuttings, etcetera. The banner reads, 'Augustin Community Garden Welcomes Sherry Oliveri To Its Board.' Within the article is a quote from Poppy calling you the town's most valuable asset. High praise from a woman rumored to be shutting down such a needed resource as the Community Garden. Maybe she wrote the words before she made up her mind to sell out."

Sherry let Chutney's leash slip from her grip. "That doesn't make sense. If she was asking for contributions in print and highlighting members of the board, the impression given is she's all for the continuation of the garden. If this ad had come out last week instead of this week, maybe she'd still be alive, unless the killer wasn't motivated to make Poppy pay for her plan to shut the garden down or, in the case of her own family, punish her for not shutting the place down fast enough."

Sherry picked up the leash as Chutney attempted to wander. "Thanks, Eileen, I'll see you later." She headed back home.

"I can think of two people who might have killed her if she *didn't* shut the garden down," Eileen called after her.

"Me too," Sherry yelled. Her legs froze in place. Chutney continued his forward pace until he reached the end of the leash and came to an abrupt halt. Sherry returned to face Eileen. "To be clear, are you talking about Tessa and Gully?"

"Oh no, dear. Although, now that you mention it, those two would be looking at a tidy sum of cash if Rohan's land was sold. Certainly is lovely property in a perfect location in the heart of Augustin. A savvy buyer would snap the land up in an instant." Eileen looked skyward before settling her sights back down. "No, I'm talking about the couple who lives next door to the garden property on Whale Watchers Avenue. Champ and Bunny Westerfield."

"I know them. They've been Ruggery customers for many years."

"No doubt you know everyone," Eileen pro-
claimed. "When Rohan Robinson died, Champ
and Bunny. made public that Rohan had given
them first right of refusal for the purchase of his
property, which they had every intention of acting
on, but, instead, it was passed down to the children through his will."

"That's disappointing for them, but you're suggesting they took it to the next level to get revenge
on Rohan's renege? Why would they have waited
so long after his death to act?"

"Not for that reason." Eileen folded the newspaper article in half and tucked it under her arm.
The pompom trim of her cherry-red sweater
danced to the beat of her movements. "The Westerfields went so far as to provide a written agreement signed by Rohan. Poppy wouldn't budge.
The couple bought newspaper space and published the document. Poppy stayed strong, despite
the urging by Tessa and Gully to sell. The Westerfields were even promising to keep the original
house on the property so their daughter and her
new husband could live close by when they could
afford to do so."

"And that's why you think they took it to the
next level?" Sherry knew Eileen savored story
buildup and she also feared a good ten minutes
might go by before the point of the story was
reached. With gentle coaxing, maybe she could
speed things along. "I don't think that's a strong
enough motive."

"I'm not there yet." Eileen slowed her words to
an excruciatingly sluggish pace. She lowered her
voice to a breathy whisper. "I have it on good au-

thority, Champ and Bunny threatened legal action against the Robinsons. Mayor Obermeyer intervened and talked the Westerfields off the ledge, so to speak."

"Sounds like the situation ended peacefully." Sherry began to inch backward toward her home.

"Yes, initially the dust settled. But, fast forward to the public hearing a few months later. The mayor presided over the hearing at Town Hall where Poppy, the new owner of 7 Whale Watchers Avenue, issued multiple grievances against her neighbors for everything from improper fence locations and tree damage to improper color combinations on the Westerfields' historic barn. Poppy went after the couple with a vengeance. She turned the tables on them and lawyered up, scaring them into submission. Champ and Bunny never made another peep after that, but the wall they erected between the two properties later that year would take a rock-climbing expert to scale. The structure's said to be most impressive."

"Who did you hear all this from?"

"I was afraid you'd ask me that. That's why you're such a good investigator. My memory's not as strong as it once was. Looking back, either that nice young woman who works at the Community Garden told me, the one with the glasses that make her look like an owl, or possibly Karenna Kingsley shared the info. Karenna's in my book group and a bit of a loose cannon when it comes to sharing gossip. Don't tell her anything you wouldn't mind broadcast on the nightly news. That's my advice. Most likely Karenna, because I can't even think of the other gal's name at this moment. The only reason there's a chance it might have been the younger woman is I recently volunteered at the Outreach Center and was assigned her classroom for the afternoon. At break time, we grabbed a cup of coffee together. Nice person, very well versed in plants and town happenings and such, but someone needs to tell her, her glasses swallow up her face. We talked about this, that, and the other, so we may have touched on the Robinson affair. As a matter of fact, I'm positive we did discuss the issue."

"Thanks, Eileen. I need to get a move on. I'll see you soon." Sherry scooted across the street and up the slate pathway to her house.

"I do hope so. I'll keep an eye out for you, as always," Eileen called after her.

Seated under the library's pergola, Sherry and Madagan had the perfect view of two white swans courting on the river below. The birds strutted, trumpeted, and flapped their enormous wings as they romanced one another. A moment later an errant peck to the head led to a lover's spat, and the offended party took flight, leaving the jilted bird paddling solo.

"Nature's rough." Sherry watched the squawking swan swim away.

"I know we could have skipped the face-to-face meeting, but I think this early in the process I'd like to get together in person and witness your reaction to my ideas. I'm batting a thousand so far since you like my design for the cook-off entry form. I'll contact the Better Off Bread Company and use my powers of persuasion to solicit sponsorship for the cook-off." Madagan batted her makeup-free lashes and puckered her unpainted lips. "That's, of course, a joke. I'm the last person who'd use feminine wiles to get the job done. I'm known at my office as being a 'rustic' girl, which is code for 'doesn't give a darn about makeup.' Don't let my lack of splashy exterior fool you, I can debate my way out of a paper bag. I'll employ my power of persuasion to get the bread company to supply the patty buns."

Sherry giggled. "Madagan, you're one surprise after another. I've been wrong about you from day one. You're so nice, funny, and smart, and I'm glad we've gotten off to a great second start."

"Thanks. That means a lot to me. I spend my workdays untangling serious disagreements ranging the gamut from noisy neighborhood roosters who start crowing before the break of day to scary contamination allegations, so I love to get complimented on sides of me I don't get to exercise much. This cook-off has been a welcome distraction from my daily grind."

Sherry waved her notebook. "I have to admit, me too. Oh, and I've got a lead on an artist for the cook-off advertising and entry form artwork. What would you think if we asked Gully Robinson? His credentials are fairly extensive, and, even though the work's a volunteer situation, I'd think the exposure would be beneficial to him." Sherry studied Madagan's expression, but the lawyer kept her reaction neutral. "I'd like to ask him today, but is the timing off, being that his sister's death was so recent? I did see his other sister out at dinner last night, and she didn't appear deep in mourning, so maybe he's not either."

"I think you could ask Gully today. Sometimes an opportunity like this is just what the doctor ordered." Madagan pulled her phone from her slim-fit pants and hit a key. "He's in my contacts. Here you go." She handed Sherry the ringing device.

"Won't he know the call's from your phone?" Sherry asked.

"I blocked the caller info," Madagan replied. "A simple procedure."

"You'll have to show me how to do that," Sherry added before the call was answered. "Sounds like something that could come in handy."

"Gully here."

As Sherry was formulating the words she would use, the call was answered on the first ring. "Hi. You don't know me, but I recently worked with your sister Poppy and I met your other sister Tessa last night. I was wondering if you could be persuaded to provide some artwork, on a volunteer basis, for the inaugural Augustin Star-Spangled July Fourth Cook-off?"

"A cook-off needs artwork? And who am I speaking to exactly?"

"Forgive me, I'm not making myself clear. Let me start over. My name's Sherry Oliveri. In an effort to improve Augustin's Fourth of July celebration, the town council will be hosting a cook-off at Town Beach as an opening act for the new and improved fireworks. If I could tempt you to contribute artwork to be used for advertising purposes and on the cook-off entry forms, I would be most appreciative. As a member of Augustin's art community, you are our top choice for the project."

A low, drawn-out sigh reverberated from Gully's end of the phone. "*The* Sherry Oliveri? The queen of cooking contests?"

"I don't know about that description, but if the success I've had in my hobby helps persuade you to contribute, I'll accept the accolades."

Hushed conversation filled Sherry's ear before Gully's reply was delivered. Sherry struggled to interpret the gist of the conversation but couldn't make out more than "ironic" and "town council."

"I'll do the work. My schedule is tight, but what you're asking for doesn't sound too taxing and"—Gully inserted a gap of dead air before continuing—"may be even fun."

"Of course, I also want to offer my condolences to you and Tessa on the death of your sister Poppy. I should have said that right off the bat. I admired her commitment to helping others."

Was that a chortle that Sherry heard?

"I appreciate your sentiments. I will pass on the word to Tessa when I see her next."

"And to her husband too."

"No husband for Tessa. No spouse for any of us. Not sure what that says about our compatibility ratings."

"Tessa's last name is Yates. That's what confused me." Sherry side-eyed Madagan, whose head was bowed. "I'd like to drop the cook-off information packet by your place if that's convenient. We don't have anything up online yet. I need an address and I'll make the delivery."

More hushed conversation. "Uh, no. I'll meet you somewhere. How does outside the library at four this afternoon sound? You'll recognize me, I'll be the one dressed in rock wall climbing gear."

"Whatever that looks like. Yes, that works." Sherry waited for further instruction. None came. "It'll be nice to meet you in person."

Gully agreed and the phone call ended.

"The library's beginning to feel like a second home, I'm there so often." Sherry made a notation on her pad. "Artwork, sponsor, location, entry form, judges, check, check, check, check, check. This is really happening. Thanks again, Madagan. I'm heading to the Ruggery now. I'll let you know how the meeting with Gully goes. Wish me luck. And knock 'em dead when you make contact with the bread sponsor. They won't turn you down. You could charm honey from a bee. Bye." Sherry gave Madagan the thumbs-up sign as she headed to the parking lot.

Chutney led the way through the Ruggery's back door. Sherry followed the sound of voices to the showroom, where Amber was engaged in a conversation with a woman leaning on a cane. Samples of colorful area rugs lay side by side in front of the duo.

"Good afternoon, Mrs. Camponella. Isn't Amber the most wonderful help, especially when there's a choice to be made?"

"She really is. I'm having a hard time not buying all three rugs. But I really only need one, so why don't you help that young lady first while I mull things over." Mrs. Camponella pointed her cane in the direction of the cash register.

Sherry's gaze followed the tip of Mrs. Camponella's cane.

"This is a surprise." Sherry willed her hesitant legs to take her over to the woman whose gold-braceleted wrist clutched an expensive-looking purse. As Sherry neared, the woman's glossed lower lip protruded and she squinted her mascara-lined eyes.

"Nice to see you again, Sherry. You do have your fingers in many pies, don't you? How do you find the time?"

Sherry extended her hand. "Too many pies, heavy on the crust, light on the filling. Nice to see you, Tessa. What can I help you with?"

Tessa made a quarter rotation, leaving Sherry's hand dangling.

Without turning back, Tessa lowered her head. "Your rugs are as beautiful as I remember. Last time I was in your family's store, I must have been seventeen or eighteen and Rohan brought all three of us kids in to pick out a Mother's Day gift. He called the oval rugs floor toupees and we had a good laugh over that. He was lighthearted in those days. Mother loved the rug we chose, which was covered in roses of all colors and served as a focal point in their solarium until that house was sold. I'm not really sure what happened to the rug, but I wish it had gone to me. My apartment could use some color."

"It's never too late to consider a new rug. Any

one in particular I could show you?" Sherry inched closer to the rug she thought Tessa had her sights on.

"Thank you. Maybe next visit." Tessa rubbed her palms together. "What I'm about to say is kind of awkward. I got a call from my brother, Gully. He mentioned you reached out to him for help with an art project for the town. I had an errand in Augustin, so I thought I'd stop by to tell you a few things about him, face-to-face."

Tessa raised her head and met Sherry's gaze. "Gully would never say no to someone in need, but I don't think the best time for him to take on a new project is right now. Especially one that has a connection to Mayor Obermeyer. They haven't always seen eye to eye on issues, and the collaboration may be harmful for both parties."

"I'm meeting Gully this afternoon. He can make up his mind when he sees what's involved, which, in my opinion, isn't a huge time commitment. What a perfect opportunity to showcase his talents while doing good for his community. Mayor Obermeyer is on the oversight committee but won't have any direct input, other than the occasional yea or nay. As a matter of fact, I didn't even mention the mayor's name in the initial conversation with your brother. Gully wouldn't have much, if any, interaction with Mayor Obermeyer. And if you have any concerns, I can ensure they have no interaction. The mayor's left the details up to myself and another woman who is co-organizing with me, Madagan Brigitti."

Did Tessa's eyelid seize up for an instant?

"I'd be most appreciative if they do not. I'm

sure you were wondering what I was doing eating out with Cooper?" Tessa gave the first syllable of the word "wondering" a ride on a thick pillow of breath.

"It's none of my business." The words took flight before Sherry knew what she'd said. "I work with the mayor and when I saw him at the restaurant, I felt obligated to say hello. I had no idea who he was dining with."

"I don't live in Augustin anymore. I live in New York City, where acting coaches are in high demand. Cooper's known our family for years and has been a most helpful resource since the passing of my sister. My brother is in his own little world and useless at making memorial arrangements. That's what I was talking to the mayor about at dinner. Cooper has no idea I'd reached out to you for your help in clearing Gully's name. Neither does Gully, and I'd like to keep it that way."

"I can't imagine the subject will come up. Our relationship is all business. But I'm curious whether you were in Augustin the night of Poppy's death? Were you with your sister that night? To me, seems a bit odd she would be in the garden, off season, after dark." Sherry held her breath, hoping she hadn't overstepped investigative boundaries.

"I'm not sure if you're aware, Poppy went to the garden after dinner nearly every night, year-round. After Rohan died, I learned not to call her cell phone at that time. She would never pick up while she was there. She didn't like to disturb the peace and quiet. I don't know what she did day in and day out, but I knew where to find her at seven in the evening. To answer your question, yes, I was in Augustin that night. Poppy and I had an early dinner and we unfortunately got into an argument. I regret that. At the time, I believed our bitter exchange was the worst way to end the evening and we'd have to figure a way to make up. That was until I learned I would never see her alive again. Then the fight took on a whole new meaning, especially when I'll never have the chance to hear and accept Poppy's apology."

"Apology from Poppy, not the other way around?" Sherry uttered under her breath.

Sherry flinched with a tap on her shoulder.

"Excuse me," Amber said. "I need to interrupt for a moment. Mrs. Camponella has a concern about the types of rug padding we offer. Her cane causes even our best anti-slip padding under a rug to slide, which is so dangerous."

"I'm on my way out. I've said what I came to say. Have a great day, and I'll be back for a rug in the near future." Tessa switched her purse to her other forearm, waved, and let herself out.

"A no-sale?" Amber whispered.

"Actually, Tessa was the one doing the selling. I'm not sure I'm buying."

Chapter Eleven

Sherry threw up her hands. "I'm realizing I need to bring my laptop everywhere to keep track of gathered information. I started a file named 'S-Info' and Tessa's info has to be added. Now I know why Detective Diamond is on Ray's back to go high-tech."

"What does the S stand for in the file name?" Amber asked.

"Suspect, or maybe I'll change that to suspicious."

"Sounds like you're all in."

"My desire to be all in is about as on par as a clam wanting to be all in a pot of bouillabaisse. Even if I were, the file is awfully lacking in the 'info' department, proving I don't have much to go on."

Mrs. Camponella made her way to the checkout table using slow, deliberate steps.

"I need to swap out all the anti-skid pads under the sample rugs with the highest quality ones we offer. I don't want to lose any of our most loyal customers to a tragic fall."

Amber nodded. "We'll change them all as soon as we're done with Mrs. Camponella. So you think Tessa might have had a hand in Poppy's demise?"

"Tessa has no alibi. She had an argument with Poppy that night, but I'm not convinced. The nagging question is what was Gully Robinson doing the night his sister was murdered? That's what I'd like to find out. He had to be aware of Poppy's habit of going to the garden every evening," Sherry whispered as she rolled up the sample rug Mrs. Camponella had chosen to purchase. The aqua blues and moss greens of the seahorse motif were Sherry's favorite color combination.

Amber tied a cord around the pink tulip and yellow daffodil rug the woman had asked to see but didn't purchase. "Why didn't you ask Tessa that question when she was here?"

"Too many questions directed at her might shut her down. I also got the impression she was embellishing the truth and I wasn't getting the full story from her. I took everything she said with a grain of salt."

"Are you young ladies talking about the murder of the Robinson gal?" Mrs. Camponella rested a hand on her rug choice when she reached the sales counter. "My stride may be slow, but my hearing's as sharp as ever. You know, I knew her father, Rohan Robinson. We went to high school together. He was quite a looker in those days, and I was no shrinking violet. He courted me for a while before Vernon Camponella caught my eye. The rest is history."

"Yes, you heard correctly. We were talking about the murder. We were discussing the different scenarios that may have taken place that night and the cast of characters who may have played the leading roles." Sherry tipped her head toward the front door. "That was Rohan's daughter, Tessa, who left a minute ago."

"For heaven's sake," exclaimed Mrs. Camponella. "Isn't that amazing. I'd heard she was a fancy Hollywood type. You never know what kind of kids people will raise until you connect the dots."

"What do you mean?" Sherry asked.

"Rohan was an actor in college." Mrs. Camponella heaved a sigh. "He made the most divine leading man, but life and responsibility got in the way and he put his dreams aside to support his growing family. He raised one child who inherited his business sense, one with his thespian talent, and Lord knows what the boy does for a living. I've heard he dabbles in art and climbs walls. Call me old-fashioned, but how either of those vocations puts food on the table, as opposed to a nine-to-five job, is beyond me. The Rohan I knew would, on one hand, encourage the creativity, but, on the other hand, be horrified at the lack of income-earning potential the boy's professions have."

"Stands to reason Gully needs money if he didn't inherit any from his father. Desperate times call for desperate actions. If Gully was strapped for cash, who knows what he would do to get an injection of capital from a most-familiar source."

"Good luck getting to the bottom of things, Sherry. Rohan's up above"—Mrs. Camponella pointed her cane to the heavens—"rooting you on, unless you discover one of his other kids has misbehaved, in which case, you're on your own." The woman raised her fingers and framed the words "his other kids" in air quotes. "Rohan would never approve of infighting if he hadn't masterminded it."

"Enjoy the rug, Mrs. Camponella. Amber will carry it to the car for you."

The woman shuffled through the open doorway, followed by Amber, hugging the bundled rug.

"No need. My husband's waiting for me right outside the door," Mrs. Camponella called out.

"She has her husband trained well," scoffed Amber when she returned a minute later. "He was waiting outside the car with open arms. Your phone's ringing." Amber snapped her fingers to the beat of Sherry's custom ringtone.

"Thanks." Sherry passed the picture window and reached across the table toward the cash register to collect her phone. "Blocked number" was displayed on the phone screen. She tapped the accept button. "Ray Bease, you must be a mind reader. I was going to call you in a minute."

"My number is supposed to be private and shouldn't come up with my name attached on caller ID. How'd you know I was the caller? Is this a good time to stop in? I have a question."

"My powers of deduction are sharpening. I put one and one together to make two because I can see you through the store's picture window. Your hat is a beacon of familiarity. You don't need to call before you come in. If the 'Open' sign is on the door, it's fair game to step inside. See you in a minute."

The door bells tinkled.

"Hi, Ray." Sherry winced at the level of sweetness injected into her greeting. Before the detective could attempt a return greeting, she asked, "Have you spoken to Gully Robinson?"

Ray removed his hat and tucked it under his armpit. "Sherry, I'm the one with a question. But yes, I have, and I can't elaborate any further about that." Ray shifted his gaze to the woman tapping her shoe on the wood floor. "Hi, Amber. Good to see you again."

"Good to see you too. Sherry, I'll be in the back. Holler if you need me."

"What's your question?" This time there was less sugar, more vinegar in Sherry's tone.

"A small bag of seeds was found in Poppy Robinson's sweater pocket. Unmarked, they had no fingerprints on them or the bag they came in. I brought the whole kit and caboodle to the lab for analysis. I have three of the seeds with me, and I'd like to know if you can identify them. The lab can be a bit backed up at times, and I assume you know, as well as the lab techs do, what these critters are." Ray plunged his hand inside his blazer and pulled out an extra-small clear plastic bag. "I ask that you keep them in the bag, please."

Before she began her inspection, she eyed the detective. "Kit and caboodle? Ray, the fifties called and they want their snazzy lingo back."

"Very funny. You know what I mean. Maybe you can exercise your extraordinary powers of deduction while you concentrate on the seeds, please."

"Nothing extraordinary here. These are your garden-variety lemon seeds, which is strange. Poppy would never have attempted to plant lemon seeds in the garden. First of all, she would have known enough to not plant any seeds outdoors at this time of year because the danger of frost isn't over until the end of next month. Second, lemon trees don't grow well, if at all, outdoors in New England. When is the last time you saw a citrus tree with luscious lemons, limes, or oranges gracing someone's property within a hundred-mile radius of southern Connecticut? You'd need a greenhouse to have any success. I think every kid growing up imagined planting a lemon seed and sprouting a tree. Growing citrus is very difficult. Requires prolonged warmth, numerous sunny days, and adequate rainfall. None of which can be counted on in New England." Sherry dropped the seed bag back in Ray's hand. "Okay, maybe not every kid. I was the complete child gardener geek and tried to grow a lemon tree from a seed, an avocado tree from a pit, and an apple tree from a half-eaten core. All failed attempts. But, who knew those experiments would come in handy one day in a murder investigation?"

"That was a very long answer to a very short question."

"Wanted to be sure I gave you the whole kit and caboodle."

Ray's facial expression remained blasé.

"Did Poppy have any gardening tools with her?" Sherry asked.

"Only the shovel she was clobbered with. A new four-foot-long metal shovel with a wooden handle. Clean as a whistle, except for the dent and a minimal amount of dried blood. Not a fingerprint or particle of garden soil to be found. Yes, the perp probably used gloves, but why wouldn't Ms. Robinson's prints be somewhere on the tool if she brought it to the garden, which Ms. Robinson clearly did not. There were no gloves on the scene in her size."

"Anyone who was a member of the garden would never dare bring a shovel like that onto the premises, and Poppy would never, ever use a long-handled shovel. Poppy was adamant about not allowing a large shovel near her raised beds to protect the untreated cedar boarding and to keep the soil from being deeply tilled, which she advocated was the best way to kill beneficial worms, destroy the natural layering of the soil, uncover dormant weed seeds, and encourage their growth. Members are all required to use handheld trowels no longer than twelve inches. If she caught you with a full-length shovel, you were barred for the entire season, and possibly forever. No one made that mistake after the first offender was punished."

"Do you have the name of the aforementioned disobedient gardener?" The detective pulled his notepad and pen from his inside pocket.

Sherry eyeballed the antiquated recording system.

Ray shifted his weight from one leg to the other. "I know what you're going to say, but don't bother. Laptop's in the car. Wasn't planning on taking any notes."

The corners of Sherry's mouth hiked up. "I'm guilty of using pen and paper myself, so I'm not passing any judgment. I'm embarrassed to say the purveyor of the oversized shovel was Reverend

Hak, but if you're considering him as a suspect, don't bother. He returned to his native Sweden after Christmas. Not sure if the incident with Poppy had any influence on his departure, but, in his final sermon, he extended an invitation to his congregation to visit him in his, quote, less restrictive homeland, unquote. Last I heard, he was all settled in and doing well."

"She's one tough cookie. Clues are adding up that Poppy didn't go to the garden that night to actually garden. And the fresh tire marks in the parking lot indicate she had more than one other car to keep her company."

"Who joined her is the question? Besides Romie and Mayor Obermeyer and possibly Gully."

"My question not yours, correct?" The detective was stern.

"I'm voicing what everyone's thinking."

"That's what the facts will reveal. They always do." Ray pinched his eyes shut. He opened them. "I went to the America's Good Taste recipe contest website in search of your recipe, and there it was, front and center. Connecticut Crab Cakes, Oliveri Style. Nice picture of you too."

"I forgot to send you the link, I'm sorry. Good job finding it on your own." Sherry tucked a lock of hair behind her ear. "Thanks. I was having a good hair day. Connecticut Crab Cakes, Oliveri Style wasn't the name I christened my recipe with, but the sponsor's at liberty to change the recipe title to their liking. Now that I say the name out loud, I kind of like it."

"I can't wait to try it. Crab cakes are a step up

from my current signature dish, Cobb Salad à la Bease. While I was on the website, I scrolled around and noticed an interesting coincidence between the cook-off and the murder scene."

"What could that be?"

"One of the sponsors of the cook-off was Ceci's Produce, featuring lemons."

"That's right. The contestants were required to incorporate either lemon juice or lemon zest into their recipe and Ceci's Produce supplied the fruit for the contest. The fruit was so fresh and tart, I had to be careful to try to not get squirted in the eye when juicing them, which, of course, I managed to do on the very first squeeze."

Ray crossed one leg over the other and leaned up against the counter. He shot a glance at his wristwatch.

"I couldn't have been happier when I found out lemons were a required ingredient in my recipe entry. Even a small amount of lemon juice brightens any recipe and enhances the seasoning. You need to use less salt with the addition of lemon because the acid intensifies the seasoning magically. Heaviness and fattiness are cut by the acid and, in my case, the crabmeat tasted sweeter after a squirt of lemon."

"I understand. You love lemons."

"No need for sarcasm. Doesn't hurt to share my lemon knowledge with you. That *is* a coincidence since Poppy had lemon seeds on her, but that's a stretch, I'm thinking. Poppy wasn't down in Orlando the day of the cook-off. Unfortunately for her, she was up here about to be murdered."

"Coincidences are often events that become more and more related the deeper they're studied, so we'll see."

"Anything else, Ray? I need to get back to work."

Ray peered around the store before settling his gaze back on Sherry. "I heard a rumor you're organizing a cook-off for the Fourth of July."

Sherry nodded. "More than a rumor. It's fact."

"Do you suppose I could enter a recipe? I'm not an Augustin resident, but I do enjoy the town. I'm working on a recipe for steak salad with goat cheese and arugula." Ray delivered the question with as much delicacy as a chef handles phyllo dough.

"Of course. All nonresidents are encouraged to enter. The contest is open to anyone with a recipe for a patty made out of whatever tastes good and holds up well on grill grates and is tasty between two halves of a bun. So, you need to grind that steak, form the meat into a signature burger, make arugula salad à la Bease, and melt the goat cheese under the bun. If you can tantalize the judges' taste buds with your culinary artistry, you've got a winner on your hand. Oh, and you didn't hear that recipe transformation suggestion from me." Sherry's eyes widened as her enthusiasm steamrolled. Her phone rang, breaking her momentum. "Excuse me one second, while I take this call."

"I thought my steak salad was a great idea. Guess I'll have to reconsider." Ray stepped back, crossed his arms, and leaned against the picture window.

"Hi, Kayson. Thanks again for dinner." Sherry turned her back to the detective.

"I was hoping we could go see a movie some night soon. Does that work for you?" asked Kayson.

The look on Sherry's face broadcast her lack of interest in any future get-togethers after dark with the radio personality. "A movie?" Sherry paused. "How about lunch instead. Say, day after tomorrow? I could pack a picnic. The weather should be nice enough to sit out at the beach."

"Lunch? If lunch is the only meal on the menu, beggars can't be choosers. Let's meet at the beach at one. See you there."

"Thanks, Kayson." Sherry set her phone on the counter.

Ray uncrossed his arms and stepped forward. "The famous radio host?"

"Yes. We're having lunch."

"Isn't he a lucky guy. Word is, he's considering a run for mayor in November."

"That's interesting because he and I got into a tiff over Mayor Obermeyer's political style at dinner, but Kayson never mentioned his own possible bid for election. Makes sense now. Kayson didn't have many kind words for Mayor Obermeyer, who is indirectly my boss. But, we live in a free country. Let the voters decide." Despite the fact spending more one-on-one time with Kayson was something Sherry wasn't sure she could generate excitement about, she had a nagging feeling it was important to keep him accessible. She was certain he knew more about the people Poppy came in contact with than he, thus far, had shared. "Is there anything else I can do for you, Ray?"

Ray scuffed his hard-soled shoe across the floor. "No, but I'm going to issue a soft warning. I feel like a broken record, but here I go. I ask for your patience. This investigation is moving at a healthy pace. No one can speed things up for the sake of their personal preference. Interference is not appreciated and will hinder my efforts." Ray placed his hat on his head and ran his finger around the rim, smoothing out kinks.

"Yes, sir. If I hear of such a person, I'll pass on your warning."

"As always, thank you for your time, Sherry." He turned toward the door, then looked back. "I'll let you know how the blue-ribbon Oliveri crab cake recipe comes out."

Sherry watched the detective leave the building. Behind her the floorboards creaked, alerting Sherry to Amber's tiptoeing approach.

"Is it safe to come out of hiding?" Amber had her hands cupped around her eyes, forming makeshift binoculars. She scanned the room. "I don't see the detective anywhere."

"He's gone, but not without the mandatory, 'keep your distance but stay close enough to answer my questions,' warning." Sherry pulled a blank sheet of paper from the drawer. "Because the detective's mixed message can be interpreted in a few ways, I'm putting one foot in front of the other for the sake of Poppy Robinson and her father. How can I not? Each one has said some pretty nice things about my cooking and me. Want to hear what I've come up with?"

Amber hopped onto the edge of the table. "Ready."

"Tessa wants me to find the killer because Gully's on Ray's list of suspects, thanks to a threatening note found next to Poppy's body. On the flip side,

Tessa Yates could easily be a suspect, so for her to try and speed up the investigation may not make the best sense. She was at odds with Poppy the evening of the murder. Tessa has no alibi." Sherry had yet to put pen to paper.

"The Robinson kids have something to gain from their sister's death. Sounds like there was a fair share of conflict between all three," Amber stated.

"Not so fast. There's more." Sherry tightened her grip on the pen. "Mayor Obermeyer wants me to find the killer because he's running for reelection. The discovery of a body in the garden he promised to maintain for his constituents casts a shadow of fear on the place until the killer is found. Yet, he's trying to steer me in the direction of suspecting Poppy's siblings for unknown reasons, which makes no sense because the mayor fraternizes with them socially and has reaped the benefits of their campaign contributions. If one more person warns me not to put Gully and Mayor Obermeyer in the same room, I'm going to invite both of them over to my next recipe contest taste-testing dinner to witness the fireworks between the two with my own eyes."

"Obviously some undocumented history there. But what happened between them?" Amber pointed to the paper. "You're not writing anything down."

"We haven't said anything noteworthy." Sherry twirled the pen between her fingers. "Romie Green wants me to find the killer, pronto. Ray's questioning led her to believe she's a suspect because of her argument with Poppy, witnessed by fellow board members. Romie has no alibi, and she's apparently dating Gully, which complicates things further."

"And Gully? Does he have an alibi?" Amber stared at the blank sheet of paper.

"If Romie was in the garden's parking lot, I wonder if Gully was with her." Sherry hailed the heavens with her hands. "There are so many moving parts. The one that's spinning the fastest is the truth or lack of truth about Poppy's character. Problem is, the truth to some is not the truth to others."

Amber stared at the paper. "What about the cook-off connection Ray was talking about?"

Sherry grimaced. "A weak connection. He may be trying to throw me off the scent. But, Ray thought the contest's use of lemons is a connection. I can maybe see what he's talking about." She glanced at the ceiling before returning her sights to her paper. She wrote some words and considered others.

"Gully had a job in Florida. He was an artist in residence for a time," Sherry murmured before raising her voice. "Amber, if I said something about someone else's children, let's say, 'look how well that mother treats her kids,' and I put air quotes around the words, her kids, what would you think?"

Amber closed her eyes for a moment. "I'd think the children in question weren't kid-aged or the children weren't her actual kids. That's a strange question."

The front door swung open and barking pandemonium ensued. "Mail's here. Package for Ms.

Oliveri," Quentin bellowed, as he stepped across the threshold. His blue uniform accentuated his eggplant physique as the buttons strained to stay fastened across his middle. Silver hair spilled out of his cap and flowed without interruption into his extensive silver sideburns.

"Thanks, Quentin. You're the best." Sherry tossed a broad smile the mailman's way in hopes he'd return the gesture. She was in luck. She was rewarded with a grin that revealed a dimple the size of which could house a cherry pit on the only patch of skin on his cheeks that wasn't sprouting hair. "There's the smile that's been lighting up Augustin's mail route for the last thirty years."

"Have a great day, ladies. And I'm closing in on forty years, come this August."

"Wow, congratulations."

Quentin didn't make a move to leave.

"Is there something on your mind?" Sherry asked.

"Evelyn, Augustin's head librarian, mentioned you're organizing a July Fourth cook-off, and I was wondering if I should enter my famous lobster mac and cheese burrito recipe. I've been making the gooey delicacy as long as I've been delivering mail. Back then, the cost of a stamp was a nickel and a gallon of gas was thirty cents. Lobster meat was practically free in those days, compared to today. That's how come I invented the recipe that now has become so hoity-toity with the cooking snob crowd. America can thank me for that yummy dish."

Sherry bit her bottom lip. "Might be hard to prove you were the first to cook lobster mac and cheese, but I, for one, am impressed you incorporated the burrito twist. Unfortunately, as tasty as that sounds, the cook-off theme is going to be grilled patties. If your ingredients can be formed into a patty, grilled, and served on a bun, you're eligible. There's plenty of time to come up with something."

"Easy for you to say. Your greatest joy in life is inventing new ways to put ingredients together and have the result judged by experts who hand you a huge check for your creativity." As Quentin did with every delivery, he set two dog biscuits on top of the letters for his favorite Ruggery canines. "Here you go, boys. No treats until you sit for the lady. Mind your manners. Have a good day, all."

"Bye, Quentin." Sherry leaned down and delivered the crunchy goodies to the obedient pups. Then she rifled through the stack of letters and pulled out a large padded envelope addressed to her. "Looks like another seed donation. Perfect." She scissored the package open and slid a plastic bag out far enough to confirm her suspicions. "I'll take this home and add it to the collection." She tucked the package in next to her purse behind the counter. At the same time, her phone rang.

Sherry searched her overstuffed purse for her ringing phone. "Did you know the song I use for my ringtone was inspired by a boat mishap out at sea that forced Jimmy Buffet to eat only peanut butter and canned goods for an extended length of time until he and his crew were able to find a safe landing to come ashore? Even though he was trying to improve his diet at the time, all he could think of was, 'if I survive, get me a thick and juicy cheeseburger.' Every time my phone rings, the song reminds me to do what's important. Fundamentals before frivolities."

Amber chuckled. "Only you could get a life lesson out of food and a ringtone."

"Hello?"

"Hi, Sherry. I wanted to give you a quick heads-up about something. By the way, this is Madagan."

"Right, hi. How's everything going?"

"I left a phone message for the Better Off Bread customer service rep, and I heard back from her. They're very interested in sponsoring Augustin's cook-off in July. That's the good news."

"That's great, but is there bad news?" Sherry held Amber's elbow as she helped her hop down from the table.

"Kind of. The woman I spoke to was confused at first about why I was calling again, because she said she had already replied with a yes. Then I became confused and explained to her the phone call was the first time we had spoken. She proceeded to search her records and realized the message wasn't a request from Augustin, rather from the town of Hillsboro to sponsor their Fourth of July cooking competition."

"No! That can't be," Sherry wailed. "This can't be a coincidence. Someone over there must have thought we had a great idea. Is there anything we can do to stop Hillsboro? If two cook-offs are held on the same night in neighboring towns, one of the events will suffer, and I don't want it to be ours. Why does that town always have to do everything bigger and bolder than Augustin?"

Chapter Twelve

Sherry returned home after work with two items left to accomplish on her day's to-do list. After mulling through her recipe files, she found a couple she wanted to print out. She studied the sheets. "Bacon, bacon, bacon. What to make with bacon? For the bacon national championship, the dish has got to be bold. Might be a good contest to enter my Sticky Peppered Maple Chicken with Spiced Pumpkin Pancakes. No, doesn't showcase bacon enough. The recipe I choose has got to scream bacon. Maple Bacon Sweet Potato Biscotti. That's the one. The judges will have to give me high marks for originality, if nothing else. Even I was surprised when I came up with that flavor combination. Three things that aren't on anyone's radar as belonging together, bacon plus biscotti plus sweet potato. I've held on to this recipe until the right contest came along. I have a feeling bacon in a cookie form is the right fit, even though no one else would believe it at first glance. I'm going with my gut on this one." Sherry decorated the selected recipe with an ink star and placed the paper on her worktable.

Next, she unearthed the year-to-date seed contributions housed in organized compartments.

"Let's see. We have plenty of early summer plantings—string beans, edamame, pumpkin, cucumbers. Some seeds that need fostering next month to get started indoors—tomato, broccoli, Brussels sprouts. We definitely need more early planting seeds." Sherry pulled the package delivered by Quentin and nestled it next to the box she'd received while in Florida.

The rustling of the paper and plastic alerted Chutney to possible treats being prepped for the offering. He trotted over to Sherry's feet. She ruffled his ear fur, which did nothing to ease his eagerness to be pampered with a crunchy delight.

"I'll get you a biscuit in a minute. First things first, I need to record these seeds. I'm a bit behind in my duties with all that's been going on." Sherry tore off the remainder of the brown paper from the box. She flipped the paper over in search of a return address but found none. She was left staring at a small shoebox. She lifted the lid, revealing two bags of seeds. They were nestled in shredded paper with a note written in block letters attached.

Sherry,

Please accept my seed contribution to the Community Garden. You, of all people, will appreciate the care I have taken to preserve a lineage of plants that have brought me so much joy in their journey from germination

to harvest. These are fifth generation heir-
loom seeds of plants I treasure, and I want
them to be carried on by a group of gardeners who know the value of a good yield. I had
no time to pack more this time, but if I can, I
will send in the near future. If I cannot,
please put these to good use and carry on
the lineage.

"No signature, no return address. Looks like eggplant and spinach. Yay, spinach! An early planter.
Spinach is very popular. Everyone will love these
seeds. Eggplant is a tough sell. As a matter of fact,
I can only think of one bed of them growing on
the entire plot of land last season at the garden."
Sherry retrieved a Sharpie from the drawer and la-
beled the seeds. She folded the note and set it
aside.

Sherry set her sights on the second package.
Chutney's ears pricked up as Sherry widened the
slit she'd previously made in the padded envelope.
With a shake, a bag tumbled out. She held the
clear plastic bag up and inspected the contents.
"What the heck are these? They don't look like any
seeds I've ever come across."

Sherry found her phone in her purse and clicked
the FaceTime icon. "Romie, hi, this is Sherry."

"Hi. Wow, FaceTime is not my friend without ad-
vance warning. If you don't mind, I'm not turning
my camera on me. I look like a wreck. I'll just give
you a nice view of the wall. What can I do for you?"

"Come on, you're so young, you have nothing to
hide, even with the terrible camera angle. Don't
worry about how you look, all that matters is if you

can see what I'm showing you. Is this a good time?" Sherry waited for hushed conversation in the background to die down before she continued.

"Sure," Romie replied.

Sherry held the bag in front of her phone's tiny camera lens. "I figured if anyone can identify the variety of seeds I received in the mail, you can. I'm usually pretty capable, but with these, I'm stumped." Sherry adjusted the camera to get a closer shot. "Can you see these clearly? I could take one out of the bag, but I never like to touch seeds without gloves. The oils on my hand can affect their ability to germinate. Can you get a good look?"

The gasp Romie produced startled Sherry, and she dropped the bag.

"Whatever you do, don't touch those seeds. I'm pretty sure those are rosary pea seeds. Latin name, *Abrus precatorius.* They're very toxic to the touch and, if ingested, deadly. Who in the world sent them?"

Sherry eyed the bag on the counter. "I have no idea. That makes two unmarked shipments I've received. The postmark on both is Augustin, but that could be where they were dropped in the mailbox. No return addresses. One contained a vague note about the contents but was unsigned. That group I was able to identify. The seeds you say are deadly had no note, just this bag inside an envelope."

"First things first, get on some gloves and get that bag out of the house and safely disposed of. Are you okay, otherwise? That's a scary delivery."

"I'm okay. Thanks for your expertise. I'm getting rid of this right now. I'll talk to you soon." Sherry lowered her shaky hand and set the phone on the counter. She put on rubber gloves from under the sink. Using the tips of her protected fingers, she pinched the envelope and bag and walked them outside to her garbage can. She returned and scrubbed her hands until they ached.

"That took a turn and not in a good direction. Good riddance to this rubbish." Sherry gathered the empty shoebox off the counter and walked it to the recycle can. As she dropped the box in, something shiny fell out and clanked on the floor.

"What's this?" She scraped the metal item off the floor before Chutney beat her in a foot versus paw race. "You can't eat a key. That's not good for you. Here's a bone." She opened the cabinet and tossed the dog his favorite snack. "What in the world is this key to? Someone must be missing this. Yet another reason a return address would have been helpful."

Sherry took out a large sandwich bag and placed the key and note inside. Returning to her desk, she lifted the lid of her laptop and began to type in the "S-Info" document. She filled in the meager facts she'd learned about Tessa and Romie's whereabouts on the eve of Poppy's murder. She stared at the list of three persons of interest with no alibis but plenty of motives to want the woman quieted or worse.

Sherry stared at Gully's list of employment. She highlighted his Florida employment in bold and saved the document. "I need to pay a visit to Town Hall before seven o'clock closing time. Want to take a ride, boy?"

*   *   *

Sherry approached the oversized wooden desk positioned inside an open cubicle. The dark wood was polished to a high gloss, reflecting the face of the woman shuffling a stack of papers. Behind her an ornately paneled door the color of roasted chestnuts sat ajar, allowing a view of a sapphire-blue rug.

"Hi, Tia." Sherry's chipper greeting was met with a blank stare. "Sorry I didn't call ahead, but I was wondering if Mayor Obermeyer was in?"

"Hi, Sherry. You caught me daydreaming. I was thinking about how to spend next weekend. You're probably in a cook-off or some exciting cooking event, right? My life is so boring compared to yours." Tia held her gaze on Sherry until Sherry took a step closer to the secretary's desk.

"Nothing special this weekend. Although, I'm hoping to get started on my next contest entry."

"What's the contest? Maybe I can help?" Tia's face lit up.

"I'm going to try my hand at the National Bacon Championships. I know I'll get plenty of willing taste testers for that. Thanks for the offer. I'll let you know if I need your help."

"I'm so jealous," Tia chirped. Behind her a man's baritone voice leaked out of the open door. "Yes, the mayor is in. I know he's not busy if he's singing *Mama Mia*. Let me ring him. One moment please."

Tia picked up the receiver on her phone and pressed a button. The mayor's rendition of the Abba tune ceased. "Sir, Sherry Oliveri is here and would like a meeting with you. I don't think you should keep her waiting. The woman is very busy. I bet she's concocting a winning bacon recipe for her next contest in her head right this very minute. I'd give anything to be a judge in that contest. All I have to do is say the word 'bacon' and I start to salivate." Tia paused. "Yes, sir, she'll be right in." Tia stood and swept her arm in the direction of the open door. "No need to knock."

Sherry glanced at the brass nameplate on the door as she passed through. The length of the name, Cooper Obermeyer, and the monstrous size of the chosen font, required the plate extend from one edge of the door to the other. Mayor Obermeyer stood up and jutted his hand across his desk. As he leaned forward, Sherry was offered a bird's-eye view of the two-tone pattern of his hair, a milky brown around the fringe and a dull overprocessed color similar to a chocolate pudding toward the hairline. The absence of silver hair didn't mesh with his lined sagging jowls, crepey undereye bags, and overgrown nose, which taken in all together, visually screamed, "over sixty but in denial."

"Have a seat. What can I do for you, Sherry?" The mayor shuffled papers on his desk and squared them up in a neat pile.

"Two things. First, the cook-off details are coming together nicely, in large part thanks to Madagan, who is a human dynamo."

"She is a dynamo at that. I've known her for a few years now. She's someone you want on your side professionally and personally. She has the capability to eat you alive if you cross her. I'm glad to hear you two have been getting along."

"There's an issue, though, and I'm not happy.

Did you know Hillsboro is planning a July Fourth cook-off? That could kill our attempt to draw big numbers to ours. I'm betting they stole our idea. Hillsboro has always prided itself on doing things bigger and better than Augustin. Remember the Art of the Oyster Shell Festival Augustin held two years ago as a fund-raiser for seeding the oyster beds offshore? A month before the bivalve celebration was held, Hillsboro, out of the blue, began full throttle advertising on the Grand Slam Clamboree to be held the day before. That deflated our town's festival to the point where we had to cut ticket prices in half. I mean, how many clams and oysters do people want to eat two days in a row?"

The mayor pounded his fist on his desk. "We're going to have to make ours the best cook-off this town has seen since, well, I'll have to check the archives because I'm not sure we've ever had one. Don't get discouraged. We won't let Hillsboro steal our town's thunder. Consider this a wake-up call for us to put our best foot forward. Or should I say, our best recipe. You and Madagan have everything under control, I'm certain of that. What's the second issue?"

"I thought so, but now I'm not so sure. I hope you're right." Sherry scanned the papers on the mayor's desk. "Would you mind checking into what type of permit we need to hold the event? The firehouse needs to be notified, the police obviously, traffic control, etcetera." Sherry watched as the mayor scribbled on a sheet of paper.

"Permits are on the agenda. I've been meaning to look into them. If I can't handle that assignment, I'm not a very good mayor." Mayor Obermeyer lifted his chin. "Any news on Poppy Robinson's murder investigation? I don't like the scuttlebutt I've been hearing about the Community Garden being haunted by Poppy's ghost. I wouldn't put it past that woman to reach down from the great beyond and do a thing like that to keep herself amused in the afterlife. This investigation needs to get a move on."

"I'm trying to get a handle on what went on that night. If I could find someone who was in the vicinity of the gardens after six, maybe he or she saw or heard something they really didn't understand was important." Sherry held her breath to steady her heart rate. "Were you in town that night?"

"I certainly was. The murder was the same night I began my new fitness regime. My fitness tracker has the date in bold, marking the day my commitment to fitness began. I commit to be fit is my new motto. I say those five words first thing every morning. I walk three miles every other night after work, instead of eating potato chips and drinking orange cream smoothies. I do miss those treats, but they were going to be the death of me. I've lost two and a half pounds already. Coincidentally, my route takes me right by the garden . . ."

Of course. I'm not surprised. The vicinity around the garden must have been as crowded as the Connecticut Turnpike at rush hour. Seems like everyone was on the way to the garden that night.

". . . but I didn't see or hear anything peculiar. I do admit I keep my eyes trained on the sidewalk because the sidewalk isn't well lit around those parts, and a misstep can be a leg breaker. As a matter of fact, the sidewalk is in real need of repair on that block."

Sherry squinted. "I would think you, of all people, could do something about that."

"Ah, yes. I did mention in my newsletter column I was upgrading some neighborhoods. I can't address all the neighborhoods' needs at once." The mayor lifted a small bedroom-style alarm clock from his desk to eye level. "Sherry, is there anything else? I have a zoning meeting in ten minutes and nature is calling. I sure hope dinner is included."

"Yes, that reminds me. There is one more thing. The Community Garden board has decided to take a look at how the properties that share a border with the Robinson property have been zoned throughout the years because we feel the productivity of the soil may be affected by how the neighbors treated theirs. We should have our soil tested for purity if a neighbor has ever, say, been a commercial site or a farm site that used pesticides. I would need to take a quick look through the history records of a few properties. I brought the two addresses with me. Maybe Tia could show me how to do that."

"You gardeners are a meticulous bunch. Sure, follow me and we'll tell Tia what you need."

Tia met Sherry outside the mayor's office and the two women climbed the marble staircase to the second floor.

Tia opened the door to room 202. "What you're looking for should be in here. Kathleen will assist you as soon as she wraps up her phone call. If you have any other questions, I'll be downstairs. We do close up at seven." Tia gave the woman seated at a desk behind a thick wood counter a wave and dismissed Sherry with a fling of her hand before heading back downstairs.

Sherry neared the counter that separated her from Kathleen. While speaking into a phone headset, Kathleen nudged a visitor log sheet in Sherry's direction.

Kathleen held up her index finger and mouthed, "One minute."

Sherry rotated away from the woman and took in the Zoning and Planning Department office décor. On one cream-colored wall was a charcoal drawing of an ancient map of Augustin. Sherry took a step closer and studied the yellowing parchment paper. When she heard the tapping of shoes closing in, Sherry spun on her heels and found herself face-to-face with Kathleen.

"Almost the whole town was farmland in those days. Properties were acres and acres and not well cleared on the property borders. Fences were stones piled masterfully on top of one another. The time and attention to detail of those stone walls was the seed of the idea that fences make great neighbors. What can I do for you, Ms. Oliveri?"

"So true. I'd like to take a look at the history of two of the properties that border the Augustin Community Garden. Might as well take a look at the garden property file itself, too, if you wouldn't mind." Sherry reached in her purse and pulled out her wallet, from where she removed her Community Garden membership card. She pointed to the fine print in the corner that listed her as a board member. "I'm representing the board and we're interested in whether any neighboring property has ever been a working farm. I realize this wall map indicates nearly every property has been a farm at one time or another, but how recently, is our concern. That knowledge will guide us in this year's soil testing program." Sherry's heart rate quickened as she considered how easily the white lie rolled off her tongue. Her cheeks tingled with warmth.

"Sure, I'll pull the files for the numbers five and nine Whale Watchers Avenue properties. I'll pull the number seven file too. Have a seat, I'll be a few minutes." Kathleen turned to leave.

"Would there be information in those files as to whether those properties had ever been involved in a . . ." The terms Madagan used in reference to the Robinson land collided in Sherry's head. ". . . dispute or grievance of any nature?"

"Look for red sticky notes. They indicate disputes, hearings, complaints, and beyond. You can document any papers on your phone or we can photocopy what you need." Kathleen made her way to the edge of the room, which housed shelf upon shelf of files. Before Sherry was able to fish her phone from her overstuffed purse, Kathleen returned with three file folders bulging with paperwork.

"Use this table." Kathleen piled the folders on a substantial farmhouse table in the corner of the room. "I'll be at my desk if you have any questions."

Sherry opened the 7 Whale Watchers Avenue file. Owners: Poppy Robinson, Tessa Yates, Gullickson Robinson. Five grievances against the address, filed in the last seven years.

"Noise nuisance complaints. Parking nuisance complaints. Here's another and another. Both files have made the complaints. Lots of back and forth, but most initiated by number seven Whale Watchers. Nothing pending, so the issues must have been dealt with. I can't figure out what the outcome was." Sherry realized she had been thinking out loud when she lifted her head and locked gazes with a scowling man at the next table. "Sorry."

Sherry captured shot after shot with her phone's camera until something, or rather a lack of something, caught her attention. Sherry set her phone down and walked over to Kathleen's desk. "Can I bother you with a question?"

"That's the beauty of my job. No questions bother me. The last call I fielded was from a man wanting to know if he would need special zoning for an airstrip in his backyard." Kathleen threw up her hands. "An airstrip. Now that beats yesterday's issue du jour. A couple wanted to file a grievance against their neighbor because of an elaborate tree house being built, the size of a single-car garage, that was obstructing their view of the Long Island Sound." Kathleen shook her head. "Some people have too much money. My job cracks me up sometimes. What's your question?"

Sherry blinked, and the thought she had nearly lost returned. "If there was a rezoning inquiry, either newly filed or pending outcome, on a property, would that be noted in the files you shared with me or are there separate files for motions in progress?"

Kathleen rolled her chair away from her desk and wheeled around until she faced Sherry's direction. "Those would be in the files. If there aren't any in there, nothing's currently in progress or has ever existed. If the owner was testing the waters, he or she may have verbally inquired at our offices, but we don't keep notes on speculative questions. There isn't enough paper in the world for that. You can't believe the questions callers present us with."

"Okay, thanks." Sherry returned to her work area. She continued clicking photos with her phone.

The second file she opened was 9 Whale Watchers Avenue. Owner: N. L. Pechman. Sherry picked up two survey maps and carried the papers to Kathleen's desk.

The woman lifted her gaze from the computer screen. "I was reading the newsletter. Nice job, as always. In particular, I enjoyed the blurb about your cook-off win. Really broke up the monotony of the town's business, since I know all that, for the most part. And that prep tip you offered when making summer sandwiches was great. Who knew canoeing out a sandwich roll so the sandwich filling sits more securely inside, makes for a yummier, more portable, and less bready picnic lunch? Genius. Do you have a question?"

"Thanks. Yes. I want to make certain I'm reading these maps correctly." Sherry pointed to a solid line on the eastern side of the Pechman property. "Obviously, this is the edge of number nine Whale Watchers Avenue. On the other side of this line, in very close proximity, is the Community Garden, which is outlined in the Robinson file. The garden's parking situation is very tight to the property line too. What is this dotted line that I see part of on this map, while the remainder that fits like a puzzle piece is on the Robinson map?" Sherry pointed to the dotted lines on both maps.

"That is the location of a shed. The building was substantial in size and build, so a permit was required and the structure's footprint added to the map."

"How can the shed be on both properties? It either belongs to one or the other, right? From what I've seen, these property owners don't strike me as the types who would share anything, let alone a substantial structure." Sherry shrugged. "Except maybe a right hook to the nose."

Kathleen leaned in and ran her index finger around each map. She stood and left Sherry staring at the maps before returning a few minutes later. "You're correct. These maps haven't been updated since Rohan Robinson's death. Earlier than that actually. The shed is now entirely on the Robinson property. I dug into the files further. A grievance was filed to have the shed moved." Kathleen waved a piece of paper in front of Sherry. "I found this letter signed by Mayor Obermeyer enforcing the urgency of the decision paper clipped to the complaint against the structure in Pechman's file."

"I'm glad the shed wasn't completely removed because the garden members need an onsite storage shed for their tools and supplies. What I noticed was N. L. Pechman wasn't a happy neighbor until about ten months ago. Then the complaints completely ceased," Sherry stated.

Kathleen sat back down at her desk. "Hard to say why. People get tired of complaining. They run out of steam. Or they have something else up their sleeve."

Sherry carried the maps back to their appropriate files. She opened the third file, 5 Whale Watchers Avenue. Owners: Champ* and Bunny Westerfield. Sherry trekked back to Kathleen. After a few minutes, it was evident Kathleen was in a deep conversation the end of which was nowhere in sight.

"What could the asterisk after Champ's name mean?" Sherry muttered as she returned to her table.

She pushed the folder aside and reopened the 7 Whale Watchers Avenue file. She snapped a photo of Rohan Robinson's death certificate filed on behalf of his children, in order to transfer the land title to their names, and flipped the folder shut. She stacked the files on top of one another and carried them back to Kathleen.

"Thank you. I think I've gathered all the information the board needs to make a proper judgment. You've been very helpful, Kathleen."

Kathleen stood and lifted the files from Sherry's hands. "You are most welcome. Tia mentioned you were organizing a July Fourth cook-off. Will there be a prize? There has to be a prize. I've got some recipe ideas in mind I'd like to enter. My chicken and broccoli casserole is my go-to potluck recipe that everyone raves about after the first bite. I'm glad I've been stingy about giving out the recipe. Let's hope the few I gave the recipe to don't show up at the cook-off with my casserole." Kathleen's words cascaded out of her mouth, picking up momentum as she waved the files for emphasis.

"Sounds delicious, but the contest's a patty-themed cook-off, meaning veggie burgers, turkey burgers, hamburgers, anything patty shaped you can grill and serve on a bun. Maybe you could do a chicken patty of some sort?"

"I guess that makes sense if it's going to be held at the beach." Kathleen paused. "Tia just sent word Hillsboro's having a cook-off. Maybe they would accept my casserole."

"No, no, you have to enter Augustin's. We have great cash prizes. Should be a blast."

"We'll see. So nice seeing you, Sherry. Can you find your way out?" Kathleen tossed her head in the direction of the staircase.

Sherry found Tia browsing on her computer as she approached her desk. "Thanks, Tia. You've been very helpful."

"Quite an amazing collection of records, wouldn't you agree? Goes to show, be careful what you do in public because words and actions become permanent history for all to see."

Chapter Thirteen

"I'm making French lemon and tarragon chicken salad sandwiches on split croissants. Mixed berries and lemonade will be our side dish and drink, if that works for you. Still fine if we meet at the beach at noon?" From her seat on the couch, Sherry spied her neighbor Eileen through the front window, performing her daily weed-plucking routine. When Eileen lifted her head from her dormant flower patch, she saluted Sherry, who waved her phone in return. Eileen pointed at the azure-blue sky and flashed a smile. Sherry popped her thumb upward. "I don't know how she finds the time to weed every single day, rain or shine."

"Who are you talking about?" Kayson asked.

"My neighbor. She's out plucking prolific plant invaders every day while I can hardly find time to get out to my garden more than twice a week. How could there even be any weeds at this time of year?"

"Listen. I'm worried that if our lunch date isn't

centered around a cooking competition, the food might not be up to your highest standards. Do you cook your best if there aren't any prizes at stake?" Kayson chuckled. "I'm only kidding." Dead air. "Sherry, are you there?"

"You know I'm kind of sensitive to your brand of humor, right? It's so hard to tell when you're kidding around or when there's a drop of truth injected."

"Here's the truth. I'm honored to be sampling your award-winning cooking. I look forward to tomorrow's lunch, no matter the quality. Should I bring a bottle of wine?"

"If you do, and you're certainly welcome to, I won't be indulging with you. I have my first tennis league match later in the day, and a glass of wine isn't a friend of my killer forehand. And don't you worry about the quality. Like your dear mother, I put my heart and soul into every meal I prepare. Prizes or not."

Kayson murmured something incomprehensible. "Speaking of friends and killers, I'm interviewing Mayor Obermeyer on my afternoon show later today. Feel free to call in. You could ask him why he so often says one thing and does another. Aren't you curious why he was out to dinner with the Yates woman when he has publicly criticized the Robinson family, stating Rohan Robinson's land was charitably designated to be used as a garden not for his spoiled children's financial gain? On the flip side, the mayor doesn't seem to have any problem cashing the family's campaign donation checks. How you can work for a man with such a low level of ethics and morality is beyond me. If I can get him to spell out his agenda for the remainder of his term, without any contradictions, I'll eat my hat for lunch instead of your *très bien* chicken salad."

"Sounds like the mayor's in for a fun time with you. Reminder. I work for the town, not the mayor. If a new mayor is elected in the fall, I hope to keep that job. I'll let my ballot do the talking as to who I prefer to see in office." Sherry allowed silence to wash over the conversation. *Kayson's not going to tell me he's running for mayor, I guess.* "Speaking of the Robinsons, I'm curious where Gully lives in town. I can't find him listed anywhere. The property on Whale Watchers Avenue no longer has a house on it, so he can't live there. The only public records I found for him have a post office box number listed as his address. Do you know him personally?"

"Nope. None of them. But I have boned up on the bullet points of the family's time in Augustin so I can sound somewhat knowledgeable when I announce the latest bulletins on the case. The Robinsons are a family most everyone knows the name of but few know on a more personal level. Rohan raised the kids in a bubble. They were home-schooled through high school and each was brilliant in their own way, but socially they were extremely private. Some would say isolated. Their inner circle was microscopic. I have no idea where Gully lives, nor do I need to know. Is there a reason you need to know?"

Sherry took another look out the window.

Eileen waved again.

"How does she always see me see her."

"Who?"

"My neighbor again. She has a sixth sense to always know when I've stepped outside, looked out my window, or even sneezed so she can say 'bless you' from across the street. It's uncanny. Anyway, Gully's doing some artwork for the July Fourth cook-off I'm organizing and I'd like to become more familiar with his background."

"So you've decided to do a bit of investigating on your own, Detective Oliveri?"

"That's not what I said and please, don't call me that. You'll get me in trouble with Detective Bease. He wouldn't be happy if he knew I was doing some snooping; although, I think he's coming to grips with the idea I'd like to find out who killed Poppy Robinson and what there was to gain in souring her reputation to boot." Sherry sighed. "I wish I had peeled back a few of the woman's layers to get to know her better when I had the chance."

"I'm on in ten minutes, so I have to go. Have a listen at five. That's when Mayor Obermeyer and I will have a meeting of the minds. Or when we butt heads. See you tomorrow. I'm starving." The phone went silent.

Sherry tossed her phone on the seat cushion next to her, disturbing her dog's nap. "There's not going to be any picnic if I don't run to the store and pick up tarragon, lemon, capers, chicken, and arugula, boy. Then you and I have to meet Gully at the library." Sherry patted Chutney's hindquarters and he perked up. She collected her purse and her reusable shopping bag and carried both to the car, where Chutney made an astonishing leap through the open door.

Once at the Au Natural market, Sherry loaded

her basket full of the items on her list. On a whim, Sherry decided to visit the prepared sushi counter to pick out her dinner. She eyed the Augustin Rockin' Rolls, which consisted of sesame panko-crusted white fish, toasted seaweed, and avocado, before making a split-second decision to swap them out for the brown rice tempura shrimp rolls.

As she reached forward to gather the package of rolls, a weight landed on her shoulder. Sherry jerked back and fresh sprigs of tarragon were launched from her basket.

"Dinner for one? I'm shocked you're not cooking tonight. The prepared section isn't for expert cooks, such as yourself. The cold grilled salmon and pasty mashed potatoes are for wannabes like myself."

Sherry twirled around toward the deep voice.

"Ray. You surprised me. Don't underestimate the power of the prepared food aisle. I consider eating takeout research for my next potential recipe creation. I've gotten some of my greatest inspiration from meals I've discovered here." Sherry peered in Ray's handbasket. "I see you share my craving for sushi. That eel roll is a pretty adventurous choice."

Ray thrust his face toward his basket. "Eel? Is that what I chose? I'm glad you caught my error. I thought those white cubes were tofu. I'll perform a little switcheroo for my old favorite California rolls."

"Or you could expand your palate and try something new. Nothing ventured, nothing gained."

Ray shook his head. "Maybe next time."

Sherry took his eel rolls from his basket and

swapped them for another package. "I'm going to make an executive decision and choose these smoked salmon cucumber rolls for you. The taste is best described as subdued adventure. If you don't like them, I'll buy your next package of boring old California rolls."

Ray smiled. "Deal."

After she stepped away from the refrigerated sushi case, Sherry squeezed her eyes shut and held her breath. "I got a warning in the mail. May have to do with the Poppy Robinson murder." She opened her eyes and pursed her lips. "I'll save you the effort by answering what's sure to be your next question. Yes, I may have been doing a little rogue investigating and someone may be telling me to back off."

The noise Ray generated deep within his throat could only be described as a muffled wail of agony. "Sherry. What. Kind. Of. Warning."

Sherry opened her eyes to the sight of Ray's mouth collapsing and his mustache being dragged toward his chin.

"I liked it better when you were smiling." Sherry examined Ray's face for a twinge of softening but found none. "Hear me out. I put out a call for seed donations for the Community Garden throughout the winter and have been receiving some on a regular basis. Yesterday, the mailman delivered an envelope to me at work and when I opened it, I didn't recognize the species of seeds inside. I showed a fellow board member, who is an expert at plant identification, and she told me if I touched the seeds with my bare hands they could poison me. They're deadly. The seeds are now in my outdoor garbage pail, if you want to take a look. I had to get them out of the house in case Chutney got any ideas about going near them."

"Sounds more like a threat than a warning. You realize the extra work you make for me? If I didn't have to run around cleaning up your messes, I might have some time to cook my own dinners instead of eating out of plastic containers."

"Come on, Ray. You're being a bit dramatic."

"I'll swing by and grab the seeds. With my thickest gloves on, that is."

Sherry lowered her chin. "You have one day before the garbage man makes his rounds. Ouch!"

"Jules, say you're sorry." A woman in a figure-hugging sweat top directed her son toward Sherry. "Are you hurt? You look a bit dazed. I thought my son was old enough to drive the shopping cart, but clearly he's not."

"I'm fine. Let him keep his learner's permit." Sherry laughed as she teetered on one leg while rubbing her sore shin that had been whacked by the metal shopping cart. She turned to face Ray. "Turns out the grocery store is where the real danger is." She tugged the corners of her mouth north.

Ray's frown didn't budge.

"Can you come pick the seeds up around five this afternoon?"

"That should be fine." Ray took a step toward Sherry. "Do you know if the seeds are from a plant native to Connecticut?"

"That's a great question. I don't know anything beyond the fact the seeds are poisonous." Sherry raised her head. "Before you repeat yourself yet again, I'll save you the effort. I consider myself warned, by you and that person out there who's not too happy with me."

"Good. Save me that effort at least. Since we're on the subject, I know you said Poppy's siblings weren't members of the garden board. That fact aside, did Tessa Yates or Gully Robinson ever make an impromptu appearance at the board meetings or at the garden itself, that you're aware of?"

"Never at the meetings, but, from time to time, I did see a man, from a distance, walking the perimeter of the garden. It was common knowledge he was Poppy's brother. He never came close enough for me to get a good look, but people talked. I imagine he was there to see Romie Green, who I recently learned is his girlfriend, besides being a very active member. As for Tessa Yates, she lives and works in the city, and I don't know how often she ventures to suburbia, but my first meeting with her was a few days ago. We didn't meet at a board meeting or at the garden."

"May I ask where you ran into Ms. Yates?"

"I was out to dinner and she was at the same restaurant. Dining with Mayor Obermeyer."

"During my initial round of questioning, an aforementioned garden board member, Romie Green, stated she watched a local news broadcast last week during which Mayor Obermeyer was overheard on a hot mic labeling the Robinson children spoiled."

"I'm beginning to think that might have been intentional."

"Intentional Romie watched the broadcast?"

"No. Intentional that the mic picked up the mayor's comments for all to hear."

Ray squared himself up to Sherry. "Conjecture

isn't admissible evidence, but you're entitled to your opinion. Now, from here on out, will you proceed with caution? Someone thinks you're sticking that cute nose of yours in places it doesn't belong."

Some early summer heat visited Sherry's cheeks. "Ray, people have pegged Poppy Robinson as a villain, and I've discovered she was completely misunderstood. Behind the scenes, she has been doing charitable work she never sought credit for. I can't let her slandered character be the first thing people think of when they hear her name."

"The facts of the case will sort themselves out. Under my watch, they always do." Ray lifted his sushi package and tipped his head. "Bon appétit, or should I say *kanpai*. That means cheers in Japanese." His smile returned.

On her way home, Sherry added a stop, bypassing the fastest route and instead merged onto Liberty Avenue. When she arrived, she parked in the "10 Minute Visitor" parking slot located next to the mayor's designated spot. She hooked Chutney up to his leash and made her way to the two-story brick colonial building trimmed with oversized dentil molding and boasting four two-story columns framing the entrance. The marble steps leading up to the paneled wooden double doors were well worn from the footsteps of over a century of visitors. Chutney bounded up the steps with youthful vigor because through those doors was a desk that housed crunchy dog biscuits.

"Sherry, you're back." Tia opened her desk drawer. She gave Chutney the sit command and rewarded him for his obedient behavior. "I'll have to double my order of dog treats if you're coming this often."

"Yep, here we are again. I need one more minute in the Zoning and Planning Department, if that's okay."

"You know the way. I'll call up there and warn them." Tia giggled as Sherry left for the stairs.

After reaching the second floor, Sherry made a turn into room 202.

"I heard you were on your way up," Kathleen sang out as she rose from her desk. "Do you need another property file?"

"I'd like to take one more look at 7 Whale Watchers Avenue, please."

"You're in luck. The file's still out on the table waiting to be refiled by our high school intern. Mayor Obermeyer was going through the contents." Kathleen pointed to the table by the shelves of files. "He warmed the seat for you."

"Did I hear my name?" Mayor Obermeyer poked his head through the office doorway. "Sherry, I heard you were back again. You didn't get the information you were looking for on your earlier visit? Kathleen mentioned you took plenty of photos."

"I need to double-check something. You know, so my report to the garden board is accurate." Sherry sat down in front of the file, with Chutney at her side. She glanced over her shoulder and noted the mayor hadn't moved from his position by the door.

His hands were in his pockets and he was leaning against the doorframe.

Flipping through the file contents, she reached the sheet she had photographed, but poorly. She squared the letter up in her phone's viewfinder and clicked. Her hand lingered over the manila covering. There was something different about the file. The papers were in the same order, but the entire file was less bulky. She turned the papers over one by one until she reached the last sheet. The collection of grievances was missing. Sherry aligned the file up with the back edge of the table and stood.

"If you're all done here, I'd be happy to walk you downstairs." Mayor Obermeyer's voice was as mellow as chamomile tea.

Judging by the mayor's stance, Sherry gathered a refusal wouldn't be accepted. She met him at the door.

"Kathleen mentioned you were looking over the Community Garden property file. I'm amazed one of the Robinson children didn't move into Rohan's house after his death. Instead, they tore the main house down. What do you make of that?" Sherry held Chutney's leash in one hand and the stairwell bannister in the other as she glanced at the mayor descending the steps beside her.

"Tessa has stated she doesn't want to live outside the city. That's where all her work is. Gully couldn't afford the upkeep and Poppy couldn't bear to live there in her father's absence is what I heard. Until her death, Poppy managed the land remotely. Due to the increasing value, I'm sure the remaining siblings will unload the parcel of land, despite Poppy having maintained the façade of representing her father's desire to have the garden there. Such a shame. She was going to pull the rug out from under the community sooner rather than later."

Sherry swung her head, ever so slightly, side to side. "Why do you have such a negative opinion of Poppy? And you haven't said too many nice things about her siblings, for that matter. I would have thought the Robinson family was one you would want to sidle up to, for lack of a better term. Rohan Robinson must have been well connected and, by association, his kids must be too. All good resources for a public-office holder. Did something happen between you and them?" Sherry envisioned Mayor Obermeyer at dinner with Tessa, handing her the breadbasket.

When they reached the base of the stairs, Mayor Obermeyer's shoulders rounded and his double chin declined, puckering the skin on his neck. "On the contrary. No one can deny Poppy and her family have been very generous to the town. I even hired Tessa to coach me in acting skills so I could improve my public speaking and overall public persona. She's the best at what she does. But I can't let people know that. If I do decide to run for reelection, that's not information I want out there. The family comes with too much baggage. I know I can trust you to be discreet with what I'm telling you."

"And Gully?"

"I think highly of Gully, who's a talented artist. His rock climbing skills are gaining him national recognition." He lowered his voice to a near whisper. "What's happened in the past should stay in the past. Water under the bridge."

"I assume you mean the property grievances I found in the files?"

"Look at the time," Mayor Obermeyer said as he checked his watch. "Duty calls."

"So, it's an act the way you bristle when their names come up? The acting lessons are paying off. I was certainly convinced." Sherry lowered her gaze to her dog standing poised to lead his owner back to Tia's desk for another treat.

"I'll take that as a compliment. As it turns out, I enjoy acting so much I'm trying out for a play in a week. I may have found the career I was destined for. I hope Tessa isn't the one who murdered her sister because she and I have formed a real connection, and, at this point, I'd be lost without her."

Chapter Fourteen

"This is your day off. What are you doing here?" Amber finished the last bite of her chickpea salad and replaced the lid on the container.

Sherry opened her Augustin Rockin' Rolls packaging and nimbly plucked one up with her complimentary chopsticks. "I have a meeting with Gully Robinson coming up, but I have something to ask you."

"I'm nervous if you had to come ask me face-to-face."

"Don't be." Sherry managed a lighthearted smile. "An idea has dawned on me. Hear me out. You've been in a recipe contest. You're a veteran now."

Amber groaned. "That's a stretch. I was a finalist in the OrgaNick's Cook-off, which is noteworthy on many levels, one being, that's where you and I met. Two being, a judge was murdered at the contest and three being, the fact I wouldn't have moved down here and started a new life if I hadn't participated in the cook-off. But, by no means, would I label myself a veteran of cook-offs. With that being said, please continue."

"My feathers are really ruffled over the fact Hillsboro has the audacity to hold a cook-off the same day as Augustin's. I think there's something I can do about the situation if I can drum up some evidence their organizer was tipped off to our plans. Yes, word our contest is taking place has gotten around town now. Our plans for a cook-off weren't a secret, but Hillsboro seemed to know almost at the point of inception. Who spilled the beans so early in the planning stages? That's where you come in." Sherry aimed the tip of her chopsticks at her friend.

"In a strange way," Amber said, "I'm relieved because I thought this was about Poppy's murder investigation."

Sherry stayed silent as she poked at the green mound of wasabi with her wooden eating utensils.

"Sherry? Your question isn't about the investigation, correct? Because, what I learned from the last two you were involved in was, I should stay as far away as possible for safety's sake." The pitch of Amber's voice rose to an intensity level that brought Bean trotting to his owner's side.

"I can safely say what I'm about to ask you has nothing to do with Poppy's murder investigation."

Amber's face relaxed.

"I was hoping I could convince you to pay a visit to the Hillsboro Town Hall in the guise of nominating yourself as a qualified judge for their contest. The goal would be to engage whoever is in charge of the event over there in a conversation to get to the bottom of how they came up with the cook-off idea in the first place. Names. I want names. What do you say about that?"

"I say I'm hesitant, but I'll do it." Amber glanced at the wall clock next to the front door. "What time is your meeting with Gully?"

"Four."

"It's two twenty. I can be back in an hour if I get going before the school busses start rolling and clogging up local traffic. Does that give you enough time to get to your meeting?"

"Yes. My meeting with Gully's only five minutes away. My car practically self-drives to the library by now, I've been there so often recently."

"I'll get going. Wish me luck." Amber grabbed her quilted coat off the wall hook and slipped out the front door.

"Amber, did you forget something?" Sherry called from the back room where she was finishing her last roll.

"I don't see Amber anywhere."

Sherry slipped through the break room door. "Romie. What a nice surprise. You caught me finishing a late lunch." Sherry quickened her steps as she wiped her hands on a napkin. "What can I do for you?"

Romie jabbed at the bridge of her glasses, tightening them against her face. "Did you throw away the rosary pea seeds? I'm worried sick over the possibility you might be harmed by them."

"No worries. They're safely contained. I definitely owe you a big thanks."

"Any ideas about where they were sent from and by whom?"

"Detective Bease couldn't tell me fast enough to

interpret the delivery as a warning to stay out of Poppy's murder investigation. But I don't understand. I'm not out on the streets actively searching for clues nonstop. Why is someone picking on me?" Sherry balled up her napkin and tossed it in the direction of the wastebasket. When the paper came up short, she found herself in a foot race with Bean to keep him from eating it. The dog won, and Sherry had to pry it out of his clenched jaws.

"On the contrary, if I were you, I'd take the delivery as a sign things need to move at a faster clip. Who knows what the next warning will be and what extent someone will go to to get their message across. But, Sherry, if I've put you in harm's way, don't spend one more minute on the case. I know I couldn't live with myself if something happened to you because I asked for your help." Romie lowered her head.

"I'm sure I'll be fine. Don't worry about me."

"Good, because something's come up that's making me extremely anxious."

"What's that?"

Romie lifted her chin until her gaze met Sherry's. "Would you be surprised to learn I'm dating Gully Robinson?"

"I think I'm the last to know, but the relationship does make sense, considering how often he was seen at the garden, when he isn't even a member. His being there did create a bit of a buzz amongst the gardeners."

Romie kneaded a lock of hair between her fingers. "Well, what would you say if I told you the reason I was at the garden the night of Poppy's murder was I followed Gully there. I was worried about his plans to confront his sister."

"Confront her? About what?" The image of a body lying next to a note with Gully's handwriting all over it flooded Sherry's brain.

"Gully told me Poppy had every intention of running for mayor in November and, as a result, after previously agreeing with her siblings to sell the land Rohan left them, she was reversing her word and pulling out of the sales agreement. Since all the kids' names are on the land's title, the deal was off unless the other two could buy her out, but that would be complicated. Gully had plans for the money he'd be making from the sale of the property to developers and saw her actions as a betrayal to her family. He went to the garden that night to tell her as much. When Detective Bease reconstructs those components, Gully will be in some serious hot water." Romie ran the back of her hand across her nose and sniffed in.

Sherry eyed the young woman. "Poppy was running for mayor? The field of candidates is getting crowded." Sherry softened her tone. "I'm sorry, but the circumstances don't sound good for Gully. You know, Tessa has approached me to find the killer because she also felt Gully was in the detective's crosshairs. I'll be as delicate as I can with what I'm about to say, but maybe he wasn't able to control himself that night and things turned ugly."

"I know things look bad, but he would never become violent. I can't say I found him by the time I drove to the garden. The night was cloudy, no moonlight, and I was hesitant to shine my flashlight for too long. Yes, he needed money. I've suggested, ad nauseam, he find a job that pays more than the measly commissions he makes on his artwork, but he's as stubborn as every single Robinson I've met. To go to the extent of harming his sister, absolutely not. I won't believe that theory." Romie began to whimper. "Have you had any luck uncovering any clues that lead in a different direction?"

Before Sherry could answer, Romie's pocket buzzed.

"Excuse me one second." Romie plucked the phone from her pants and checked the screen. "Gully's calling, speaking of the devil." Romie made a forty-five degree turn and answered her phone.

"Hey, Gull." Romie groaned. "I'm sorry, I'm not at home right now, but wait there. Do you think you have time to get that key made so this doesn't keep happening? I have to take mine with me, and I don't like to hand out copies." Romie tipped her head forward and rounded her shoulders. "I'm at the grocery store picking up a few things. Can you hang out for a bit? I should be there in about twenty minutes? See you then." She stuffed the phone back in her pocket and turned to face Sherry. "I can't tell him I'm here with you. He's in a vulnerable state, and, to make matters worse, he lost his backup key to the place where he's staying. He's locked himself out, and I'm not going to give him a key to my place. He's so scatterbrained. So, he'll have to be patient. The trouble with artists is they're too free-spirited and disorganized for their own good. I'm the one with the common sense in the relationship. He provides the whimsy."

"Why would he be upset to know you were here with me?" Sherry asked.

"Maybe I'm overreacting, but his behavior has been off recently. If I didn't know any better, I'd say he was tracking my every move. If I'm not where I said I was going to be, he gets upset. So, better to keep things simple by telling him I'm at the grocery store. I'm sure his moodiness is in part a reaction to the shock of his sister's tragic death." Romie nodded her head slowly. "Do you have any new leads you're following? Have you given any consideration to Mayor Obermeyer having a part in this mess?"

"Nothing to hang my hat on, yet. Sorry."

"I want to show you a quote the mayor gave to the *Hillsboro County Gazette.* The mayor was asked by a reporter for a comment on Poppy's passing and the impact her death may have on the Community Garden." Romie removed a folded paper from her back pants pocket. She opened it to full size and began to read. "'The mayor replied, "I can only hope the remaining Robinsons feel a monkey has been lifted off their backs as I'm sure most of Augustin does. Poppy held the town hostage while she made up her mind whether to continue bringing joy to the needy or sell out and be greedy.'" She refolded the paper. "I, for one, don't appreciate being manipulated by his opinion in this way. Mayor Obermeyer had to have had an inkling Poppy was considering a run for mayor. I think he was in the midst of a full-on character assassination gone awry and there was only one way out."

"Ugh. I had a talk with the mayor about the

message he's putting out concerning the family. I don't understand his animosity because he says one thing but does another." The words she uttered stung her ears as she quoted Kayson's sentiments exactly. "Dirty politics is one thing. Murder is another. Let's not jump to regretful conclusions. Like I said, if I discover any leads that'll help Gully, I'll let you know, but he's not doing himself any favors by getting bent out of shape." Sherry scrunched her eyes closed. "May I ask where he's locked himself out of?" When she opened them wide, Romie was studying her canvas slip-ons.

"I'm sorry. Gully's keeping his whereabouts under wraps for the time being because he claims, until recently, he's had people show up at his door to get him to change his sister's mind about selling the property on Whale Watchers Avenue. I have to respect that."

"Careful. Watch the door." Sherry motioned to Romie to move away from the door that had swung open. "Madagan. Welcome to the Ruggery. Is this your first time here?" Sherry's head pivoted from Madagan's ruddy-cheeked face to Romie's pale complexion. "Romie, do you know Madagan? She's a lawyer in town and is guiding me through the cook-off organization process. I'd be lost without her."

The ensuing silence became awkward. The moment Sherry couldn't stand the void anymore, Madagan offered, "Sure. Romie and I met about a year ago, I'd estimate. In my office."

"That sounds about right," Romie mumbled. She checked her phone. "I'm late. Good to see you, Madagan, and we'll talk soon, Sherry." She headed for the exit without waiting for a reply and was gone.

"Is Romie a client?" Sherry framed the question in an air of nonchalance.

Madagan set her bike helmet on the table. Her braided pigtails were sprouting wisps of hair, lending them the look of fuzzy plant roots. "Romie came into my office with Gully. It was his appointment, but she insisted upon staying by his side. Technically, Gully never became my client, so I'm not breaching client confidentiality when I tell you Romie had his arm twisted the entire meeting. They were seeking my help to force Poppy to sell 7 Whale Watchers Avenue, but I was already working with Poppy and saw that as a conflict of interest. More importantly, I don't take clients I don't trust are telling me the truth."

"Strange. I've had nothing but a warm relationship with Romie. But I guess I can see how she could be an arm twister if the cause was worthy enough. I admit my assessment of her character is only based on our time together on the board. But I'm beginning to be haunted by what you said about things not being what they seem." Sherry shook her head. "Anyway, that's not why you're here." Sherry's attempt at a laugh died, due to lack of effort.

"I took a chance you'd be working here today. I came in to buy a welcome rug for my office, the more nature themed the better, and to have a quick word about your upcoming chat with Gully."

Madagan took a walk over to the rug display rack. Her footsteps were muffled because she had taken off her mud-caked biking shoes and left them by the door. Madagan pointed to a rug. "This country road scene is perfect. Reminds me how much I adore biking. The greens, browns, and golds will go perfectly in my office. That's the one for me."

Sherry met her at the rack. "Fastest decision on record. Once again you've impressed me to no end."

"Thanks. I know what I like, and I don't bother with the rest. No one's ever accused me of wasting time trying to convince myself I can be open-minded. I can't." Madagan lifted the lush wool rug off the display bar and carried it to the checkout table. "Now, about Gully."

"He's a popular subject today. I've heard so much about him, I feel like I've known him for years. What have you got to say about him?" Sherry fussed with the rug, plucking off stray wool fibers and dust particles that time and curious customer hands had deposited.

"Unless things have changed, I recommend you not bring up Mayor Obermeyer in any capacity when you meet with Gully. Gully may not be so willing to volunteer if you do." Madagan's tone was serious.

"You're not the first person to make that request. I have to ask why? Not that I was planning on mentioning the mayor, but if I know why I shouldn't, there's a better chance I won't make that faux pas."

"Over the years, the Robinsons have had a few run-ins with the Town Council addressing grievances filed against them. The mayor led the hearings and always got the conflict to go away, but one day Gully waited for the mayor after a meeting. The resulting altercation didn't end well, and Gully spent the night in jail. Seems he didn't like something the mayor kept doing throughout the proceedings. The matter was settled quietly, and I wasn't involved in any way, so I don't know the details. Poppy told me she advised Gully to keep away from the mayor while the land was in the family's name, and, as far as I know, he's kept to her wishes. I want to honor Poppy's suggestion since she's no longer here to oversee Gully's behavior."

"Do you think Gully and Poppy had a healthy sibling relationship?" Sherry visualized the note Detective Bease mentioned, found at Poppy's side. "Tessa told me about a note found next to Poppy, signed by Gully. It said Gully wasn't happy with the direction Poppy had taken the land their father left them."

"I'm aware of his sentiments. Poppy was my client and she shared her brother's feelings with me. I have a hard time believing he would threaten his own sister beyond mere words, though." Madagan unzipped her belted waist pouch and pulled out a credit card. "Charge it, please. On the other hand, when Poppy refused to make an exception to Rohan's wishes and let Gully join the garden membership, they stopped talking. A note may have been his only acceptable means of communication."

"Why wouldn't Poppy let Gully join the garden? That doesn't seem fair." Sherry swiped Madagan's credit card in the card reader.

"He only wanted to join to be with Romie and, to Poppy, that was an insult. That's what led Gully and Romie to call a meeting with me in hopes of changing Poppy's mind, but I couldn't act on their behalf. Legally, there was no forcing Poppy's hand. She had it in writing that Rohan's wish was only Poppy be on the board, not Gully or Tessa. The rift between Gully and Poppy was created by that document and continued on until Poppy's death, as far as I know."

"I won't bring up the mayor in my meeting with Gully. Sounds like that would be opening a can of worms, not to mention there's a good chance we'd lose our cook-off artist. I'd sure like to know how that note found itself next to Poppy. If it was hand delivered to Poppy in the garden that night, Gully has some explaining to do." Sherry held up the rolled rug. "Do you need a bag for the rug? How are you going to get this back to your office if you rode your bike? I would be happy to make a delivery."

"Thanks for the offer, but I have a rack on the back of my bike, and I manage more unwieldy items than this rolled rug." Madagan secured her helmet and rescued the rug from Sherry's clutches. "Thanks again for this beauty. And be sure to let me know how the meeting goes."

As Madagan exited through the front door, in walked a trio of women chatting over each other with a frenzy of words, accentuated by hand gestures and head wagging.

"Hello, ladies. Welcome," Sherry greeted, knowing the words were most likely drowned out by the ongoing banter.

"Sherry, so nice to see you. Your ears must have been burning. We were discussing recipes to enter for your July cook-off," Ruth said. "Never too soon to start tinkering in the kitchen."

"Can we run a few ideas by you, dear?" Frances shifted her baby-blue and silver beaded handbag from one forearm to the other.

Sherry shook her head. "You can run ideas by me, but I can't comment one way or another. If word got out I influenced any part of the contest, my reputation would be compromised. Also, if you're on the planning board, I'm not sure you should be eligible to enter. You understand, don't you?"

"That's exactly what Erno said you'd say," Ruth lamented. "You can't fault me for trying."

Frances and Bev bobbed their heads and murmured in agreement.

Frances clicked open the gold-plated kissing-lock on the top of her purse. "There's another reason we came in." She rooted around and retrieved a wrinkled sheet of paper. "As you might recall, the night of your father's birthday we all had dinner with Mayor Obermeyer."

"Not all of us."

"Right, you and your sister chose not to attend. But that's beside the point. Before we arrived, the mayor had been working on his column for the newsletter. He said you had enforced a deadline that had gotten away from him, but he hoped he had completed his assignment. He read us what he hoped was his final draft." Frances unfurled the paper. "After he was done, the silence was deafening. He squashed the paper and tossed it in the garbage, realizing none of us approved. When he went to the men's room, I rescued the paper, in case." She lifted the paper to eye level.

"You mean stole the paper, don't you, Frances?" Ruth added.

Sherry shrugged her shoulders. "I don't know why I'd be interested in his discarded draft. I'm not his personal editor, only the newsletter's."

"Maybe the part about Poppy's death will be of interest to you, since you're on the case." Frances smoothed the paper as best she could against her ribs. Raising the words to her face, she pushed the paper to arm's length before lowering her hands. "Oh my, I can't see a thing without my reading glasses. Why do I think my eyes will magically see twenty-twenty if they haven't in thirty years?"

"Here, Frances. Let me." Bev secured the paper from Frances's grasp and ran her finger down to the section highlighted in neon-lime ink. "Here we go. The mayor writes, '. . . and, in conclusion, I'd be remiss not to mention the passing of Poppy Robinson. As a caller in to WAUG this morning so succinctly described, it's harsh to speak unkindly of the dead, but the woman may have been deserving. On a side note, that caller had a very nice speaking voice, if I do say so.'"

Chapter Fifteen

"Thank you, ladies. Would you mind if I keep that?"

Frances dropped the rumpled paper in Sherry's extended hand.

"At the time, none of us thought too much about what the mayor may have been implying, but as the days went by, we put our heads together and decided we might be sitting on a clue powder keg."

"Maybe," Sherry said.

"Ladies, if we're done here, I need to get back to the city by dinnertime." Bev checked her sparkling diamond watch. "Sherry, I'm coming back soon to work out a design for a guest room rug."

"Sounds good," Sherry replied as the women neared the front door. "Have a nice rest of your day."

Each gave Sherry the return good wishes and together they flowed through the doorway.

A moment later the door burst open. Amber strutted inside. "Guess who's one of the official cook-off judges for the Hillsboro Independence Day Cook-off?" Before Sherry could open her mouth, the answer was provided for her. "Yes, that would be me."

"You're not serious, are you? You were supposed to collect some information by inquiring about becoming a judge, not actually take the role."

"I went to Hillsboro Town Hall, which I must admit is a tad nicer than Augustin's, as you instructed. The man behind the information counter seemed thrilled when I described, what I think, is my limited experience at cooking contesting and told me to have a seat. He sprinted up the stairs and returned with the mayor of Hillsboro."

"The mayor? He went and got the mayor to speak to you?" Sherry's voice raised two octaves by the time she finished spitting out her words.

"I'm not kidding. I got the red carpet treatment. I wasn't exactly forthcoming about the fact that I rent in Augustin because I wasn't sure how they'd take the fact I lived in their competing town. Let's say, since they didn't ask, I didn't tell. Next thing I knew, the mayor had me agreeing to be on the judging panel."

"Okay, okay. That can be remedied, but did you get to the bottom of who put the cook-off bee in Hillsboro's bonnet?"

"First of all, let me preface my story by mentioning Mayor Whinnery may be the most charismatic human being on Earth. When he enters a room, he commands the space with his presence. His perfectly buffed bald scalp shines like a lighthouse beacon and all heads turn toward him in hopes he graces them with a proclamation. He's got these

eyes that bulge out a bit like a pug and when you
make eye contact with him, you sense he's burrow-
ing into your soul."

"What about the cook-off? How did the concept
come about? Did you get the answer?"

"After I gave him my judging sales pitch, I figured I'd hooked him. I tried to create an appropriate segue. Not sure I succeeded when I blurted
out, 'Augustin isn't too happy Hillsboro is having a
July Fourth cook-off. Where'd you get the idea to
steal their thunder?' "

Sherry's mouth fell open. "You said that?"

"He was making me nervous with those eyes."
Amber pursed her lips. "Believe me, I was as surprised as anyone those words gushed out of my
mouth. I pride myself on being cool, calm, and
collected most of the time."

"Understandable. What was his answer?"

"His wife."

"His wife?"

"His wife. Her name is Colette Darbonne. Does
that name ring a bell?" Amber asked.

"No way." Sherry threw up her hands. "Her show
on the Oven Lovin' network is the best. *Honey Buns
and French Quiches.* I never knew he was married to
her. She's on her way to becoming the next big
celebrity chef. So she came up with the idea?
There goes my theory of the origin of their cook-
off being a spiteful move on the part of Hillsboro."

"The mayor said his wife came home from her
acting class all hopped up on the idea. He was a bit
dismayed when she announced she was way too
busy to help organize. Must have been why he was
so happy for any volunteers, like myself."

Sherry picked up her phone and checked the time. "Acting class. Did he mention where the class was or who the teacher might be?"

"He did say his wife spends most of her time in the city, shooting her show. I imagine taking the class there would be most convenient. Why would that be important?" Amber asked.

"Mayor Obermeyer takes an acting class in the city and Tessa Yates is the instructor. Might be a stretch, but if Colette's a fellow student, there's a possibility the mayor was discussing the concept and Colette picked up on the idea."

"More than a possibility. Mayor Whinnery specifically said a fellow student gave Colette the suggestion. His wife told him Augustin was motivated to outdo Hillsboro's July Fourth festivities. Then the student went on to suggest, 'Wouldn't it be a shame if Colette let the outdoing happen with all the resources she was privy to.' That would be a funny thing for Augustin's mayor to say. If the suggestor was Mayor Obermeyer, why would he try to gum up the works on his town's festivities?"

"All sorts of things seem to be gummed up. Thank you so much, you've done a great job. I have to get to the library to meet with Gully." Sherry removed Chutney's leash from the wall hook and clapped her hands. Her pup scampered over, Bean not far behind. "Call me if you need me. Otherwise I'll be home around five."

Amber held the door open for Sherry. "Very good. Glad I could be of service."

* * *

Sherry gathered her papers and Chutney from the back of the car. As she neared the library, she observed a man dressed for a workout but decided his oversized shirt and slouchy sweats wouldn't work for scaling rocks without snagging. Upon further inspection, he had too many years under his belt to be Gully's age.

Passing Workout Man, Sherry made her way over to a picnic table under a pergola, a popular after-school hangout for children. Thankfully, there seemed to be an organized activity happening with the kids and they were over on the riverbank gathered around a lecturer.

"Any of those belong to you?"

Sherry turned toward the voice. "Not a single one."

Sherry scanned the man who stood a head taller next to her. Brown hair, restrained with a headband covered in cartoon renditions of mountain goats, framed a rugged face blooming with scruffy facial hair. Cutoff sleeves promoted two of the hairiest arms Sherry had ever seen. Pant legs, ending below his knees, exposed bruised and scraped shins and ankles. The man's sandaled feet boasted more than one blackened toenail.

Sherry's cheeks ignited after she lifted her line of sight back up to the man's extended hand.

"You must be Sherry Oliveri. And who's this?"

"Yes, that's me, and this is Chutney."

The man pointed to the papers in her hand. "I saw the word cook-off on your literature. I'm Gully Robinson."

His forearm, the shape of an oversized yam,

reached closer to Sherry. She grasped his hand and pumped. The feel of the callouses on his fingers reminded her of the few times she'd handled a whole flounder before the fish monger scaled off the abrasive skin.

"Yes, that's me. So nice to meet you. Let me start by saying, I'm so sorry about the passing of your sister Poppy. Have I already said that over the phone? If not, please accept my deepest sympathy. From the little time I spent with her, I learned to appreciate her passion for her interests. I admire that." Sherry realized she still had Gully's hand in hers and was shaking to the rhythm of her words. She released the calloused digits only to find she had a white powdery substance on her palm. "Powdered sugar?"

"Thanks for the sentiment." His gaze dropped to Sherry's hand. "Chalk. A climber's best friend. Keeps my hands dry. If I don't have a good grip on the rocks, I'm a goner. I was rooting around in my gym bag and must have gotten some on me. Here's a wipe." Gully lowered his bag from his shoulder, removed a chamois cloth, and swiped Sherry's dusty palm. "You've been rock wall baptized; although, being a cook, you'd probably prefer powdered sugar." He smiled and winked. "Let's take a look at the material you brought."

The two sat down at the picnic table, where Sherry spread the papers out in front of Gully. "Thank you for volunteering to do this. The cook-off needs a catchy logo for the entry form, T-shirts, advertisements, aprons, you name it. I would love a full poster advertisement also, if possible. The theme is grilled patty on a bun. Venue is Town Beach, event date is the Fourth of July. After that, your imagination is the only limitation."

As Gully scanned the material, he rubbed his facial scruff, and the sound, similar to sandpaper smoothing wood, resonated in Sherry's brain. She shivered.

Gully lifted his head and looked into Sherry's eyes. "I'm getting some good ideas. Doesn't seem too difficult. You know, Rohan was a big fan of your cooking. He worked full-time until the day he died and his family urged him to balance his life with outside activities, but I think following your wins was the only hobby he ever pursued. He would have loved to attend this cook-off."

"I had no idea. I only met him once at a cooking demonstration."

Gully's eyes narrowed. "He'd have been so excited hearing you won the cook-off in Orlando. He clipped articles from the newspaper about you."

"You're being too kind."

"I wish he'd accepted my interests as readily as he embraced odd ones from others he didn't even know." His voice had an edge that triggered a chilled ripple down Sherry's spine.

"Was your family close? What I mean is, did you see Poppy and your other sister, Tessa, often?"

Gully's fingers curled inside his palm until two fists were poised on the table. "I know you've been asking some questions. Tessa told me. I like to keep my personal life private, Sherry, and if you're on some self-motivated hunt for Poppy's killer, you'll have to look elsewhere rather than to our immediate family. At least I know I didn't kill any-one, and I told the detective who's on the case ex-actly that. I'm willing to offer my relationship with Poppy has been rocky at best. I feel extremely guilty I arranged for her to meet me at the garden that night. If I hadn't, she may be alive today. That's all I want to say on the subject of my family." Gully's voice cracked on the final syllable.

Sherry lowered her gaze. "If I need to drop off any more material, that's easy for me, if you live right in town."

"Right now, I'm in between residences, so that's not a good plan. Text me and I'll swing by."

"But you haven't traveled far for this meeting, have you? What I mean is, I don't want to inconve-nience you with this project if you're not a local. That wouldn't make sense."

"Nope. It's all good." Gully twisted up the cor-ners of his mouth. "If there's nothing else to dis-cuss, I need to get back to the gym for flexibility training. I'll stick this folder in my bag, work on the design as soon as possible, and text you when I'm done, if that works for you."

"That's fine," Sherry acquiesced as she helped Gully pack away the papers. "Need a ride?"

"No thanks. My ride has arrived." Gully clutched the folder to his chest and tilted his head toward a car in the drop-off zone.

Through the tinted car window, Sherry made out a silhouette barely a head above the steering wheel. The window rolled down and Romie waved. Sherry offered a semi salute and returned to her car, Chutney in tow.

"That was a cat and mouse game, and I don't think I was the winner," Sherry commented as she steered her car out of the lot and onto Main Street. "Chutney, I think you would have an easier time sorting the who, where, when, and why of the night Poppy was murdered than I'm having."

Chapter Sixteen

"If you've joined us for the first time after the commercial break, welcome. I'm in the WAUG studios having a one-on-one with Mayor Cooper Obermeyer. To recap, he has cited his accomplishments as mayor over the last seven years served, which didn't take long. Mayor, can I get you some water? Sounds like you're coughing up a hair ball."

"I'm fine. There's a ton of dust in here. Does this studio ever get cleaned?"

Sherry shifted her body as a weak smile crossed her lips. She repositioned her computer as the sunlight streaming through the window glared on the screen. "Do you want me to turn the volume up?"

Detective Bease continued to stare at his crossed legs. "I can hear perfectly fine. I'm running out of time, though, and listening to a rehash of Augustin politics is as dull as the California rolls I ate for lunch. Are you sure this is worth my while?"

"You didn't buy California rolls. I picked out

smoked salmon cucumber rolls for you. Did you swap those out for your safe tried-and-true roll? I'm ashamed of you, Ray. Nothing ventured, nothing . . ."

Ray put his finger up to his lips and shushed Sherry. "They're back on. Here we go."

"We're going to open up the phone lines for the remaining minutes, so please call in with comments, questions, and concerns for Augustin's mayor." After no more than a few seconds of silence, Kayson continued, "That didn't take long. We have our first caller. Good afternoon, you're on the air with Kayson listening to *Shore Things*. Who am I speaking with?"

Sherry put her phone down to her side and whispered, "I wasn't counting on getting straight through. I'll put it on speaker."

Ray jutted his chin forward. "Well, you did get through, so speak."

Sherry wrestled her dry tongue off the roof of her mouth. "Hi, this is Mary from Augustin."

"Thanks for calling, Mary from Augustin," Kayson sang out. "What's your question for Mayor Cooper Obermeyer?"

"He knows I'm the caller," Sherry mouthed to Ray.

The muscles around Ray's jaw bulged and his eyes narrowed. "That's impossible. How could he? You haven't said anything yet."

Sherry straightened her posture and took a deep breath, summoning her inner thespian. She concentrated on producing a honeyed bawdy voice. "Mayor Obermeyer, two questions. First, do you think there should be a term limit for the office of mayor in Augustin and second, is there anyone running for mayor this November who can beat you if you decide on a bid for a third term?"

The detective signaled Sherry to cover the phone. "How are those questions in any way applicable to the murder investigation? I couldn't care less if the guy runs or not."

Sherry uncovered the phone and raised her index finger sky high.

"Good questions, Mary," the mayor replied. "May I first say, you have a lovely voice. If we ever meet on the street, please introduce yourself to me. And that goes for any caller today. To address your first question, who wouldn't want more of my administration? What I've gotten accomplished in my one and three-quarters terms has been remarkable. Walk the streets of Augustin, swim at Town Beach, watch with confidence as the police and firefighters keep the community safe, and read at the library. I dare you to not admit you live in the best town in America. If more of me brings more of that, who would want term limits?"

Sherry shut her eyes for a moment, not wanting the detective's grimace to convince her she had taken the wrong approach.

"And your second question is a beaut. One of the benefits of working at Town Hall is I'm aware of applications submitted by potential candidates. Still early days right now, but, thus far, I'm aware of two applications on file. I won't name names, but one is a local on-air personality who could inflate a blimp with the hot air he spouts and the other tragically passed away since her paperwork was filled out."

Kayson interjected, "Are you suggesting Poppy Robinson was a candidate for mayor?"

Sherry wished she could see the look on Kayson's face as he must have feigned surprise.

"I never mentioned her by name but since you did, yes, it's more than a suggestion. She had every intention to run for mayor, beat me, and take this fair town back to the Land of Wishful Thinking by promising to create a utopia without explaining the horrendous sacrifices involved."

"Speaking of utopia, the wonderful Augustin Community Garden was her baby, right? Don't you believe that's been a great legacy of hers?" Sherry squirmed in her seat when she realized she had reverted to her normal voice halfway through her question.

"Sorry to interrupt, but we only have time for one last question from, Sher . . . , uh, Mary. We've got to give some other callers a chance. Let's wrap this up, Mayor," Kayson added.

"Mary, the garden has served its purpose. Maybe Ms. Robinson's death is a sign that time has come to move on. I know I promised the voters the garden would have longevity, but I couldn't control the longevity of the owner and now that she's out of the way, let me rephrase that, now that Augustin's lost an esteemed citizen and the rest of her family has neither the interest nor means to continue, the land should be put to an alternative use."

"Thank you, Mayor Obermeyer," Kayson said before Sherry could respond. "Have a nice day, Mary."

Sherry put her phone down and fixed her gaze on Ray. "The mayor doesn't come across as saddened in any way about Poppy's death. He was walking by the garden the night Poppy was shoveled and he has a motive. I don't want to believe Kayson may be on to something when he suggested Mayor Obermeyer has more to gain from a dead Poppy than an alive Poppy. If the mayor knew Poppy was gunning for his position and the garden was the pawn in her bid, he may have felt backed into a corner and lashed out. I wanted you to hear him state the reasons himself because I know how you are about hearsay and assumptions." Sherry's phone buzzed. "Let me check this text." She gave a soft snicker.

"Something you'd like to share with the class?"

"The text is from Kayson. He says he doesn't have to eat his hat because the mayor contradicted himself about the Community Garden, promising in one breath to provide for his constituents and in the next breath telling Kayson the garden has outlived its usefulness. An inside joke."

"Funny, I'm sure. I was wondering how you were going to get any information out of the mayor, you took such a roundabout route getting to the meat of the matter," Ray teased.

"Even I understand coaxing people to talk takes patience. As my father would say, you can't make a fluffy omelet without separating the eggs."

The detective cocked his head to the side. "Meaning what?"

"Better results come by taking extra steps. I didn't want the mayor to shut down by attacking him with an aggressive first question, so I massaged his ego before I went in for the kill."

"Don't enjoy this too much. I only agreed to witness this phone call because I trusted your judgment, but I'm, by no means, in favor of any further sleuthing on your part."

"Message received, as always."

"One more thing." Ray opened his briefcase and removed his computer. "I did some internet searching, per my assignment."

"More recipes?" Sherry asked.

"Nope. I searched Rosary Pea Seeds and guess what state they're most often found in?" Ray flashed the screen in Sherry's direction. "Florida." He closed the lid and placed the computer back in his briefcase.

Sherry groaned. "Florida," she regurgitated. "A-plus, Ray. You're a good student."

Ray glared at Sherry. "Could be yet another co-incidence, but I'm wondering, had the murderer been to your cook-off? And if he or she had been, was the takeaway some sort of inspiration to commit the heinous act?" Ray punctuated his words with a tip of his frayed hat.

"You can't drag me and my cook-off into this. I had nothing to do with Poppy's death. I happen to know a few of her relatives and acquaintances, but that's the extent of my involvement." Sherry's breath ran out as the last hasty word was spat out.

"Calm down. You're being a little oversensitive. My job is to explore all leads."

Sherry stood and joined Ray, who had made his way to the front door. "Thanks for your time." She opened the door for the detective.

Ray studied his leather dress shoes, which were in need of a good polishing. "That Bradshaw character is running for mayor?"

"Yep. I think he'd be a decent mayor. He has some good ideas, he only needs to take off his talk show hat that ignites controversy and put on his servant of the people hat. That new outfit could take some getting used to."

"Hmm. Have a nice evening." The detective placed his hat on his head and left the house. As Sherry was closing the door, he turned back midway down the porch steps. "Oh, and I'll pick up the seed bag from the garbage can on my way out. I brought a hazardous materials container."

Sherry closed the front door, picked up her phone, and walked into the kitchen. She opened the cabinet that housed her seed collection and, one by one, placed the donation packages on the counter. The only envelope she spaced a distance from the others was the one containing the key and note. Sherry searched her contact list under the letter *G* and found Romie's number.

"Hi, Romie. I know it's late in the day, but I was wondering if I could meet you at the Community Garden parking lot in a few minutes. I'm painting my kitchen this weekend and I was hoping you'd babysit the seed donations for a week or so until the cabinet I keep them in is redone. Would you mind?"

On the other end of the phone, Romie uttered, "Uh, I guess so. I can be there in five minutes."

"Five minutes, well, sure. The sun sets soon, so the earlier the better. See you soon." Sherry clicked off the call and reached into a drawer for her supply of large paper sacks. She scooped up the seed bags and placed them inside. "Don't look at me that way. I told a little fib. I do plan on repainting the kitchen one of these days."

Chutney turned tail and pranced away.

The short drive to Whale Watchers Avenue gave Sherry the time she needed to organize her plan. Plan wasn't exactly the right word, more like wild notion. As she parked her car in the gravel lot, her heartbeat quickened. Scanning her surroundings, she saw hers was the only car in sight. The sun was setting and the sky was swabbed with more shades of turmeric orange and paprika red than blue. Bag in hand, Sherry stepped out of the car and surveyed the empty lot. Bats were taking flight overhead as the light dimmed. An owl let loose a forlorn but piercing hoot.

"That owl has been here for years."

Sherry jerked her head around and came face-to-face with Romie. "I didn't hear you coming. Where did you park?"

"Gully's borrowing my car to go to the gym. I walked over." Romie tipped her head toward the edge of the lot. "I was surprised you called. Almost as if you knew I was nearby." Romie's voice took on a brittle quality Sherry hadn't heard her use before.

"I took a chance you'd be available. You're doing me a big favor. I don't want to expose the seeds to paint fumes, and my house is so small I don't have much storage area."

"Of course, happy to help. I'll keep them cool, dry, and out of the light until you want them back." Romie reached out her hand and choked the collar of the bag.

"Can I give you a lift? It's getting dark and a little unnerving out here." Sherry pointed over Romie's shoulder. "I wonder who left the light on in the shed."

"No thanks. I'm heading back over to my friend's house next door. I cut my visit a bit short to meet you, so I should spend a little more time there." Romie turned toward the direction Sherry indicated. "I'll take a look on my way out. I know some members have been itching to get planting and they may have found a way into the shed to check how their tool supplies fared over the winter. We do keep the building locked, so I'm a bit concerned the lights are on, but I'll take care of it." Romie backed up until she reached the Belgium block border of the parking lot.

"I wonder if your friend next door is ever annoyed by the comings and goings of the garden. I mean, the most ardent of members hang out until midnight watching their bean plants grow minute by minute. Can be an obsession with some. Members bring family and friends, crank up boom boxes, and have picnics in celebration of summer solstice, national tomato day, and world vegetarian day. Any excuse for a party."

"He's resigned himself to being neighborly." Romie's tone was clipped. "Thank goodness. Our friendship would suffer if something that gives me so much pleasure brings him pain. I hear the neighbors on the other side have done some complaining." Romie displayed the bag. "These seeds are safe with me. See you soon."

Sherry's gaze followed Romie as she strutted

across the bluestone slates imbedded in the lawn. She eventually folded into the enveloping darkness. A moment later, the shed light went out.

"Romie, can you hear me?" Sherry called out. "Everything okay over there?" A rustling of branches produced two shadowy figures and one thin stream of light crossing in front of the shed.

"All's well," delivered a hoarse voice before the light bounced out of sight.

Chapter Seventeen

Sherry's father lay a sample rug across the display rack.

"The way you take so much care to present those rugs with perfection always reminds me of the first time I presented my recipe to a panel of contest judges. The National Crepe Cook-off was the contest, and I was so nervous about the presentation of my tray of French Chicken and Mushroom Crepes, I rotated the tray in measured increments on the judges' table until I was finally satisfied Chef Saint Pierre had the optimal view. Whereas you're always happy with the final result, I second-guessed myself for the next couple of months because I came in second, not first."

"That's a very nice story, sweetie. As I always say, 'put your best foot forward, and you'll get a hand.'"

"I've never heard you say that, Dad. You don't mind if I leave Chutney here with you and Bean during lunchtime today, do you?"

"No problem. You're having lunch with that radio DJ fellow today, is that right?" Erno asked.

"He's not a DJ. I'm not even sure that's a profession anymore. He's a talk radio personality, and yes, that's what I'm doing at lunchtime. I should be back by two, maybe sooner."

A noise in the back of the store grabbed Sherry's attention.

"Do I hear wedding bells in your future?" Amber emerged from the storage closet.

Sherry shot a grimace back at Amber. "If you do, you should get your hearing checked."

At the same time, the front door swung open and the copper bell overhead tinkled.

"Right on cue," Amber said. "A definite sign of things to come."

Sherry sweetened her tone. "Good morning, welcome to the Ruggery. What can we do for you?" Sherry's breath hitched in her throat.

The man with the ample head full of graying hair shifted his gaze from Sherry to Amber before landing back on Sherry. "Good morning. I was hoping to have a word with Sherry Oliveri."

"I'm Sherry." Sherry examined the eyes and nose of the man who appeared to have lost his razor for the last day or two. "You look so familiar. Have we met?"

"Funny you asking me that, because I feel like I've known you forever." The man's voice was as smooth as molasses on a summer's day. "Anyone who's followed your contesting career feels the same way, I'm sure. I did have the pleasure of meeting you personally one afternoon."

Sherry inched sideways in Amber's direction.

"Really? Give me a clue where I might know you from."

"The pilot abruptly turned on the return to your seats sign, and I absconded an empty seat next to you until the turbulence calmed down."

"The flight from Orlando, of course, yes. Now I remember. You said you were in the audience at the America's Good Taste Cook-off. I'm sorry, I know we introduced ourselves, but, for the life of me, I can't recall your name."

"That's all right. You've probably met so many fans. How could you possibly remember my name?" He extended his hand. "Let me reintroduce myself. I'm Nolan."

"Ah, yes. Nolan, this is Amber and over there is my father, Erno. He owns the Ruggery."

On the other side of the room, Erno pitched a wave.

"What can I do for you?" Sherry asked.

Nolan peered from Sherry to Amber before settling back on Sherry. "Would you mind if we stepped outside for a moment?"

"Sure. Let me give Amber her to-do list. I'll be right with you." Sherry touched Amber's elbow and guided her to the display rack where Erno was fretting over an oval rug that wouldn't hang correctly. "Amber, I don't remember much about this guy. He sat next to me on the plane and said he's followed my contesting for years, which is flattering, but I don't want to take any chances. If I'm not back inside in ten minutes, would you make up an excuse to call me back in? Make that five minutes."

"Do you really think it's smart to be alone with him?" Amber croaked. "Someone's out to get you. What if he's that someone?"

"In broad daylight? Nothing's going to happen. Call me in five, please," Sherry whispered.

Sherry shuffled by Nolan as she exited through the doorway he held open for her. She stopped outside the picture window, in full view of the inside of the store. She peered back inside the store's window and was reassured when she saw Amber fidgeting with something on the sales counter, in between glancing back at her every few seconds.

Nolan turned to face Sherry and drew in a deep breath. "I'll get right to the point. I have a friend who's in trouble. She told me she's come to you for help. She doesn't know I met you and she would be very upset knowing I am here, but I can't help myself."

"Who's your friend?"

"Romie Green. She seems to think she's on the suspect list of that woman Poppy Robinson's murder investigation. She said you're some sort of amateur sleuth who relishes solving murder mysteries and would be able to find the murderer faster than the investigators. You're shaking your head. Am I wrong?"

Sherry sighed. "At this point, I should hang out a shingle with 'murderer finder for hire' emblazoned on it, so you're not entirely wrong, and you're not entirely right." Sherry's head jerked around when the Ruggery's door swung open and out walked Amber.

"Hey, Sherry, I'm going to need you very soon. How much longer will you be?"

"Two more minutes."

Amber remained in the doorway.

"Three at the most." Sherry delivered the words with a subtle shoulder shrug.

"Is she worried about you being out here with me?" Nolan asked.

"Not at all. Today's been a busy day and we're having trouble keeping pace." Sherry willed someone, anyone, to walk into the store to give the illusion of activity. No such luck.

"As you've said, Romie's already approached me to speed things along and I'm trying."

"I've had my run-ins with the Robinson family. I live next door to Rohan Robinson's property."

Sherry's jaw dropped open. "Are you the N. L. Pechman living on 9 Whale Watchers Avenue?"

"Someone has been doing their research. Yes, that's me. Hope I'm not on the suspect list. I'm not, am I? For the mere reason I live next door to the garden? It's bad enough knowing there's a madman running around the neighborhood, let alone anyone thinking I could have something to do with the murder. I'm here to help Romie. That's all." Nolan stuffed his hands in his corduroys.

"No, no, you're jumping to conclusions." Sherry's sight darted in all directions. *Where are the shoppers today?* "I was looking at the property files of the houses abutting the Robinson land and found the N. L. Pechman file, I mean your file. And now here you are." Sherry peered at the storefront. She saw Amber's back to the window. *Turn around, turn around.* "I'm sure Romie mentioned we know each other from the Community Garden board. I was doing research on the properties to see when and if the land parcels were ever farmland. If the land was farmland prior to World War Two, pesticides probably weren't used, but after World War Two chemical pesticides became all the rage because they killed every bug in sight and no one would know of the consequences for years to come. That information affects how we would test the soil this year."

Nolan propelled a pebble down the sidewalk with the toe of his boot. "Makes sense."

"When I was browsing the file, I couldn't help but notice the grievances that went back and forth between you and 7 Whale Watchers."

"The Robinson group became a difficult neighbor when the garden was first created a few years ago. I don't think they knew the monster the garden had grown into. There wasn't much sensitivity to the noise and parking overload, and I felt I was being ignored when I nicely suggested they enforce the hours and general behavior of the members. Think about it. All hours of the day and night, groups working outside, having picnics with musical accompaniment, kids playing games like hide-and-seek spilling over to my backyard, nonstop activity. The only saving grace was I wasn't the only neighbor perturbed. A fence wasn't much help, and I wasn't going to go to the extent the Westerfields on the other side of the Robinsons went to. They had a devil of a time once they began filing grievances. For them, the effort didn't pay off in the end. Lawyers got involved, the mayor stuck his nose in, a big hoopla. The commotion took a toll on the couple and also on the three Robinson kids. From what I've heard, they were all at each other's throats over the situation. The family began bickering and that continued up until Poppy's death. That's the group you should be looking at when you're snooping around, I mean gathering information. The Westerfields and the Robinsons. Romie's quarrel with Poppy the night she was murdered was solely a case of bad timing on Romie's part."

"At this point, I'd like someone, anyone, to find the murderer so I'm not the one he's setting his sights on next." Sherry craned her neck to locate Amber's silhouette. "I need to get back inside. Would you like to come in and have a look around?" Sherry edged backward toward the store.

"You have every right to be nervous. If the murderer catches wind of an amateur investigator hot on his or her heels, there'll be hell to pay. There is one more thing on an entirely unrelated tangent. In hopes I won't humiliate myself, I'm planning on entering the July Fourth cook-off I hear you're organizing." He held his unblinking stare on her face.

"That's great. Everyone's encouraged to enter. The entry form should be out by the end of the month." Sherry halted her backward progress when she reached the storefront. She slid her hand behind her back to feel for the doorknob. As her hand made contact with the cold brass knob, the door gave way. She lost her balance and tumbled through the doorframe, landing in Amber's outstretched arms.

"Look what I caught," Amber said.

Sherry freed herself, straightened up, and searched through the open doorway for Nolan, but he was gone. "Thanks for saving me. I was going down for the count." As she shut the door, Sherry scanned the area outside but saw no sign of Nolan. "No good-bye?"

"Everything go okay?" Amber asked.

"He gave me the creeps," Sherry stammered. "His idea is that the Robinson family has turned on themselves and the Westerfields may have been their undoing. I don't know. I have a nagging feeling Mayor Obermeyer is playing the role of his life right now in some sort of cover-up. I'm going to give Ray a call, even though it may be my undoing when he gives me yet another lecture."

Phone in hand, Sherry headed to the break room.

"Bease here."

"Hi, Ray, this is Sherry."

"Since when do you make calls from a blocked number?" Ray asked.

"Yay, I was successful. I was practicing a new skill I recently learned."

"No doubt from that Bradshaw big shot. He's the type who needs to make anonymous phone calls due to his overwhelming celebrity status."

"Wrong. Someone else. And need I remind you, more often than not, you call from a blocked number," Sherry responded.

"I'm not even going to dignify that with a response. Now, what can I do for you?"

Sherry heard shuffling paper and keyboard tap-

ping through her phone. "I'm afraid Mayor Obermeyer is playing the Robinson family against one
another for the sake of his political ambitions and
things have turned deadly. I have every reason to
believe he helped the couple who lives next door
to the Robinson land on Whale Watchers Avenue
harass Poppy over the existence of the garden.
The mayor presided over Town Council hearings,
where neighbor was pitted against neighbor. He
only put a Band-Aid on their issues so the conflict
continued to fester until one night Poppy was
killed." Sherry stared at the phone. "Are you there?"

"I'm here. On one hand, you say Mayor Obermeyer is running for reelection with the promise
of the continuation of the Community Garden, and,
on the other hand, you're telling me behind the
scenes he's rallying for the garden's demise. You're
also telling me, Mayor Obermeyer told you how he
holds the Robinson family in high esteem one moment and bashes them verbally in public the next.
You work for Mayor Obermeyer, correct?"

"I work with him on the town's newsletter, not
technically for him. Believe me, I wouldn't be
putting this bug in your ear if I weren't absolutely
confident he and the Westerfields are at least, in
some way, responsible for Poppy's death. The
mayor's putting on a good act that the Robinsons
are awful people, but he's not fooling anyone, especially when he's so careless as to be seen sharing
dinner with Tessa. But why go to all that effort? Enemies or allies, make a choice. Unless there's
something for him to gain from a fast sell of the
land while he maintains he's a man of the people.

His campaign to slander Poppy all over town before, and even in the wake of her death, is the low-
est of the low and smacks of a man desperate to
clean up a mess he's made of things." Sherry blew
out an extended breath. "Didn't you hear him say
on Kayson's radio show that, with Poppy gone, the
time had arrived to put an end to the Community
Garden? That means he was planning all along to
not follow through on his promise to voters. But
why? What would he have to gain if the family sold
the land?"

"I'll take all that under advisement."

"Is that all you have to say?"

"I do have one more thing to say and don't take
this information as any form of encouragement.
Don't waste your time looking any further into
one of the Robinson neighbors. The couple you
mentioned, the Westerfields of 5 Whale Watchers
Avenue, is no longer a couple. The husband,
Champ, had a fatal heart attack two weeks ago
while on vacation in Hawaii. Iron-clad alibi. She
and his remains didn't return from Hawaii until
two days ago."

"I had no idea." Sherry lowered her voice.
"Maybe that explains the asterisk next to Champ
Westerfield's name in the property file I was look-
ing at."

"Have a good afternoon, Sherry." The detective
ended the call.

"That man is obnoxious." Sherry joined Amber
at the sales desk. "This whole scenario is infuriating. Tessa wants the case solved to clear Gully.
Romie wants the murderer found to get herself

and Gully off the suspect list. Nolan wants Romie cleared as well. Mayor Obermeyer thinks a fast find of the murderer will save his campaign, even if he has to take everyone down in the process. The cherry on top is Poppy made plans to reach out to me before her death, as if she knew her time on Earth was nearing its end, as if she believed I could make sense of her death. Poppy's reputation and legacy are on the line until we find out what really happened and why."

Amber opened her hand, revealing multiple yarn strands. She lay them side by side across the table until there was a rainbow of woolly colors. She separated the strands into groups. "See these? The blues go well with the browns and the teal makes sense with the gold. But when they're all combined, the blend is confusing and distracting." She stirred the yarn together until the combination was a blur of muddled colors.

"When people ask me how I come up with recipes to enter in a contest, thinking there couldn't possibly be any original pairings of ingredients out there, I tell them, 'start with the simplest idea and go from there. Don't overthink.' Like your yarn demo. And maybe the same goes for Poppy's murder. You're brilliant, Amber."

Amber reached for a piece of blue yarn and set the strand a distance from the others. "Poppy." She separated the jumbled yarns and arranged them as rays around the blue yarn. "The Westerfields, the mayor, Gully, Tessa. Am I forgetting anyone?"

"You can take out the Westerfields' strand. I was

informed the Westerfields have an iron-clad alibi."
Sherry removed the yellow yarn, leaving only one
green, one brown, and one orange ray projecting
from the blue yarn. "The ingredients just got a tiny
bit simpler. Should only be a matter of figuring
out if any remaining suspects complete the recipe."

Chapter Eighteen

"Madagan, I got a text from Gully. He's completed a mock-up of the cook-off logo, the advertising poster, and the artwork for the entry form. All overnight. How amazing is that? If I'd known how easy the steps to organizing a cook-off are I'd have done it long ago. I'm kidding. Competing in them is where my heart lies. I got extremely lucky teaming with you and now Gully. Can't wait to see what he came up with." Sherry looked past the store's sales desk and caught a glimpse of her father hard at work scribbling customer notes on index cards. "My only worry is his artwork needs to be more eye-catching than what Hillsboro puts out on their advertisements. I didn't want to put any undue pressure on him, so I didn't tell him he had a competitor."

Madagan grumbled something undecipherable. "I'm curious when Hillsboro will run their cook-off entry form."

"I dread the day. If only there was some way we

could wave the white flag, make nice, and convince the town to move their cook-off date. As soon as I get the artwork from Gully, let's meet up."

"Sounds like a plan," Madagan replied.

"On another subject, I have a question for you. I'm pretty sure you can't give me a straight answer because of client confidentiality, but here goes. The six-million-dollar question is was Poppy moving forward with plans to sell the property and if she was, who knew and who didn't? If she was, plenty of patrons would be upset, though murder seems a bit excessive. If she wasn't, her neighbors had to live with the continuing nuisance. Again, murder doesn't seem the best way to resolve issues. One of those, combined with a deeper motive, makes the most sense to push someone over the edge. Say, a brother who is strapped for cash, living an expensive lifestyle, who feels his pot of gold was within his reach, only to have the treasure suddenly yanked away. Or a mayor who believed his career depended on the decision going a certain direction." Sherry waited, but the phone stayed silent. "Madagan, what do you think?"

"I think you know I can't elaborate. But I will say I'm worried for both of them. Be careful. No one reacts well when they're backed into a corner with no way out."

"I'll let you know when I've got Gully's work in hand. We'll talk soon."

"Sherry, you okay?" Amber approached. "You look very distracted."

"I need to get going if I'm going to pull together a picnic lunch to wow a guy I'm not sure how interested I am in impressing." Sherry sighed.

"Who am I kidding? I want Kayson to think my food is right up there with the best home cooking he's ever had on a picnic or anywhere else." Sherry collected her purse from under the sales counter and slung her sweater over her shoulder. "I'll see you later."

"Knock 'em dead," Amber called after her friend before the door slammed shut.

"Would you mind sitting somewhere else? Are you listening to me, Chutney?" Sherry high-stepped her dog as she carried a bowl filled to overflowing with tarragon, chopped chicken breasts, scallions, chutney, and mayonnaise. "Don't get up. I'll risk life and limb so you can have your coveted spot to recover any dropped ingredients."

Sherry placed the bowl on the counter next to her other ingredients. "Dijon mustard, flaky croissants, chopped pickles. Lemon. I forgot the lemons. What's lemon tarragon chicken salad without the lemons? That's right, simply tarragon chicken salad." Sherry handed her dog a morsel of cooked chicken, which he gobbled up.

After combining the meat with all the ingredients, except the bread, she canoed out two baguettes to provide deep beds for the chicken salad to nestle in. She scooped in the chicken filling, set the bread lid on top and stepped back to admire her work. "Perfect. Ready to pack up." Sherry opened the drawer organized with food storage items and located the foil.

Chutney began an insistent bark.

"Okay, okay. Calm down." The doorbell's incessant chiming demanded Sherry put everything on hold to see who was so impatient.

Foil in hand, Sherry peered through the side-light window. Seeing the man in uniform waiting on her porch was a delivery person, she opened the door wide enough to accept what he was presenting. Chutney's bark began to fizzle as his enthusiasm to protect his master waned. His teeth remained bared.

"Thank you." Sherry accepted a box from the man, who kept his gaze unwaveringly on Chutney.

"No problem."

Sherry studied the small box wrapped in white paper. On the top left the words: "America's Good Taste Cook-off."

"My favorite part of cook-offs, the gift baskets. Never ceases to thrill me the sponsors make that extra effort to express their appreciation." Sherry returned to the kitchen, set the foil down, and slid a knife down the seams of the wrapping paper. "Good things come in small packages, like you, boy."

Chutney didn't seem impressed with the compliment delivered without an edible treat.

Sherry waded through the packing peanuts and scooped up a decorative bottle embedded within. "Organic lemon zest. I could use this on the sandwiches." She unscrewed the lid of the blue glass bottle and waved the fragrant contents under her nose. "Smells strong. Maybe I'll only try a sprinkle on one sandwich and let the taste tester decide between the two."

A pinch of the zest was added to one of the chicken tarragon fillings and Sherry used a Sharpie to mark the letter *L* on the foil she wrapped the sandwich in. She finished packing her wicker basket with the new-and-improved sandwiches, along with fruit, lemonade, and sugar cookies. She donned her windbreaker and left the house, with hopes for a warm breeze at the beach.

"Sorry I'm late. There was breaking news at the station, and I had to adjust the news hour copy." Kayson joined Sherry at the picnic table.

"Hope it wasn't something awful. The news these days keeps getting worse and worse. Makes me want to never turn on the television." Sherry continued unpacking the basket.

"You should, instead, listen to the radio," Kayson said in his most professional announcer's voice. "I'm kidding. No breaking news. I'm late because I stopped at Mason's Wines and Spirits and picked up a rosé. The line for lunchtime indulgers was long." Kayson reached inside the basket and collected the melamine plates and the individual bundles of utensils, forks, spoons, and straws tied together with gold yarn. "You put a lot of effort into this. I feel special."

"It's in my nature to give it my best for anyone, whether they appreciate my gesture or not."

"Have I already done something wrong? When will I ever learn to think twice before I speak?" Kayson plopped down on the bench and tucked his face in his hands.

"You did it again. For some reason, you feel the need to come out swinging. If you're late, say sorry but don't make up a silly excuse. You could have told me the real reason you were running late is bad planning and I'd accept that, but now I'm once again left wondering if half of what you say is the truth." Sherry passed the fruit container and sandwiches to Kayson, who perked up. "Here, make yourself useful." Sherry lobbed a half-hearted smile in his direction.

"I can't wait to get my foot out of my mouth and replace it with the taste of your cooking. Can I pour you a glass?" He held up a bottle with pink liquid inside. "You did bring cups, I'm hoping."

"No more than a small splash for me, please, otherwise I'll be snoozing on the tennis court later. Doubles tennis is a fast game. I need to be as alert as possible or I'll have a giant circle bruise dead center on my forehead."

"Lucky guy or gal who gets you as a partner." Kayson volleyed a grin back at Sherry. "And that's the truth."

"Thanks. Now, let me tell you what I've made. And I have a surprise, since I can't resist the urge for cooking competition. I created an opportunity for you to be the participant. I've made two chicken sandwiches, one with a slight variation. Not only do I want you to judge the better sandwich, I want you to identify the mystery ingredient that makes up the difference." Sherry pushed a plate adorned with two half sandwiches and a side salad of spinach leaves, dried cranberries, and toasted pumpkin seeds toward Kayson.

"If I can guess the ingredient, will you share the recipe with me?"

Sherry gave Kayson a side-eye glance as she

handed over a glass for his drink. "I can tell you the recipe but then I'd have to kill you."

"Harsh. Who's coming out swinging now? Seems as if I've met my match." Kayson raised his hand high until Sherry clapped her palm against his. "Let's eat. Do you know which is which?"

"I do. Try the one on your left first."

Kayson took a bite of his sandwich. After he swallowed the morsel, he sipped a generous amount of his wine. "Very nice. Chicken, some kind of herb that reminds me of mild licorice, I'm thinking tarragon, and those crunchy pickles you make. Really delicious. Do I win?"

Sherry shook her head, no. "We're not done yet. You're only halfway through the taste test. Try the next sandwich."

Kayson took a bite of the sandwich half on the right side of his plate. "Wow, that's unmistakably lemon. Lemon on steroids, I'd say. So much lemon I can't taste anything else." He reached for his glass, took a noisy gulp of wine, and swished the liquid around like mouthwash. "Not my favorite flavor, if you don't mind me being brutally honest."

Sherry grimaced. "I'm so sorry, I didn't even taste the filling after I seasoned it. I ran out of time. Big mistake. I'm so embarrassed. Here, give me the whole sandwich. You can eat the other half of the un-lemoned sandwich. I'm not hungry anymore." Before Kayson could act, Sherry nabbed the offensive sandwich off Kayson's plate and took it, along with the uneaten half, to the garbage drum on the edge of the boardwalk.

"Let me rephrase. The taste wasn't that bad, if you like a zesty sour slug in the face. Don't beat yourself up. If I were a real judge and this were a real sandwich contest, I'd vote for number one, though."

"I accept when you say the sandwich wasn't too awful, but now I'm getting a strong message the company you're keeping is boring you to sleep. You could at least put your hand over your mouth to mask those yawns." Sherry squinted and studied Kayson's melting face. When she saw his pallor becoming washed, Sherry raced to his side. "You don't look so good. How do you feel?"

Kayson raised the back of his hand to his mouth. "I'm sorry. I must not have gotten a good night's sleep last night. I've hit a wall."

"Kayson, are you all right? What's the matter?"

Sherry shook Kayson's shoulder, causing his head to collapse forward until his forehead came to rest on his plate in a pillow of chicken salad. She touched his ashen cheek with a trembling hand.

Chapter Nineteen

Sherry leaned her hip against the sales desk. She ran her hand across the soft wool of a wildflower rug a customer had brought in to have the Ruggery experts mend. "The only thing I could think of was to dial nine one one. I couldn't lift him by myself to get him in the car, let alone get him to the ER somehow. He was passed out and, at that point, became dead weight I couldn't budge." Sherry threw up her hands. "He wasn't in pain as far as I could tell. Simply unconscious after eating my sandwich. I was having flashbacks of the cook-off where the judge tasted my entry and promptly expired."

Amber clasped her face with her hands. "What a mess."

"When I gave the ambulance crew Kayson's name, you should have seen the looks on their faces. I think they assumed I was an assassin of some sort until I showed them the picnic basket. That didn't exactly convince them I was on the up and up, so I described the taste-off I invented that had taken a turn. I couldn't explain fast enough how Kayson went from lively lunch date to sluggish sloth in a matter of minutes. Realizing I had backed myself into a corner by admitting my food made Kayson sick, I gave the ambulance crew my name in hopes they'd heard of me. The young EMTs weren't impressed at all. Part of me wishes I had given them an alias so I'm not associated with sickening food."

"This is bad. I don't like the situation one bit."

"We rushed over as soon as we heard what happened. We thought you'd need support." Ruth draped her arm around Erno. "Frances sends her regrets. She couldn't get out of her farmer's market vendor's meeting. One missed meeting and she could lose her pickle table to someone on the waitlist lurking to take a spot. That's exactly what happened last year when Aww-gustin Custom Pet Sweaters missed the location assignment meeting because their road was the last to be plowed after a freak spring snowstorm. A day later the little company, run out of a garage, was notified their vendor table was replaced with Punch in the Gut fermented fruit drinks."

"I do love those probiotic drinks," Erno added. "Gets my engine started."

Bev held up the hand she had clasped in her husband's grip. "But we're here for you, dear. Erik and I dropped everything to make sure you were okay."

Sherry nodded. "I'm really fine. You all didn't need to make a special trip over."

"Is the young man going to be all right?" Erik asked.

"He'll be good as new very soon," Sherry replied. "The EMTs eyed the wine bottle on the table, which was three-quarters full, and the third-degree questioning began. You know me. I can't keep my answers short, especially if I'm nervous. I gave them a lengthy explanation about how we were in the process of judging my sandwiches for a mystery ingredient and how I hadn't taste tested my own cooking, which is one of my cardinal rules in a contest. Taste as you construct your recipe so you can continually adjust the seasoning and build layers of flavor."

Ruth narrowed her red-lined lips. "Dear, are we making you nervous? You're getting off track."

"Sorry. Long story short, once at the hospital, heart attack, stroke, and panic attack were immediately ruled out, thank goodness. Kayson was so embarrassed when he woke up in a hospital bed with nurses hovering all around him. He probably didn't mind the nurses hovering part too much. After a comprehensive round of testing, doctors determined he consumed enough of a knockout drug to have had an acute reaction combined with the wine he drank. He's home now, with a major headache and a vow never to eat my cooking again. He's well enough to joke the guess-the-secret-ingredient contest I created was rigged because the secret ingredient in my recipe was impossible for him to identify since it was purchased at the pharmacy, not the grocery store. He also couldn't resist mentioning he'd rather lose a bet to me and have to eat a hat than one of my sandwiches. An inside joke."

"I'm sorry that happened. You're positive the

lemon zest you received and used in the sandwich was tainted?" Amber asked.

"We'll know for sure soon enough because Detective Bease said he'd swing by to collect the remains. But, yes, I'm certain that's what zonked poor Kayson out."

Amber pulled a stool up to the checkout table and sat down. "You're not fooling yourself in any way by thinking that dose of knockout powder, or whatever it was, wasn't meant for you, right? I think you're getting too close for comfort to the murderer and you might be served up next on the menu. Skewered, flambéed, or worse. I'd like to say I don't mean to scare you by saying this, but I really do mean to scare some sense into you."

"Do you have any idea who the guilty party might be?" Bev asked.

"The person trying to warn me off is doing a good job of telling me I've gotten a whiff of his or her scent. My gut feeling keeps bringing me back to Gully Robinson. I mean, when I gave him the background material for the cook-off artwork, his mood swung from elation to near fury in a matter of minutes. He sensed I was sniffing around, and he didn't hold back telling me his privacy was paramount. He has a big problem with his relationship with Rohan and Poppy, even now after their deaths. He might have had enough of the way his feelings were dismissed by them and acted out, but I haven't come across any damning evidence yet." Sherry paused. "At our meeting, Gully brought up my Orlando cook-off, which leads me to believe he could have sent the lemon zest and put the return address down as the America's Good Taste Cook-off to entice me to open the package immediately. And maybe even the rosary pea seeds. Most importantly, where's the proof?"

"Sherry," Erik began, "have you asked that Romie Green gal he's dating?"

"Asked her what?" Sherry replied.

"Erik's on to something, dear," Bev added. "She may be one of the reasons he's experiencing mood swings."

"How do you mean?"

"We saw Romie Green," Erik continued, "out and about, cavorting, as you youngsters say, with someone who didn't appear to be Gully. The night we went to the mayor's house for dinner, we stopped at Mason's Liquor Store for a bottle of wine, a fine Malbec, if I'm not mistaken. You know the red pairs so nicely with steak."

"Erik, dear, stay on point." Ruth waggled her finger at her friend before winking at Sherry.

Bev heaved a breath. "What Erik is taking the roundabout route to tell you is, Romie was leaving the store as we pulled into the parking lot. She hoisted her petite self into the passenger side of a pickup truck, and she gave the driver a most passionate greeting, if you understand my meaning. Having witnessed the scene, I would even go so far as to call her allegiance to the Robinson boy into question. But that's the tip of the dysfunctional relationship iceberg."

"What specifically should Sherry ask Romie?" Amber chimed in.

Erik dropped his wife's hand. "If I were asking

questions, I'd ask the unfaithful Ms. Green why she deposits a hefty check signed by Gully each week into her account at the First Augustin Savings Bank, oldest banking institution in Hillsboro County, even after the poor young man's sold his car and moved out of his rental, bouncing a couple of his payment checks along the way. Seems especially unsavory, considering her philandering."

"I know he's been having a bit of a financial issue. His sister didn't try to hide the fact, but how do you know all those details about his account?" Sherry's gaze darted from Erik to Bev, whose wifely sights were trained on Erik.

"Erik, darling, would you care to explain the situation to Sherry?" Bev ran her hand across the colorful gemstones adorning the front of her leather handbag.

Erik remained silent.

Bev's fingers drifted up to the aqua-blue and gold silk scarf draped around her neck. "As you know, our MediaPie operations have expanded into the area. Erik opened a rather voluminous account with the local bank to ensure good communication with the institution. Shortly after doing so, Erik was asked to sit on the bank's board. My husband never accepts a position without discreet but intense scrutiny of the business and, after thorough analysis of the bank, Gully Yates's account activity, along with Romie Green's, were highlighted as cause for concern."

"Robinson," Sherry corrected. "Gully Robinson, not Yates."

"Actually, Yates is the correct name," Erik interjected. "Let me complete my wife's thought. The end result of multiple withdrawals from Gully's account, which was under the name Gullickson Yates, not Robinson, into Ms. Green's, his account balance dwindled steadily until the balance was below the minimum required. Not noteworthy, except for the fact the account was opened with a huge deposit check from Rohan Robinson. The man hadn't completely cut off the boy's finances, as rumors may have suggested. Gully was forced to close the account, only to reopen another not long after, under the name Robinson. Whether he was paying Romie back for something or loaning her money, all appearances indicated he could barely afford the arrangement."

"I'm trying to follow along. But this is getting confusing." Erno sighed. "As the old saying goes, 'the dirtier the water the better the soap worked.' "

Ruth peered over her reading glasses at Sherry's father. "Well said."

All heads turned to face Erik as he cleared his throat. "About the young man's last name. Seems Poppy Robinson was the only legal child of Rohan Robinson."

Ruth unleashed a moan. "That's ridiculous. Tessa and Gully may be a number of years younger, but they are his children." She hesitated. "I believe. I didn't know his second wife. She never came out of her house, as far as I heard. But I pride myself on knowing details about the citizens of Augustin."

"Sorry to burst your all-knowing bubble, Ruth, but this is a situation that may have slipped past your inquisitive eyes and ears," Erik responded. "Rohan's second wife, Geena, came into the marriage with two youngsters in tow from a previous relationship with a Mr. Yates. Gully took the Robinson surname, but not legally, and Tessa refused to give up Yates. Common thought was she made up Yates as a stage name, but that wasn't the case. Explains why Rohan didn't treat the younger children as equals of Poppy. Sometimes parents have trouble warming up to their stepchildren."

"Well, I'll be," Erno said.

"Back to the question about who the guilty party is. You think any of what Mr. Van Ardan described has to do with Kayson getting an unwelcome sleep aid during our lunch?" Sherry asked in a near whisper.

"No doubt meant for you, dear," Ruth added.

"That's what you need to figure out," Bev gushed.

"You do have your hands full. I'm glad I'm not in your shoes," Ruth admitted with a halt in her voice. "Remember to be careful. Your father needs you in tip-top shape so he can continue to only take on part-time hours. But do find that blasted murderer before he or she strikes again." Ruth bear-hugged Erno.

"My wheels are spinning with the voices of Tessa, Mayor Obermeyer, and Romie urging me on. Not to mention Poppy and Rohan." Sherry sighed. "What have I gotten myself into?"

The door's bell tinkled. All heads rotated in the direction of the open door.

Sherry took a step forward. "Ray. You got my message. You didn't have to come all the way down here to the store. Would everyone mind if the detective and I had a word in private?"

"Judging by the look on Detective Bease's face, yours is not going to be a friendly chat," Erno whispered to Sherry. "We'll be in the break room if you need backup assistance. Come on, everyone. Let's give them some space."

The group dispersed toward the back of the store, leaving Amber stocking paper bags at the sales counter and Sherry wringing her hands.

"Yours wasn't the only call I received. Confirming the message you left me, the Augustin police network put out a notification your friend Kayson Bradshaw was admitted to the emergency room around lunchtime, suffering from what appeared to be ingestion of a tranquilizer strong enough to put a horse in a coma. Bradshaw was approached by officers but chose not to initiate an investigation. Thanks to Detective Diamond's new position in Criminal Data Analytics, I think that's what it's called, we keep track of any hospital admissions that are suspicious in nature, whether charges are formally filed or not. Frankly, you could analyze data until the cows come home, but cases are solved faster with street smarts and intuition. Computers rule the world, so here I am following up on Bradshaw's incident."

"Excuse me, Sherry, but I wanted to mention the store closes in twenty minutes and, because we need to leave at exactly five fifteen to get ready for tennis, I'll need your help soon to put away all the wool that was delivered earlier." Amber tilted her head in the direction of four stacked boxes. "Erno and the rest of the group have fled."

"Message received. This won't take long, will it, Ray?" Sherry knew full well if he hadn't removed his hat by now the visit would be brief.

"I'll do my best. Bradshaw told the police officer he was involved in a cook-off of sorts with one Sherry Oliveri, who arrived at the emergency room shortly after the ambulance transporting Bradshaw."

"So far so good with the account," Sherry agreed.

"Cook-off? Is that what we're calling a date now?"

"Definitely not a date. Chalk that description up to the aftereffects of Kayson's medication. He was being silly. We played a game called Guess The Secret Ingredient. To his credit, he did identify the secret ingredient correctly before he passed out. Who knew the winner was destined to be the loser?" Sherry winced. She ran her hand across the loops of brown yarn that made up a turtle's shell. "Did you pick up the package of questionable lemon zest I left on my porch for you? I would have brought the seasoning here if I knew you'd be coming."

"No problem. I'm getting used to running personal errands for you. The bag is in my car and will soon be at the lab. The packaging had a return address of America's Good Taste Cook-off, which leads me to the next line of questioning. Either you made an enemy at your last cook-off or the same person who wanted you to back off your amateur sleuthing of the Poppy Robinson murder is getting more serious. Which do you believe to be correct? Or possibly both are true?"

Sherry brushed a piece of lint from the rug's surface. "Are those the only choices?"

"Stands to reason it's the latter. Would you agree?" Ray matched Sherry's nonchalant tone.

Sherry nodded.

"Lemon is a running theme. Do you have any explanation what lemons signify?" Ray put his hand on the rug, and Sherry forced her gaze up to his face.

"Lemons or lemon zest were required ingredients in the America's Good Taste Cook-off. That's all I can think of. I agree, this is no coincidence. Whoever sent the package either attended the cook-off or read the advertising about the cook-off. Doesn't narrow down the field of potential suspects. Except, if you include the common denominator of being Poppy's killer. And yes, I'm certain I didn't make any lasting enemies at the cook-off itself so I'd exclude that possibility."

Ray removed a pen from his blazer pocket and began tapping it on the counter next to the turtle rug. "Poppy Robinson had lemon seeds in her possession when she was found. Someone is obsessed with lemons."

"Gully?" Sherry asked. "He worked in Florida for a time. There are certainly lots of lemon trees in Florida."

The detective reached into his pants pocket and retrieved his phone. "Bease here. Yes. No. Right. Don't lock up until I get there. Meet you in fifteen minutes." He poked at the screen and put the phone back in his pocket. "Thank you for your time. Got to get to the lab before the end of the day." He ran his thumb and index finger around the brim of his hat and took aim for the door.

Sherry sucked in a breath. "I have a key."

Ray pivoted his head back in Sherry's direction.

"In a seed delivery I received for the Community Garden, along with a note and a seed contribution, there was a key."

"I'm listening."

"What's beginning to make sense is the seeds, note, and key were sent by Poppy before she died. The note inside was cryptic at first but is beginning to make more and more sense. The key is baffling, though."

The detective presented his palm.

"Sorry, I don't have them here."

"Of course you don't because you'd like me to start my own pickup and delivery service free of charge, with you being my exclusive customer." Ray retracted his hovering hand and plunged it in his pocket. "I'll be in touch to arrange a pickup." He left the building.

"Bye," Sherry called to the man on the sidewalk walking past the store window.

Sherry spun on her heels and headed to the back of the store. "I'm back and ready to help."

"All taken care of." Amber set the last of the yarn in the proper storage container. "I saw you were in deep out there, so I tackled the load myself."

"Sorry about that," Sherry moaned. "I don't want my search for clues to get in the way of work, but the pace is accelerating. I don't know where the information's leading, though. Or maybe I do and I'm afraid to follow."

The door swung open for Quentin and his sack of letters and parcels.

"Forgive me. I'm late. Had some engine trouble, and I almost had to amend the old saying, 'neither rain, sleet, snow, or gloom of night will slow my appointed rounds' to 'when I can't drive, your mail won't arrive.' " He chuckled until his sack swung wide and hit the table.

"Glad you made it. We were about to close up. I was worried about you." Amber patted the silver-haired civil servant on the back.

Quentin pursed his lips, causing his whiskers to project forward, reminding Sherry of a walrus. "Can I ask you a question, Quentin? Is Gully Robinson on your delivery route? Or Gully Yates? Not sure which one he prefers, Yates or Robinson, but they're the same person."

"Gullickson Robinson receives junk mail. Gully Yates receives bills and business correspondence. Yes, he's on my route."

"He's doing artwork for the new July Fourth cook-off I'm organizing for the town, and I've given him some material to guide him along. I forgot one sheet and I'd like to save him an extra trip. He doesn't have a car and, well, you know what that's like, right, Quentin? I was wondering if you could share his address so I could swing by."

"I'm not big on sharing my customers' personal information, but I can tell you he recently switched to a post box in the main Augustin post office because I had so much trouble delivering his mail to the mailbox he installed over at number seven Whale Watchers. The path wasn't lit, and I had to complain to my supervisor that the route was dangerous in winter when the sun goes down early. I miss seeing him. He's a nice young fellow."

"Thanks. I'm sure he wouldn't mind you sharing that information. I'll give him your regards when I see him," Sherry assured.

Chapter Twenty

Sherry flipped the brass key over like a delicate crepe. The bumpy edges made an indent in her skin. She tucked the key in her purse's side pocket. As she strolled to the front door, she caught sight of her image in the front hall mirror. Her new tennis skirt wasn't covering as much of her legs as she had hoped, but no time to run back to the store to exchange the sportswear for a larger size. Amber insisted they have matching team outfits, so there was no swapping her outfit out for a different look she may have in her closet. This sporty look would have to do.

As she steered her car away from the house, Sherry voice-commanded her phone to dial up Amber. "See you in fifteen. Can you meet me in the parking lot so we can walk in together?"

"You're not nervous, are you?" Amber asked.

"You know I'd do much better if the competition were held in the kitchen rather than the tennis court, right?"

"Yes, but the fuzzy yellow balls wouldn't cook up very tender, and you'd be penalized by the judges." Amber laughed. "Your only choice is to beat your opponents with the strings of your racket. I'm about to park, so I'm hanging up. See you soon."

The mega-colossal sports complex in Hillsboro that housed a wide variety of sports including basketball, swimming, figure skating, and squash was an easy drive, even at rush hour. Guiding her car into the massive parking lot, Sherry caught a glimpse of a familiar silhouette posing with her tennis bag on the front steps of the five-story glass and steel structure. Finding a spot within reasonable walking distance was another story.

Sherry rolled down her window as she drove past Amber. "I'll be right there."

"I'll be waiting," yelled Amber as she waved her tennis bag at the passing car.

Five minutes later, Sherry strolled up to Amber. "Sorry. I parked way over there. Must be something going on here. I've never seen the place so crowded."

"I saw your partner, Den Donnelly, go inside. He told me to tell you to shadow your strokes on your way to the courts. Like this." Amber swung her free arm in a mock forehand.

"He can make suggestions for improvement from now through eternity, but the only thing on my mind right now is a hot shower and a goblet of pinot grigio."

Sherry followed Amber through the glass doors, past the indoor skating rink and up one level of stairs. The volume of people filling the building increased as she neared the floor the tennis courts were located on. She was forced to bump and wrestle her way through the crowded hallway to make the slightest progress.

"Take a look at that." Sherry pointed to an observation area overlooking a towering wall of simulated rock. Draped atop the rock wall was a banner that read: Southern New England Indoor Rock-Climbing Championships. "That's where the action is. I'm sure glad all these people weren't here to watch tennis." Sherry's gaze darted from the seated audience surrounding the climbing course to the athletes unpacking their equipment bags in a corner of the competition space. "Doesn't look like the competition's started yet."

"Maybe we can catch some of the action on the way out. We should keep moving." Amber nudged Sherry forward with her bag.

"Message received." Sherry's sneakers screeched as she rotated away from the window. Before she could take a step forward, she found herself face-to-face with a whiskered man in a knit cap, an oversized bag slung across his shoulder. She recoiled. "Gully?"

"Sherry Oliveri, this is a surprise. Which one of the multitude of sports this place offers are you involved in here today?" Gully surveyed Sherry up and down. "Never mind, dumb question. Tennis, of course."

"My friend Amber convinced me to join a league and today's my first match. I'm sure you can understand when I say competition outside the kitchen is a challenge for me." Sherry caught sight of Amber's shrug. "Gully, this is Amber. Amber, this is Gully, uh, Robinson."

"Very nice to meet you. Are you competing in the rock climbing? We saw the huge banner." Amber croaked. "That's also a dumb question. My guess is you wouldn't be dressed that way if you weren't."

"Yes, you're right. I'm psyched to do well. I've been putting in extra training hours for months in preparation for this. My arm strength and overall stamina have peaked over the last month, and all the stars are aligned. I have no injuries, I'm feeling super positive, nothing to hold me back except a more capable climber, and I don't know if there is one at this moment in time." Gully drummed his bag with the palm of his hand. "Coincidentally, I have a mock-up of the cook-off poster and contest logo with me. I was going to stop by the Ruggery tomorrow, but let me give it to you right now." He unzipped a side pocket and rummaged around until he located a manila envelope, which he handed to Sherry.

She accepted his offering. "This is amazing. Thank you. I look forward to seeing what you've come up with when I get a chance to concentrate."

"I wanted to tackle the project sooner rather than later. You never know what distractions will come up out of the blue. I don't want to let you down. Once I've committed to achieving a goal, I don't let anything stop me. I'm obsessed that way."

Gully gathered his bag.

"Interesting choice of words," Sherry whispered to Amber. She turned to Gully. "Best of luck today. I'm going to channel your confidence into my ground strokes."

"Same to you." Gully hoisted his bag over his shoulder and lost himself in the crowd.

"I'll tuck the artwork under my racket so it doesn't get crinkled. I can't wait to take a look." Sherry slid the envelope inside her racket bag and followed Amber to the courts.

Sherry took a seat on the bench outside the tennis court entrance and tightened her sneaker. "If Gully killed his sister, he certainly isn't sitting around regretting his actions. He's getting on with his life."

Amber raised her arm over her head and stretched her shoulder. "Maybe he no longer feels the stress of being broke. Relief is only a land sale away."

"Did I hear something about a land sale? I hope neither one of you is moving any time soon. I'd miss you." Madagan, dressed in yoga pants and a crop top, approached Sherry. "Plus, we haven't finished work on the cook-off. Not by a long shot."

"Madagan. What a nice surprise. I didn't know you played tennis." Sherry stood and mimicked Amber's shoulder stretch.

"My husband's playing tonight. He's the team's number one player." Madagan pointed to the whippet of a man seated on the floor, pressing his head down to one knee then the other with fluid ease.

"Great chef, great athlete. Is there anything he can't do?"

"Please don't say that in front of him. He'll be impossible to live with." Madagan nudged Sherry's core with her elbow. "He's a good guy. I'm very lucky."

"Maybe I'll be partnered with him some day. I'd estimate five years and five hundred hours of

lessons should get me to his level." Sherry peered
at her racket bag. "Speaking of the cook-off, I ran
into Gully Robinson downstairs. He was heading
to a rock-climbing event. He was feeling great
about his chances."

"I can imagine he's happy. A tough week ended
on an upbeat note for him. His sister, Tessa,
bought out his share of Rohan's Whale Watchers
Avenue property, and I'm sure he'll be in the black
again once the check clears."

"Did you handle the transaction?" Sherry asked.

"No, if I had, I wouldn't be talking about the
deal. But I was contacted about the matter by
someone at Town Hall, who shall remain name-
less. That individual was double-checking with me
about the details of Poppy's will for Tessa. I drew
up Poppy's will after her father passed away. During the conversation, I was read every grievance
filed against the property, dating from the inception of the Community Garden, each of which I
was well aware of."

"Wonder why?" Sherry rolled her shoulders
while tipping her head left and right. "Oh, that's a
tight spot," she moaned as she rubbed the tender
neck muscle.

"If I was made aware of all the trouble between
neighbors, I would be a better representative of
Poppy's interests. Tessa wanted to make sure she
was doing the right thing. Too many grievances
equals a tough sale if she were to put the property
on the market, but they were all garden related,
and, oddly, there haven't been any filed for over
six months, even though I can't imagine much

changed in the day-to-day comings and goings. The Westerfields quieted down, but the other neighbor also swallowed his annoyance. So, Tessa was satisfied all was well."

"Mayor Obermeyer," Sherry said.

"I didn't hear what you said." Madagan cupped her hand around her ear.

"Nothing important." Sherry slapped her hip. "I almost forgot to mention Gully gave me the art-work for the cook-off. I'll let you know what I think when I have time to take a look."

"That's exciting. I'm going to work out while the match is on, so I'll see you after the win." Madagan flipped a wave and was gone.

Sherry sat down on the bench. "No wonder Gully was in such a good mood. If Poppy's death facilitated Gully's ability to sell out, common sense dictates he may have been involved. If he'd been banking on the sale all along and she wasn't coop-erating, his patience may have worn out."

"The timing of the sale is awfully quick. One could say premeditated. But where's the hard evidence?" Amber arched her back and drew in a deep breath.

Sherry stood and joined her friend, performing deep knee lunges. "I'll have a look."

"What did you say?" Amber straightened up and faced Sherry. "I don't like the sound of that."

A man in a navy-blue sweat suit burst through the court door. "Ladies, are you set? Sherry Oliv-eri, you're on court two with Den Donnelly, and, Amber Sherman, you're with me on court four. Our opponents are already out warming up."

"I'll see you after the match. Crush 'em," Amber called out as she followed her partner to their court.

"Tie-breakers are the worst way to lose a match," Sherry huffed as she removed her sweatband. "I mean seriously, why should a game that went back and forth from our advantage to theirs and back again for an hour and a half come down to the best of ten points. Of course I'm going to freak out and double-fault. In no time, game over. Maybe the net was too high. I should have measured. The weird thing is, I can't wait to get back out there and try again next week."

"Who knew? The girl is a competition junkie." Amber zipped up her hoodie. "Let's get out of here before the team convinces us to go out with them. My partner was so bossy I need decompression time away from him. He felt the need to hit almost every shot, even if he was encroaching on my side of the court. I'm happy we won, but he yelled 'mine' so many times I thought we were digging for gold."

Sherry and Amber hiked down two levels of staircase before reaching the ground floor. Once they stepped off the stairs, they were swallowed up by a milling murmuring throng of humanity spilling out of the rock-climbing arena.

"What's going on? Did someone pull the fire alarm?" Sherry was pinned against the wall by the oncoming crowd.

Amber struggled to get to her friend's side. "I

heard a lady say someone got hurt rock climbing and they're clearing the way for the EMTs."

Before another word came out of Amber's mouth, Sherry had elbowed her way to the glass door, using her tennis bag as a battering ram. She stood on the tips of her toes and signaled to Amber to hurry over.

"We need to get in there. I've got a bad feeling. Follow me." Sherry hustled over to a guard stationed inside the rock-wall arena. His arms were crossed against his protruding chest. "I think that's my brother laying there." Sherry aimed her bag at the circle of personnel squatting around a man splayed out at the base of the twenty-two-foot climbing wall. "Was the man who fell wearing a black shirt with an eagle pictured on the back and a gray knit cap?"

"Yep, that's him all right. Gilly or Gelly something. His emergency contact has been notified and is meeting him at the hospital, ma'am. Did you say you're his sister or mother?"

"Sister. What happened?"

The guard checked over his shoulder. "His safety rope snapped; although, to me, the rope looks an awful lot like it was severed with a sharp blade. The cut was so clean. He was almost at the top of the course when the rope gave way. Amazingly, he scaled the face of the course, literally hanging by a thread. People were calling out to him to turn back when the belayer, the safety guy below the climber, noticed the rope was severely compromised. Shows he didn't put any weight on the rope until the top, which means his technique was darn good."

"Are his injuries bad? I'll run ahead to the hospital and meet him there."

"Hard to say. Wasn't a fall many would survive, but he did all the right adjustments with his body on the way down to minimize impact damage. Sorry about the bad news, ma'am."

"Thank you." Sherry put both hands on her bag, jutted out her elbows, and muscled her way out the door and down the hall to the entrance.

"I hope he's not hurt too badly," Amber offered when she reached her car. "Are you really going to the hospital?"

"No. That was all I could come up with. I'm going to keep moving. I have somewhere I need to make a stop at. Thanks again for tonight, and congratulations on your win." Sherry peered in all directions for the fastest route to her car.

"Sherry?" Amber softly drew out both syllables of her friends name as if being careful not to startle her. "Is there something you're not telling me? Your plans were to go home and take a hot bath and now you're off to unspecified locations. Can't be good."

"You know the old saying, 'the stickier the batter the flakier the scone'?" Sherry turned to leave.

"Ah, no."

"Okay, well then, how about, I may have to get my hands a little dirty to complete the job."

"Wait, what job?"

Sherry waved her hand and disappeared behind a row of cars.

Chapter Twenty-one

Sherry clicked off her phone's ringer after the third call from Amber went unanswered. She continued her drive down the dark street. "I'll call you back soon, Amber. I can't talk now or I'll lose my nerve," she whispered to the vibrating device desperately begging for attention. "Mayor Obermeyer should consider installing lighting along Whale Watchers. If a deer jumps out of those bushes, one of us could wind up dead. A brighter entrance would sell the place faster I'd imagine, and that would make the guy happy, despite what he wants people to believe."

Sherry turned her head to get a better look at the gold house number that shone in her car's headlight beams. "Number five." She slowed the car to a crawl and peered up the short driveway. "Lights are on. Fine. I hope everyone's preoccupied at home enjoying a good book." Her foot twitched, the accelerator pedal descended, and the car bucked forward. Sherry sucked in a long breath. Her foot relaxed and the car slowed.

Sherry turned the steering wheel hard to the left and the familiar crunch of driveway pebbles greeted the car's tires. She had been up this driveway dozens of times over the past growing season, and she was always exhilarated to see others arriving to garden as well. The excitement in her gut that should have been was replaced with an icy shudder along her spine. She guided her vehicle to the farthest corner of the spacious rectangle that made up the parking lot.

Sherry flicked off her headlights and reached across to her tennis bag resting on the passenger seat. After unzipping the side compartment, she wriggled Gully's poster free and laid the paper across her lap. Through the windshield, Sherry saw the black shadows of the pine tree barrier separating the driveway pebbles from the grass. Between the trees, Sherry could make out the Belgium blocks that bordered the stepping stone walkway to the Community Garden. She shifted her head left when movement caught her eye. A rabbit darted from the driveway to find refuge under a rhododendron bush. The same bush that bloomed blood red in early summer and marked the edge of the Robinson property.

Satisfied she was alone, Sherry switched on her phone's flashlight and lit up Gully's artwork. The poster depicted a grill active with flames kissing the grill rack and burgers browning on the heat. The rendering was so alluring Sherry could smell the sizzling meat juices. The background of the poster was a beach, complete with rolling waves, sailboats, and a setting sun. The logo on the top right of the artwork was decorated with the words, "Augustin's Star-Spangled Grill-off" encircled in fireworks bursting with the colors of bananas, tangerines, and cherries.

"Gorgeous. Great job, Gully." A smaller piece of heavy drawing paper was attached to the poster with a paper clip. Sherry unclipped the paper and studied the handwriting in the flashlight's thin beam. She adjusted the light in hopes of making sense of the tiny letters.

Sherry, if you like my ideas, here's another one. You're not seeing what's right in front of you.

"Ah! What does he mean?" Sherry flipped the paper over but only saw blank space. "Gully, I hate to do this to you, but I need proof that either *you're* what's right in front of me, or is it someone else?"

Sherry set the artwork and the note on the passenger seat and let herself out of the car. The moonless early evening enveloped her when the car's interior light dimmed. In an attempt to avoid the branches of the rhododendron bush, she stepped in a depression in the driveway. Her knees buckled and the phone catapulted from her hand into the darkness.

"Ugh," Sherry whined. She made her way back to the car and opened the door. She flicked on the headlights. The bush lit up like a Christmas tree but, unlike the festive Yuletide symbol, yielded no presents at the base. The phone was nowhere in sight.

"I hope the rabbit appreciated my contribution to his technology collection." Sherry turned off the car lights and inched toward the dark pathway leading to the garden. She could only make out the first few steps of the meandering route.

"I think I'm going the right way. I recognize that tree."

With one arm overhead to steer any threatening branches away from her face and one arm sweeping forward to ward off any nighttime critters, she forged ahead. Sherry passed the dogwood tree that had suffered major damage during a late winter storm. One more turn to the right around a cluster of decades-old lilacs that played host to flocks of chirping and buzzing birds and bees in the early summer, but at this time of year were silent, and she was within striking distance of the six-foot cedar-post fence that surrounded the garden beds.

"There's a sight for sore eyes."

The limited moonlight that eked through the dense cloud coverage in the night sky highlighted the shiny metal of the mesh chicken wire strung between the fence posts. As quickly as a glimpse of the fence had her convinced she wasn't off course, the clouds smothered the moonlight, and Sherry lost her bearings again.

"I'm beginning to think this wasn't a good idea. No choice. It's now or never because Ray is picking up the key, and this is my only chance." Sherry reached in her tennis jacket pocket and touched the cold key. As she did, her foot snagged a broken branch littering the path. She wrenched her hand out of her pocket to brace for the tumble but didn't have enough time to dislodge the key from her palm. She went down hard, her clenched fist bearing the brunt of her body weight. When she righted herself, she took inventory of working body parts.

"Nothing's broken," she whispered as she wiped hair out of her eyes. Something warm and sticky kept her hand from traveling smoothly across her forehead. Close inspection of her hand in the murky darkness, revealed the key had sliced the base of her thumb and both her hand and the key were coated in blood. The cuff of her sweat jacket was torn up to the forearm. "My new jacket's ruined, but I think the gash is a flesh wound." She wiped the key and her hand with her sleeve.

Sherry kicked the offending branch aside. She looked back over her shoulder and could make out the silhouette of the old lilac bushes. She stole a glance forward and sighted the garden fence up ahead to the left. The edge of the shed that housed garden supplies lay a few yards to the right. Above her head, rustling leaves captured Sherry's attention. An owl screeched as the raptor left its perch.

"I can't do this, not even for Poppy, her father, or even an injured Gully." Sherry rotated her body and headed back to her car. She climbed in and slammed the door shut. Before the console light dimmed, she inspected her bloodied hand. Instead of turning over the ignition, Sherry reached for Gully's artwork with her clean hand. She studied the poster.

"Gully, I'm looking at what's right in front of me, but I'm obviously not seeing everything." Sherry scoured the picture from corner to corner until her vision settled on the grill. She touched the grill grates, leaving a red fingerprint.

"These aren't all burgers. This is grilled eggplant. No doubt a nod to Poppy." Her finger traced the outline of the sketched pergola to a stone wall separating the grill area from the beach. "I know that wall." Sherry pushed the poster aside and reached for the door handle.

Keeping her sights locked on her footing, she quickened her pace as she squinted to make sure every detail of her surroundings was visible amongst the dark shadows that lined the walkway. When she reached the garden fence, she looked left. There, a few yards away, was the stone wall she had seen so many times on her visits to the garden. Beyond the wall, a floodlight belonging to the neighboring house burst on, blackening the outline of the property barrier. Sherry backed away from the fence, with full attention paid to the dark void between her and the wall. She reached in her pocket and pulled out the key.

The brisk walk to the shed elevated Sherry's heartbeat, until all she could hear was thunderous pounding in her eardrums. The one-story building facing her appeared cold and uninviting. The burnt-red metal frontage of the shed was embellished with two paned windows and a double door presumably wide enough for large landscape machinery. She put her nose up to one of the windows but could see only the dark lining of a piece of fabric blocking the view inside. She shuffled over to the doors. When Sherry touched the cold door handle, she shuddered. She twisted the knob but was met with resistance.

"Come on key, do your thing." Sherry inserted the key in the lock above the knob. She flipped the key over, and a satisfying click resounded. With a gentle shove, the door gave way to the tune of screeching hinges.

"Over the winter, someone has made our garden supply shed into a pretty nice no-tell motel." Sherry tiptoed inside and was slammed with the stench of sour body odor, paint fumes, and expired food. Parked by the door was a laundry basket piled with rumpled clothes. The sink, where Sherry had washed soil off her hands countless times during the growing season, was barely visible under the mountain of dirty dishes. On the rim of the sink balanced a cup filled with various lengths of paintbrushes.

"The decoration leaves a lot to be desired. And an air freshener wouldn't be a bad idea. Wonder where all the tools the members stored over the winter have gone?" Sherry's question was answered when she clicked the wall switch. In the back corner of the room, clustered in a tall pile, were rakes, hand shovels, a broom, and gloves. "Thank goodness Rohan put electricity and running water out here. Bet he didn't count on his addition becoming a dwelling."

A scan of the room yielded a welcoming object on the floor. "That's one of our rugs. All those roses, in a variety of colors. I'd bet anything that's the rug Tessa lost track of after the family moved."

As she made her way across the space to a cot, Sherry was drawn to the wooden chest at the foot of the small bed. She lifted the lid. Inside was a helmet, ropes of all thicknesses bound up in neat loops, and a pair of the same shoes Gully had been wearing earlier in the night at his competition.

Sherry turned her attention to a book on the side table. The blue and yellow cover was a familiar sight. She picked up the publication and smiled when she saw how many pages were wrinkled and dog-eared.

"America's Good Taste Cook-off contestant cookbook. What do you know? But Gully wasn't there. At least I don't think he was." She peeled open the front cover, ripping the thick paper, as the lower half of the sheet came unstuck from another page. There, on the inside cover, five words leapt off the page.

"Happy cooking, Nolan. Sherry Frazzelle."

She set the book back on the table and picked up a crumpled white bag next to a half-filled glass of what resembled days-old orange juice.

Sherry smoothed the wrinkles and ran her fingers across the green lettering. "Orlando Rare and Exotic Seed Factory." She dropped the bag as if her fingers were singed.

"See anything you like?"

Sherry's breath jettisoned from her lungs. She swiveled her head around so fast her hair caught in her eye. She blinked to clear her vision. The man who had parked himself next to her on her flight from Orlando and later visited her in her father's store came into focus.

"You startled me." Sherry adjusted her body to face Nolan. She willed her legs not to collapse.

"Looks like you've had a bit of an accident." Nolan pointed to Sherry's red-stained hand. "Or have you been peeling beets." A harsh chortle burst out of the man's mouth. "Seems pretty late in the day for a visit to the garden."

"I had a small mishap on my way down the path, not the least of which was losing my phone, which doubled as my flashlight. I came out to see what the shed looked like after the winter. The start of a new season is right around the corner." Sherry sang out the words, but they fell as flat as her smile, which sagged to a frown. "This is the only time I could squeeze in a trip."

"I can't offer you a Band-Aid but let me cheer you up with some good news." Nolan lifted his closed hand over his head and waved. "On my way here, the old rhododendron was buzzing like a horde of angry hornets and beaming with light, as well. I know bees can't light up like a firefly, so I felt safe reaching under the bush to investigate the flashing, noisy creature. Turned out to be a phone receiving a text. Yes, I admit to reading the message. Thought maybe I'd get a clue as to who owned the phone. Seems your friend Amber thinks you may be in a bit of hot water coming out here by yourself, and she wonders how you are and why you haven't answered her last seven attempts at calling and texting." He continued to hold the phone over his head while holding an unblinking glare. "I'd text her back on your behalf that all is well, but that would be a lie."

"She's a worrywart." Sherry's gaze darted from Nolan to the door. "I should get going. I see the tools I was looking for over in the corner. No one told me there was someone living in the shed, which sounds funny to say." Sherry forced out a tee-hee. "So, I'll be advising the board we need a Plan B for members' tool storage. Thanks for finding my phone."

Sherry extended an open hand while side-stepping toward the door.

Nolan shoved the phone in his pocket. "You won't be needing this anymore. I'll keep it safe. And I don't think you'll need to advise those board members of anything because there won't be a garden after today." Nolan widened his stance and crossed his arms. "Following the tragic accident, everyone will agree that the garden is cursed, should be discontinued, and the property sold."

Sherry pried her tongue off the parched roof of her mouth. "Tragic accident?"

"You didn't have to get involved. You could have let the natural order of things occur. But Miss Celebrated Cooking Contester couldn't keep out of other people's business and now you're the one who's getting cooked." Nolan reached behind him and collected a plastic container with a long spout off the floor. "The plan was to let Gully take the fall and now your interference spoiled everything."

Sherry was having trouble hearing Nolan because the words were accompanied by a rushing sound in her ears. Tiny spots began dancing across her vision. She shook her head and the white noise cleared.

"Believe me, I was onboard with Gully being the guilty party, right up until the time you sent him off to his competition with a compromised safety rope. But why? And why did you have to kill Poppy?" Sherry corralled a lint ball with the toe of her shoe.

When Nolan's gaze shifted to her foot, Sherry counted the number of steps needed to reach the door at full sprint.

"Like you, Poppy stuck her nose where it didn't

belong." Nolan swung the plastic bottle by the lid, until drops of liquid dripped out of the seal.

Sherry winced when she caught a whiff of astringent gasoline fumes. Her eyes began to water. She blinked back the excess moisture that blurred her vision.

"Do you know how many years I had to put up with Rohan Robinson's unneighborly antics? At first I thought, 'this can't last.' But his incessant complaints and grievances about my trees, my fence, my very occasional parties, you name it, kept me busy clearing matters up at Town Hall nonstop. He was obviously trying to drive me out of the neighborhood."

"It wasn't a one-way battle. There were plenty of grievances and complaints made by you toward Rohan before his death. I saw them in your property file. The argument went both ways."

"You're right. I admit I may have enjoyed the fight at first, to a certain degree. When the mayor stepped in, events took a turn. I couldn't fight city hall when the fight became dirty."

"I saw complaints filed by Rohan the first time I reviewed your property file, but when I went back to check something, the papers had been removed," Sherry asserted.

"Huh. Another sleight of hand by our good mayor, I suppose. Now you see 'em, now you don't. I'd file a complaint and it would magically get lost in the system. Imagine my frustration. Well, at least Rohan's campaign contributions went to good use. The mayor made all my attempts to live a quiet peaceful life go away." Nolan surfed the sole of his hiking boot across a puddle on the floor. "Put

yourself in my shoes. I had every last dime invested
in my house. All's well, until the owner of the
house next door makes my life a living hell from
the time he moves in. Just when I thought I could-
n't take his endless bickering another day, Rohan
Robinson up and died. Ah! Relief!" Nolan puffed
out his cheeks. "But, no! Two months later, a sign
for the new Augustin Community Garden went up
and the gardeners started arriving with their cars,
music, yelling, and lights on all hours of the night."
Nolan raised his sights to the ceiling. "Rohan, you
did this on purpose to punish me. And Poppy
wouldn't stop the madness, all in the name of her
father. I didn't have the resources to fight any
longer. If I sold, I would have lost money I didn't
have, because no one would pay good money to
live beside such a neighbor. The result would be
selling my house at a fire sale price. I was stuck."

A screech of door hinges sent Sherry teetering
backward.

Chapter Twenty-two

"Nolan? Sherry? What's going on in here? And why do I smell gasoline?" Romie waved a key in her hand. "Gully must have left his key in the lock, although I don't know how in the world he could have done that, since he's in the hospital." She inspected her fingers. "Not sure what this red stuff is."

"If he's in the hospital, what are you doing here?" Nolan's voice was bitter. "You were supposed to be at my house not coming to see him here."

Sherry studied Romie's face. The young woman's glasses slipped down her nose.

"Gully needs a warmer set of underwear, if you really have to know. Hospital gowns can be drafty. I'm not going to deny him that," Romie spat out. "Would someone please explain what's going on here?"

"Seems Sherry is more than a decorated home chef. She's also a self-appointed amateur investigator."

Romie shifted her gaze from Nolan to Sherry. "I know. That's why I asked for her help to find Poppy's murderer. You're not joining forces with that detective fellow who thinks Gully had something to do with the murder, are you?"

"Forget the act. She knows Gully's not the murderer."

"Romie, did you know your friend here cut Gully's rope, and that's the cause of his near fatal fall?"

Romie's lip began to tremble. "Nolan? Is she telling the truth? You said he wouldn't get hurt, that you only wanted to scare him."

"Were you also aware that the money Gully deposits in your bank account every month is being monitored by bank officials and is flagged for suspicious behavior? Would you care to explain what you're charging Gully money for?" Sherry asked.

Nolan took a step toward Sherry. "Take it easy with the accusations. Romie was helping a friend out."

"You're the one who should forget the act," Romie snarled. "You had a ridiculous idea from the start, and I should have never let you talk me into joining in. Gully's way too nice to be suspected of murder. I know the ploy was to prolong the investigation. By sending the detective in the wrong direction, you'd be buying time to attract top dollar for your property before a trial taints the attraction of living on Whale Watchers Avenue. You've gone too far. You promised no one would get hurt. Sherry was almost poisoned, twice, and Gully was nearly killed. That wasn't part of the deal."

Nolan tapped the toe of his boot in a slow, steady beat. "You see, your friend Romie and I are a little more than friends. That friendly monthly deposit was an arrangement we brokered with gullible Gully as a way to, shall we say, foster loving feelings between stepsiblings."

"What does that mean?" Sherry asked.

Romie lowered her chin and shook her head. "I made a deal with Gully. Nolan would keep quiet about Rohan's unethical alliance with the mayor, ensuring his stepfather's reputation not be spoiled. Gully may have had issues with his stepsister, Poppy, but she was his extended family and he took that connection seriously. Despite Rohan's treatment of his stepkids, Gully knew Poppy would be crushed if Rohan's legacy went down in flames. Gully's such a nice guy. How could I have done this to him?"

"Yep. I got to Gully, thanks to Romie. He put up a feisty front of not getting along with the half sister he wanted to protect, but don't believe everything you see. Each month he makes a tidy deposit in Romie's account in return for my silence. He knew if Rohan were slandered, even in death, Poppy would be destroyed. When I came to see you at your store, my plan was running like clockwork. There were so many suspects being considered, thanks to the flu-like spread of gossip in this town. The investigation was at a stalemate. I was home free."

"You two never told me you had a meeting. What's going on here?" Romie turned her head from person to person.

Sherry's young friend's face blanched the color of button mushrooms.

"Did you and Nolan kill Poppy and then try to kill Gully because he was going to stop paying you hush money and expose your plot to drive the remaining Robinsons or Yateses, or whatever names they go by, to sell out, making your boyfriend's property all the more valuable?"

"Of course not!" Romie screamed. "That's absurd. Nolan, tell her. And wipe that smirk off your face."

"Interesting theory, but no. Romie had nothing but nice things to say about Poppy. And Gully, too, of course. Although, I don't know what she ever saw in him. Romie would never hurt a flea. If nothing else good came out of my frequent Town Council hearings, I did learn of the not-too-savory alliance between Rohan and the mayor. What I knew about Rohan Robinson, and his shady dealings with Mayor Obermeyer, was my ticket to shutting up the neighbors from hell. Until it wasn't."

"I suspected Mayor Obermeyer put his campaign donors' wishes over the town's needs, but I didn't want to fully believe it until I found indisputable evidence."

"At first, we were going to go to Poppy directly and get her to end that dang garden in return for my silence on her father's indiscretions, but then one day Romie let the cat out of the bag that Gully and Tessa weren't even Rohan's children. That was knowledge I could work with."

"You've been using me this whole time. I would never have shared Gully's personal information with you if I knew what your intentions were," Romie whimpered.

"Save your tears. You did a great job filling in

the blanks when my original plan was collapsing. You should be proud of your contribution." Nolan snickered.

"So you're the one who has been butchering Poppy's character?" Sherry asked.

"Ha. Good job piecing the facts together. I did my part turning the easily swayed Augustin population against the woman. On top of that, after his death, Rohan himself did a fine job of severing any allegiance his stepkids may have had to him. The will he left behind was a slap in the face to them. Poppy's reverence of her father served as an invaluable quality to exploit. All I had to do was play my hand right and let the chips fall where they may. The more widely believed it was Poppy wanted to sell 7 Whale Watchers, along with the garden, for profit, the greater likelihood she was perceived as the town villain. Even she couldn't stop the snowballing momentum, as more and more people believed she had turned on the town."

"You sent me to that board meeting in such an angry state after you filled my head with the notion she was selling imminently. How could I ever have let you convince me without solid facts? When I told you about my argument with Poppy, you must have felt like a child on Christmas morning. Knowing I was possibly a suspect and pretending to solicit Sherry's help to clear me?" Romie gasped. "Wait. The fact Poppy died that night wasn't an awful coincidence. You monster!"

"Look, Romie, I don't feel great about using you. You're a nice kid, but enough is enough. Poppy was never going to sell out. Yes, she came close until something or someone changed her mind. I know who that someone was, that buffoon mayor. She was even going to run for mayor to erase Obermeyer's negative influence over the town and rebuild her image. He made a tragic error when he stated to the media he was for the garden, when he really was against the garden and out for himself. Only a moron wouldn't see through his contradiction. He's the worst actor in the history of bad actors.

"I was hoping either Gully or Tessa would come to their stepsister's rescue when her reputation began to take a terrible beating. A conversation Romie and I had with Mayor Obermeyer about how much he stood to profit if the land was sold to a developer may have been the tipping point. A developer the mayor could secure for a, quote, un-quote, campaign contribution. Unbeknownst to me, Obermeyer's flip-flop stance on the garden ended up being his best and worst performance si-multaneously. He had no choice but to continue portraying the Robinsons as a liability to the town if he was to cash in."

"I went along with you because Gully needed the money from the land sale," Romie added.

"Gully needed the money to pay you, Romie. That's the irony," Sherry hissed. "Up until Poppy's death, that is. After that I would say the deal fell through. Why did you kill Poppy? Wouldn't her death dry up your extra income pipeline?"

Romie squealed. "You killed Poppy?"

"Killed is a strong word. I prefer to think I put a period on her misguided intentions," Nolan an-swered.

"If you believe what you're saying, you're mad!" Romie shrieked.

"The mayor, Gully, and Tessa nearly had Poppy convinced to sell the property. The papers to re-zone the land for luxury townhouses were on the lawyer's desk. Dollar signs were popping up every-where. But Mayor Uber-Liar wasn't satisfied. He jumped ahead and made the agreement with a de-veloper to win the contract. That way he could skip his reelection bid and pursue his acting ambition, all while filling his pockets with inappropriate"—Nolan signaled air quotes—"donations. Poppy got wind of the mayor's actions through her lawyer, and the deal was off."

"Good job, Madagan," Sherry whispered.

"Say what you want about Poppy, but she was an Augustinian through and through. She chose to keep the garden running and run for the mayor seat herself. Don't get me wrong, I still hated her and her father for how they treated me over the years, and if I wasn't getting what I wanted, neither was she." Nolan lifted the plastic container and flipped up the tiny cover on the spout.

"My head is spinning. There's more double-crossing going on than on my best lattice piecrust," Sherry whispered. "Did you have anything to do with the note from Gully found with Poppy the night of her murder?"

Nolan held the container over the laundry bas-ket. "The one so poetically signed, 'you're dead to me'? Pretty good job of forging his handwriting, if I do say so. I've seen so many cutie love notes from him to Romie I could imitate his cursive in my sleep."

"Have you been going through my purse? That's where I keep them. You could take a page out of Gully's 'how to be romantic' book, you know."

Nolan took a step forward.

"Nolan, let's not overreact here," Romie pleaded. "I'm sure we can work something out."

"She's right. Let's not act in haste. I was thinking. Remember how you said one day you'd like to be on the organizing side of a cook-off? Well, we're looking to staff the July Fourth cook-off, and I think you'd be perfect. Volunteer, of course. We can't afford to pay anyone." Sherry sucked in a deep breath and coughed as the gasoline fumes irritated her lungs. "Let's head out of here and get some fresh air."

"Funny you should bring up cook-offs. After I saw you compete down in Florida, I returned with newfound inspiration to take matters into my own hands."

"What would my cook-off have to do with any of this? And what were you doing down in Florida, anyway?"

"You told me you were going to buy us a place down there with the money your house would bring in. You said the value skyrocketed because the property next door was being sold to a luxury home developer. Now you're telling me you were at Sherry's cook-off?" Romie cried.

"I saw the ads for the cook-off while I was in Florida. I'm interested in domestic pursuits as much as the next guy. I'm allowed to go watch home cooks battle for the title of best home cook in America. Your friend Gully had been talking about the cook-off down in Florida for weeks. I'm pretty sure he was more excited about your competition than you were, Sherry. He said his stepfather was a foodie and he was becoming one too. When I told him I brought back the contest cookbook, he badgered me relentlessly until I lent the book to him." Nolan pointed to the bedside table where the cookbook rested. "But, yes. I was on a mission. I was buying a place and changing my name, like Sherry."

"Wait a minute," Sherry huffed, "I changed my married name back to my maiden name after my divorce, not because I committed a crime."

"No matter the reason, I liked the idea. And yes, your cook-off inspired me to act. You went after your goal and you won. I've been kicked around for so many years. When I saw you take down the competition, I knew I could too. So, don't tell me I took things too far when you're the one who should have left the investigation up to the professionals. They were well on their way to convicting the wrong person, and you ruined everything. You wouldn't heed my warning to give me space. And now I'm going to have to take care of you, which is such a shame to lose a talent of your magnitude."

"Relax, Nolan. We can work this out." Sherry eyed the container Nolan was choking with his grip. His knuckles were white.

"You're the one who should have relaxed. If those poison seeds and a trip to the hospital for your radio friend weren't enough to deter you, maybe experiencing the heat of an oven at full blast from the inside, like your best Bundt cake, will do the trick. Pretty ironic, the cook's final recipe has her roasted." Nolan grabbed Romie's slender forearm and she dropped the key. "I'll take that. Your boyfriend won't have a front door to unlock soon."

"I'm such an idiot." Romie rotated and faced Sherry. "I'm so sorry."

Nolan pushed Romie back a step before pouring the container contents over the clothes in the laundry basket. He reached behind him and produced a paper bag. "Neither one of you will be needing these. He emptied the bag onto the laundry pile.

"Our seeds," Sherry cried.

"Nolan, you said they'd be safe with you. Sherry, he's evil."

"Hope the food's good in heaven." Nolan tossed the empty container on the clothes and shoved his hand in his pants pocket. He wrenched out a matchbook and ignited the laundry.

"Bon appétit." Nolan grinned, saluted, and slammed the door behind him.

A resounding click of the lock followed. Soon after, the seeds began spitting and dancing out of the basket like exploding kernels of popcorn.

"I'll try the window." Sherry spun on her heels and raced to the window by the sink. She was halfway across her father's rug when the wool oval squirted forward on the slick synthetic floor. Sherry crashed to the ground, producing a sickening thud as the back of her head met the hard surface.

"You okay? Can you move? How many fingers do I have up?" Romie waved three fingers in front of Sherry's blinking eyes.

"If you hold them still for a minute, I can tell you."

"Sorry."

Sherry clutched the back of her head. "No more sorrys. I'm okay. Sprouting a mini grapefruit back here, that's all. Guess Gully didn't bother to buy an anti-skid pad for this rug. I wish I had one of his helmets on. We need to get out of here. The air's running out."

Romie groaned as she pounded on the window-pane. "These things are bolted shut." Romie coughed as she choked out the words. "Can you throw me one of his helmets?"

"Great idea." Sherry hoisted herself off the floor and yanked a helmet from the chest. "Here you go."

"I'm not strong enough. It won't budge," Romie screeched as the helmet collided with the window and fell to the floor.

Sherry snatched the helmet from Romie's hand. The first attempt to crack the window resulted in the helmet ricocheting off the window and careening onto the cot. Sherry gathered up the helmet, shadowed her best forehand smash, and hurled the helmet toward the glass with an effort that could crack a walnut on a sponge. Glass shattered and the pane frame split wide open.

"Ace!"

Chapter Twenty-three

"Thank you all for attending this afternoon's cook-off organization committee meeting. As Augustin's newly appointed interim mayor, it's my job to oversee the Star-Spangled Grill-off. That includes presiding over the final decision on the makeup of the judging panel, the reason for today's meeting." Kayson sat down and leaned closer to Sherry, seated on his left. "And you're sure this committee will go for the idea of the third judge when they find out who we're recommending?"

Sherry smiled. "You're not giving these folks enough credit. Trust me on this one." Her thoughts flashed back to the picnic lunch she and Kayson shared in the early spring. The meal that sent him to the hospital was her attempt to maintain a connection in case he could provide valuable information concerning Poppy Robinson's murder. Sherry still harbored guilt about how the lunch ended.

Poisoning someone, even by accident, can under-standably chip away at trust between two people.

"As most of you know, it took a few tries, but I've convinced Mayor Whinnery and the town of Hills-boro to join forces with Augustin to merge their cook-off with ours. The combo cook-off will be held at Town Beach with the same theme we had previously chosen, grilled patty on a bun. The two towns have put their differences aside for the good of the July Fourth festivities. It also made sense to ask the mayor if his wife, Colette Darbonne, would join the cook-off judging panel and she agreed. Unfortunately, she has had to pull out, due to over-booking."

"You're teasing us," Ruth scolded. "Does that mean the cook-off merger is on or off?"

"The two-town cook-off is still a go. Mayor Whin-nery is backing the concept one hundred per-cent." Kayson shuffled papers in his hands. "Right here, I have a note from Mayor Whinnery sending his regrets for being unavailable to attend this meeting. Our fault, I'm afraid, for scheduling at such short notice. He will be sent the notes from the meeting and will be fully informed of all deci-sions we make today."

Seated across from Ruth, Frances asked, "Do we have anyone in mind to step in as judge in place of Colette? And why do we need a third judge? I would think three judges, rather than two, would lead to a stalemate. Wouldn't you agree, Sherry?"

Sherry addressed the committee members. "Ac-tually, the opposite is true. Recipe contests are both hard and easy to judge. The easy part is eliminating the recipes that just aren't tasty, aren't executed properly or aren't appealing to the eye. Those ones are unanimously rejected on the spot. The hard part of judging comes when, for example, you present your best sweet potato shepherd's pie to a judge who hates sweet potatoes in any form. That's when it's important to have those two other judges instead of only one. You need majority to rule. So far, the judging panel consists of the distinguished food journalist Patti Mellitt and the husband of our very own Madagan Brigitti, Chef Vaughn Brigitti."

Ruth leaned forward. "Amber was going to judge the Hillsboro cook-off before it became a combined contest with Augustin. Shouldn't she be the third judge?"

Sherry smiled at Amber. "Amber and I have discussed the situation and she has decided she'd rather enter the contest than judge it."

Amber added, "That's right. I'm not even on the organization committee. I'm here to make sure everyone is okay with me bowing out."

"If you're not a judge you won't be attending our meetings, Amber, and we'll miss you, but I know you'd rather cook than judge so we all support your decision. Madagan and I have come up with someone we believe would be a fine addition to the judging panel." Sherry's gaze shifted from Ruth to Frances before continuing. "Gully Yates."

"Dear, did you just say Gully Yates?" Frances asked. "The same Gully Yates who was the prime suspect in his sister's murder investigation?"

Madagan stood up. "Sherry did say Gully Yates, and here are the reasons Sherry and I feel he would do a great job. During the height of the murder investigation, Sherry's gut began to tell her Gully wasn't the murderer, but like her best recipes, she had to make all the ingredients, or clues in this case, work together, even the far-fetched ones, before she could be sure she wasn't making a terrible mistake. She accomplished what she set out to do, despite the fact she almost got herself killed." Madagan grinned at her co-organizer. "Sherry not only proved Gully Yates an innocent man, she inspired him to enter culinary school. He'll also be heading up and maintaining the Augustin Community Garden. He's announced the garden will be renamed the Poppy Robinson Garden Shares. Gully convinced his sister, Tessa, to join him on the board, in the absence of two members, Poppy, of course, and Romie Green, who has left the area with her tail between her legs. The poor girl made some terrible decisions of the heart."

"I'm surprised Tessa would involve herself with the garden," Ruth commented. "I was always under the impression she'd prefer to cash in on the property rather than let the town use it."

Madagan nodded. "You're not wrong about that. At first I was skeptical about Tessa's commitment to the garden, but she truly wants to rid herself of the guilt she carries after fighting with Poppy the night her sister died. Seems Poppy challenged Tessa to tell Mayor Obermeyer he was overstepping his authority when he used his position for personal gains, but Tessa refused. She wasn't ready to lose a client with good connections. She's ready now. She claims she's all in for keeping the garden alive in her sister's name."

"Good for Gully for bouncing back after his terrible fall," Frances added. "Hard to give up a passion, but I've heard he's retiring from rock wall climbing competitions."

Madagan continued. "Sherry and I felt offering Gully a spot on the Star-Spangled Grill-off judging panel was the least we could do as thanks for his commitment to preserving the garden. When we ran the idea past him, he was thrilled to put his new culinary knowledge to the test." Madagan sat down.

"Very good," Ruth said as she nodded her approval.

"Let's take a vote," Kayson announced. "All in favor of Gully Yates joining Patti and Chef Vaughn Brigitti on the judging panel raise your hand."

Everyone seated around the conference table hoisted a hand skyward.

"I wasn't sure how the idea of Gully being a judge at the cook-off would be received." Sherry set her notebook on the hood of her car, while she fished in her purse for the car keys. "Now all we have left to do is put the entry form online and watch the recipes roll in."

Amber paused by the passenger door. "I'm excited to enter a recipe contest. I've even started brainstorming grilled patty possibilities. I was thinking about a quinoa-brown-rice patty. Any thoughts on that?"

Before Sherry unlocked the car door, she said, "You know I can't comment on my friends' entries."

"It was worth a try."

"When we were talking about Poppy's murder investigation inside, I was reminded of something I've been meaning to ask you."

Amber peered at her friend over the roof of the car. "Ask away."

"When Romie and I escaped from the burning shed, Ray and a crew of police were there to greet us. He refuses to provide me with any details as to how he was tipped off that we were in trouble. You have to admire his discretion, but I have a sneaking suspicion you played a role in there somewhere. How far off the mark am I?"

"He's a nice guy. I asked him to keep that detail from you because I was worried if you found out I called him you'd think I didn't have confidence in your ability to, and I quote the words you said to me that night, get the job done."

"I did say that, now that you mention it."

"Your exact words when I asked you where you were off to after tennis that night were, 'I'm going to finish the job by getting my hands dirty.' What better place to get dirty than the Community Garden, the scene of the murder? If I've learned anything from our friendship, it's that you can't be deterred when a goal is in sight."

Sherry tipped her head slightly as she considered Amber's words.

"You wouldn't answer my calls or texts. I had to call Ray and urge him to get over to the Augustin Community Garden as fast as his gray sedan could get him there."

"Thanks. How can I ever repay you?"

Amber yanked on the door handle. "Let's call it

even for all you've done for me. Or, on second thought, you could take a tiny taste-test bite of my contest entry."

Sherry ignored Amber's persistence. "You're right. Ray's a nice guy."

Before she got in the car, she pointed over Sherry's shoulder. "Speak of the devil. Someone's come to find you. I'll wait in the car. Take your time."

Sherry turned her head toward the approaching footsteps.

"Good afternoon, Sherry. I stopped by the Ruggery and Erno said I could find you here." Ray buried his hand in his pants pocket. "I wanted to return your phone."

"I can't believe the police department held on to it for so long. Obviously, I've replaced it with a new one, but I sure would love the stored photos back." She scrutinized the phone the detective handed her. "A little worse for wear. Still has a blood splotch on it. Thanks."

"You're welcome. I have something to ask you. Nothing to do with police work."

The look on the detective's face gave Sherry no indication what direction his question was headed.

"Would you ever have a free moment to"—Ray hesitated—"taste test a salmon burger I'm considering entering into the July Fourth cook-off? I could make a batch for a lunch or a dinner."

"I'm sorry, Ray. I would if I could. I really can't have any input in people's entries. You understand, don't you?"

"Of course." Ray's chin dipped. "I just thought." His voice drifted to silence.

"That reminds me. I have something for you. I've had it in my car since the America's Good Taste Cook-off." Sherry opened her car door and tucked her head inside. She popped back out with a pen in hand. "I knew you had Florida, so I pulled a few strings, made a trade and got you New Jersey. That's why I was concerned when I thought your Michigan pen was New Jersey. Almost spoiled the surprise."

Ray reached for the pen. "Nice. Thank you."

"I've grown attached to it. It's a lovely garden scene. New Jersey's the garden state, you know."

"I'm aware. Would you like to keep it?" Ray extended his hand.

"It's all yours. Enjoy."

Ray dunked the pen in his pocket. "It's going right in my collection. Take care, and stay out of trouble." Ray turned and headed to the gray sedan in the parking lot.

Sherry let herself in the car. As she buckled her seat belt, Amber asked, "Anything important?"

"He was returning the phone I lost the night of the shed fire. He also asked if I would sample his entry for the cook-off. Of course, I told him what I told you."

"You can't fault us for trying," Amber said as she opened the car door.

Before Sherry started the ignition, she tapped the steering wheel with the palm of her hand. "I've got the perfect solution. Why don't you sample Ray's entry and he can sample yours and may the best patty win?"

"Not a bad idea. I'll run it by Ray. Don't you feel

a sense of relief that the plans for the July cook-off are moving forward without a hitch?"

As Sherry backed her car out of her parking spot, she replied, "Now all I have to work on is making sure there is no murder associated with the cook-off, before, during, or after!"

Please turn the page for recipes from
Sherry's kitchen!

Shrimp Nachos with Artichoke Hummus

1 tablespoon plus ¼ cup olive oil, divided use
1 pound large shrimp shelled, deveined,
    uncooked
1 tablespoon apricot preserves
¼ teaspoon dried oregano
1 teaspoon sea salt, divided
½ cup canned garbanzo beans, rinsed, drained
6 ounces marinated artichoke hearts, drained
½ teaspoon minced garlic
2 tablespoons fresh lemon juice
2 tablespoons fresh dill, chopped
½ cup cherry tomatoes, halved
2 tablespoons black olives, chopped
¼ teaspoon smoked paprika powder
¼ teaspoon ground pepper
4 pita whole grain pocket bread, opened, cut in
    triangles
½ cup crumbled feta cheese

Preheat oven to 400 degrees.

Heat 1 tablespoon oil in a large skillet over medium heat. Add shrimp and cook until pink. Add apricot preserves, oregano, and ¼ teaspoon salt to the skillet and toss to coat shrimp. Remove shrimp to a plate.

Prepare artichoke hummus by combining the beans, artichoke hearts, ¼ cup olive oil, minced garlic, lemon juice, and ¼ teaspoon salt in a food processor. Pulse until ingredients are well blended. Remove artichoke hummus to a bowl and stir in dill. Set aside.

In a bowl, combine tomatoes, olives, paprika, ¼ teaspoon sea salt and ground pepper.

Line a 9x13-inch baking dish with pita quarters and bake until crispy. Spread chips across a small serving platter. Spoon dollops of hummus over the chips and top with shrimp and tomato blend. Sprinkle feta evenly across top.

Nutmeg State Cheddar Apple Baked French Toast

1 cup milk
4 large eggs
3 tablespoons pure maple syrup plus
    1 tablespoon, divided
1 teaspoon vanilla extract
¼ teaspoon sea salt
1 cup McIntosh apples, peeled, diced
½ cup shredded cheddar cheese
½ teaspoon fresh ginger, grated
2 tablespoons butter
8 slices cinnamon raisin bread
½ cup chopped walnuts

Preheat oven to 350 degrees.

In a large bowl, whisk together milk, eggs, 3 tablespoons syrup, vanilla extract, and salt.

In a medium bowl, combine apples, cheddar cheese, and ginger.

Use 2 tablespoons butter to grease a 9x9 inch baking dish. Soak 4 slices bread in egg mixture. Fit soaked bread slices across bottom of baking dish. Sprinkle apple-cheddar mixture across baking dish. Soak remaining bread slices in egg mixture and fit on top of apple blend. Pour any remaining egg blend into baking dish.

Bake covered for 40 minutes or until puffed and browned. Sprinkle nuts and remaining maple syrup across baking dish. Turn off oven and let dish sit in oven for 3 more minutes. Remove from the oven, slice, and serve.

Warm Ruby Roots Forbidden Rice Salad

2 tablespoons fresh lemon juice
¼ cup white balsamic vinegar
½ cup olive oil
2 teaspoons prepared grated horseradish
2 teaspoons sea salt
2 beets, cooked to tender, peeled cut in ½ inch
  cubes
2 scallions, diced
2 radishes, sliced thin
2 tablespoons dried cranberries
2 cups packed baby lettuce greens
2 cups cooked black rice (also known as
  Forbidden rice), kept warm
¼ cup fresh goat cheese, crumbled
¼ cup pistachios, toasted

Prepare dressing in a small bowl by whisking together the lemon juice, vinegar, olive oil, horseradish, and sea salt.

In a medium bowl, gently combine the beets, scallions, radishes, cranberries, and 2 tablespoons prepared dressing.

Assemble salad by placing lettuce greens in a salad bowl. Toss lettuce leaves with 2 tablespoons dressing. Spoon warm rice across greens. Add the beet blend, sprinkle the goat cheese and pistachios on top. Drizzle with dressing and serve with extra dressing on the side.